SPIN AND DIE

SPIN AND DIE

Stella Whitelaw

This first world edition published in Great Britain 2002 by
SEVERN HOUSE PUBLISHERS LTD of
9–15 High Street, Sutton, Surrey SM1 1DF.
This first world edition published in the USA 2002 by
SEVERN HOUSE PUBLISHERS INC of
595 Madison Avenue, New York, N.Y. 10022.

British Library Cataloguing in Publication Data

Whitelaw, Stella, 1941-
    Spin and die. - (Jordan Lacey series)
        1. Lacey, Jordan (Fictitious character) - Fiction
        2. Women private investigators - Fiction
        3. Detective and mystery stories
        I. Title
    823.9'14 [F]

    ISBN 0-7278-5831-9

Typeset by Hewer Text Ltd.,
Edinburgh, Scotland.
Printed and bound in Great Britain by
MPG Books Ltd., Bodmin, Cornwall.

To Diana and David
with love, as always

One

Winter was biting hard and I needed work. Silence drained away the last of autumn warmth. Latching pier leaned on shrunken legs. The sea was a grim grey, lashed with steely foam. Snow was not expected as it rarely snowed in Latching. It had not snowed since 1937 when toddlers looked at the white world in bemused amazement and small children shrieked with excitement, believing that aliens had white-washed the globe.

I even bought a second undervest. One on and one in the wash. Some days I wore both.

'Jordan Lacey, you are becoming a two undervest woman,' I shivered as I dressed, crouched against the wall radiator in the bedroom of my two bedsits in a muffled embrace. 'Any minute now I'll be wearing long johns.'

I'd bought a car, my spotted ladybird Morris Minor. She ate money, spewing out the oxides, but cycling was no fun when the wind took one's breath away and fingers froze on the handle-bars.

I walked the pier every day, careful not to slip on the skating rink that passed for a deck, hanging onto rails at the far end, buffeted by the wind. The sea had no memory, nor had the wind.

It was a day off. The shop, First Class Junk, was closed for renovations (new shelf). I'd just seen the show, *Little Shop of Horrors*, at the Pier Theatre and the music was pounding in my brain. Not quite my beloved big band jazz, but near enough. First Class Investigations, my private eye business, was also closed temporarily, due to lack of business. So I'd had given myself an early Christmas shopping day.

This was a laugh. My Christmas shopping list could be written on the back of two postage stamps. Cleo Carling and Leroy Anderson: decent presents. Mrs Fenwick and Mrs Drury: token presents. Joshua: zero. Derek: zero. My jazz trumpeter: zero, as he was not around. DI James: I wanted to give him the biggest, bestest present I could afford that would not give away my state of mind or frighten him off, i.e. a diary?

Money was less of a problem since an unexpected cheque had arrived from Italy as the result of a recent case I'd been involved in. It seemed that a wealthy Italian family had put up a huge sum in euros for the capture of the Scarlatti brothers, and somehow (a DI James intervention?) a percentage of it had filtered through to me. Hallelujah. As my bank did not hyperventilate at the conversion of euros into pounds, I banked it, paid all outstanding bills and was now embarking on my marathon shop.

Since I had decided the two decent presents could only come from Guilberts Department Store, the classiest shop in Latching, I wore my indigo jeans, black polo-necked jersey, black leather jacket and boots. I tied my tawny hair up into a bunch. My normal clean but scruffy look would not do. I did not want to be picked up as a shoplifter.

'So go act rich,' I told my mirror reflection. 'And don't count the change.'

Guilberts Department Store was easily the largest shop in Latching, a treble-fronted sandstone building, four storeys high, on the corner of the old high street. It was still family owned. It sold clothes for men, women and children, and in the basement was a household and electrical department. If you wanted furniture, you had to go to their other branch in Brighton. It also sold cosmetics and perfume. I was guilty of slipping in for a free squirt. Squirt now, buy later . . . very much later.

The store was mega busy. People, laden with bags, kept bumping into me. I tacked the crowd like some rudderless dingy, little runs and pauses.

'Sorry, doctor,' I said in *Little Shop of Horrors* mode. The phrase was catching.

I can shop for fruit and yogurt, hit on charity goods for my shop and clothes for surveillance. But finding these presents sent my brain into a spin. My taste is on a level with Miss Piggy's.

Two silk scarves seemed the answer. Both expensive, both beautiful, each a different design. I would decide later which suited who. The two older friends were more difficult. I'd already found a pre-war flowered teapot in a charity shop for Mrs Drury's spout and handle collection. Mrs Fenwick had everything, except a husband.

It was as I was cruising the basement of Guilberts, wondering if Mrs Fenwick had any use for egg coddlers, that I saw a young woman slip a tin opener into her pocket. She was in torn jeans, a backpack on her shoulders, hair in blonde dreadlocks. Not your average customer at Guilberts.

Dilemma: accuse, inform, or turn a blind eye?

I slid up to her, wondering if I might get a sock on the jaw. The young are unpredictable. I said in my best Bogart voice, 'Buy ring pull cans, babe.'

She went white, turned on her heel and fled up the stairs faster than a missile. There was no catching her. She was out on the street and lost in the crowds before I had time to rearrange my face. It was sad. She'd get caught one day and DI James would haul her in, handcuffed, put her in a cell and read her her rights. If it was a first offence, that is, the first time she had been caught, she'd probably get community service and probation. Shopping for old ladies would not be suitable.

The pier beckoned me. I was kicking myself for the feeble response. I should have been more commanding, taken charge of the situation. There was no solace in the waves. They were angry and cold. It was if they were storing up hatred for the entire human race. What had we done, apart from polluting the seas with every form of poison known to man?

'Don't blame me,' I said, hanging over the far rails. 'I don't even spit.' Somewhere across the horizon was France. One day I would go there on the ferry. Perhaps DI James might take me, purely on a shopping trip. I could drop hints. Brick-sized, lint-lined, disguised as a learning curve.

Jack, the owner of the amusement arcade, waved to me from behind his bulletproof kiosk. He was busy. It was the get-rich-quick season. He did not have time to talk. Pity, because I could have done with a cup of his awful coffee. Anything to warm me up. My goose pimples were getting pimples.

The solution was to open up my shop and change the two tiny windows into festive scenes. First Class Junk sold only the best junk around. There was a couple of hours to closing time. I might get lucky and snare a customer. I took down the sign, switched on the lights and tried to invoke the festive season with Mr Acker Bilk playing 'Tuxedo Rag'. Not exactly a carol but it depended on your base.

I also brewed a pot of my good coffee. The aroma filled the shop air. It fired the veins. And I hadn't eaten. What would I do on Christmas Day? Listen to the Queen's speech with a paper hat on, eating a tuna sandwich?

A man edging thirty came into the shop. I didn't know him. He was a sharp dresser, pinstriped navy suit, white shirt, subdued tie. The shoulders said, don't mess with me, buster. But his hair was stressed, his expression hung harrassed and he had a tendency to fiddle with the watch on his wrist. A bit like Prince Charles adjusting his sleeve cuffs. Half an inch out and he might lose the throne.

'Miss Lacey?' the man asked.

'Er . . . yes.' I am always cagey these days after the Italian brothers went to work on me. He did not look like a customer. His eyes flickered over my window displays with a glimmer of amusement.

'Ah, competition . . .' he murmured.

'Can I help you?' I asked on the edge of a retort.

'This is a private matter. Confidential. May we talk in your office?'

I took the man through into my back office where First Class Investigations interviewed clients. He sat on my Victorian button-back velvet chair and murmured, 'Nice.' I warmed to my visitor. He nodded approvingly at the circular Persian mat, its faded jewel colours still warm and rich. He could have a cup of my best coffee.

'You may be wondering why I have come to see you,' he said, crossing a well-trousered leg, hitching the crease. 'Or how I came to hear of you.'

'I'm sure you are going to tell me,' I said, putting bone china mugs, chocolate digestive biscuits and a pot of coffee on a tray. The aroma of coffee and chocolate was decadent. I suppose he was about my age or a bit older, teetering around thirty plus. I was twenty-seven.

'My name's Oliver Guilbert of Guilberts Department Store. I see you shop with us.' He'd spotted the mauve carrier bag on my desk.

'Occasionally.' Note: keep bag, classy prop.

'You were recommended to me by a friend, Miss Leroy Anderson, who thinks highly of your services. And you make good coffee, if I may say so.'

Again I was glad I was dolled up. He might have been less impressed by slob gear. 'Ah, Leroy,' I said, giving nothing away. I had no idea if he knew about her sister's sticky death and my part in the investigation. 'So you have some problem?'

'The store does . . . not me personally, although I am the General Manager. My father owns and runs the store. Let me explain. Some months ago a customer, a Mrs Sonia Spiller, slipped whilst shopping in the basement department. She fell, twisted her ankle and dislocated her shoulder.'

'Nasty.'

'We did all the right things, called our first-aider, then an ambulance and she was taken to Latching Hospital. I believe

5

they kept her in overnight in case of concussion, but she was allowed to go home the next morning. We sent a letter of apology and offered to pay any out-of-pocket expenses.'

'Such as?' I was making notes.

'Taxis, help in the house. Just till her ankle was fit to walk on.'

'Sounds very generous.'

'So we thought,' said Oliver Guilbert. 'But apparently not. We expected that to be the end of the incident. Then out of the blue we get a letter from a solicitor saying Sonia Spiller is going to sue us for negligence to the tune of £150,000. Her dislocated shoulder has prevented her from going back to work and she's suing us for loss of earnings, pain, trauma, and loss of social life.'

'No more bingo.'

'She says she used to play county class squash, go scuba-diving and jive dancing. Frankly we just don't believe her. She's taking us to the cleaners and it's all a scam.'

'Isn't Guilberts insured for customer accidents?'

'Yes, of course, we've comprehensive insurance but we've never had any claim like this. Before we pay out we want to make sure that the claim is genuine. That's where we want you to help. We want you to watch this woman and film every step she takes.'

A nerve end tingled somewhere round the back of my neck. Work and regular . . . for a period. My damned honesty piped up before I could stop it. 'I don't have video equipment.'

'We can lend you all the equipment you need from our electrical department. It's no problem. Leroy says your fees are very reasonable.'

Arithmetic flashed through my head, straight through and out the other side. Nine to five one person surveillance is a lot more time consuming than your average sleuthing. I normally charge £50 a day when I'm on a case, but surveillance means all day, every minute of it, no slipping out on some other investigation or doing some shop-keeping in between.

'It's £100 a day, one person prime-time surveillance, that is for a twelve hour stint, seven to seven, eight to eight, whatever you suggest.' Making it twelve hours calmed my conscience. It was a bit drastic, doubling my fee on the spot but it was boring work and I'd be out in all weathers. My ladybird would be spotted instantly. (Joke) Shopping list: sheepskin coat, Claret, brandy, handwarmers. Well, perhaps not the sheepskin. No need to go overboard.

Oliver Guilbert was doing calculations in his head. 'So a week's work would be £700?'

'If you feel that is a bit steep, I have an hourly rate but that's hardly a full cover. Mrs Spiller might well skip out for a game of squash just as I packed up,' I added.

'No . . . no,' Oliver Guilbert said hastily. 'Your daily rate is quite acceptable, especially if you save us £150,000. Less than half a percent. But I would like to have a daily report from you on what you have observed.'

'Naturally. But I should prefer to phone in a report. It would not be a good idea for me to come to Guilberts or call at your office. Mrs Spiller might get wind of what is happening.'

Also I do not want to be up half the night typing on my old portable, I could have said.

'And I can rely on your absolute discretion and loyalty in this instance, can't I?' he said, looking embarrassed.

'Heavens! What do you mean? My discretion is one hundred and ten percent. If you can't trust a private detective, who can you trust?'

'I just thought that Mrs Spiller might come to you and offer you a bigger fee for not following her. After all, you could just hang about somewhere and film a hedge for a week.'

'Mr Guilbert,' I said, slowly, counting to ten. I don't have red streaks in my hair for nothing. 'If you don't trust me, then I can't work for you. You'd better find someone else.'

I couldn't believe I was saying this, but I was. I was turning down paid work. I was tipping the Christmas Claret and brandy down the drain. It was back to hot chocolate and a small box of mints.

'I'm so sorry, Miss Lacey. I didn't quite mean what that sounded like. I've got suspicious of everyone. This business has really upset me. You don't know who to trust. Of course, I want you to take on the work. Come into the store tomorrow morning and chose what equipment you need. You can borrow it for as long as it takes.'

I let his apology sink in. It seemed genuine. His stressed hair was standing on end, like a small boy at the end of his first day at school. He had pleasant hazel eyes, flecked with winter sun. I wondered if Leroy liked him.

'What has made you suspect that Mrs Spiller could be on the make?' I asked.

'One of my staff saw Mrs Spiller out walking her dog. It's a young, boistrous dog, but the point is that the dog was on a lead and she held the lead in her right hand. Now, it was her right shoulder that she injured in the fall. It would hurt too much to allow a young dog to tug and pull at it.'

'Very true. All right, I will take on this undercover filming, initially for one week. I'll vary the timing of the twelve hours according to what seems appropriate for her lifestyle. She may well be a night bird.'

Oliver Guilbert breathed a sigh of relief. 'Good. Thank you. I'll give you a note for the equipment. Just hand it to the cashier. I won't say what it's for, just sign my authority for the loan. And this is my mobile number for your daily report. Phone anytime.'

I got out a client contract form from the filing cabinet and asked him to fill it in and sign. He used a fountain pen, a Mont Blanc, one of Guilberts' best. Then he finished his coffee and stood up. This was probably the best case that had ever come my way. It beat lost tortoises and trashed wedding cakes. I'd better not screw it up.

He shook my hand. Nice, firm grip. No sweat. 'I have every confidence in you,' he said, trying to make up for his previous gaffe.

'I saw someone nick a tin opener in your store today,' I said. He nodded with resignation. 'They'll take anything that's not bolted to the floor.'

As soon as he was out of the door and had driven off in a racy red car, I was on the phone to Latching police station, asking for Detective Inspector James.

His world-weary voice answered as if the day had been a long line of burglaries, assaults, drunks, RTAs and road rage. Yet, that gravelly voice was enough to bring sanity into my life and a reason for living.

'It's Jordan Lacey. Sorry, James, I know you're busy. Don't ask me why because I'm not going to tell you, but can anyone at the station give me a quick ten minute briefing on how to use a video camera? I need to know fast, like by tomorrow morning.'

I heard his sharp intake of breath, waited for the invective. But the reply was mild, as if soothing a ten-year-old.

'I'll put you through to Sergeant Rawlings. He'll give you the number of a film expert who works outside the police force. It'll probably cost you a bottle of Scotch.'

'I'm not going to tell you why.'

'I'm not exactly agog to know.'

'Thank you,' I said, wondering how I could keep him talking when I was obviously being dismissed. '. . . er . . . Happy Christmas.'

'And a Happy Christmas to you, Jordan. Don't choke on your mince pie.'

I heard him transferring the call. He didn't even say good-bye. But neither had he bawled me out. I suppose that could be called progress.

Two

T he man who owns the best camera shop in Latching was polite even though it was seven o'clock and technically he had closed. It was a novelty to have a meek female on his doorstep, practically begging for help.

'I have to know how to use a video camera,' I said. 'It's a big occasion. Very big. You know, something special . . .' I was making it sound like the wedding of the year. 'I also need to know how to load and unload the . . . er, film.'

'Sure, come in. It's not often I get an amateur to instruct. It's important not to abuse your equipment and most people don't know how to use them, sling their cameras about as if they are egg whisks.'

'I won't. The camera is only on loan to me.'

'So you don't know the make?'

'No, not yet. I'll know tomorrow when I get it.'

'No problem. We'll go through several different leading cameras and I'll explain how they work.'

William Rushton was a thorough instructor. I learned enough to handle any camera, with luck and a good memory. I offered some kind of payment, but he refused. I would have to drop in with an inspired gift of Highland origin.

'Thank you again,' I said, leaving.

'Anytime. Come back if you have a problem. You know, after the wedding.' Mr Rushton was keeping a straight face. I don't think he thought it was a wedding either. Perhaps Sergeant Rawlings had dropped a hint when he phoned through for me.

As soon as I left the camera shop, I sat down on a municipal bench and made copious notes. It was customary. I write everything down, always. My memory is like a colander and sometimes all the best bits slip through.

It was almost too dark to write. A sodium street lamp shone on the page of my notebook, making it shiny like wax. It was also too cold to stay out long. The wind sliced between my hair and my collar. I shivered and headed for home. I hoped no one would call on me, particularly not spongers, the amiable Joshua looking for pre-Christmas dinner nor the ferret-faced Derek looking for more than a meal. Supper was a bowl of home-made vegetable soup with all the leftovers thrown in to simmer. Lettuce, radishes, beetroot . . . I wasn't fussy even if the colour was a bit odd for soup. A few handfuls of herbs and the brew was thick and nourishing. I curled up on my moral straight-backed sofa and switched on the black and white television. The programme was wallpaper. Surveillance needs planning, venues, timing, luck.

My first sighting of Sonia Spiller was from the health club car park. I'd pencilled in Sunday morning for a personal Christmas treat of steam and sauna. The steam room is good for my asthma. If I could think of a way of earning a living from a steam room, I would. The only option is a life of sin which is hardly my style, bearing in mind my low success rate with men, that is, any decent men.

Only misfits lust after me. Must be something in my genes. But I yearn for two men. My jazz trumpeter, who is out of bounds because he is married, and DI James, who is out of bounds, full stop. Don't ask me why. It just hasn't happened. He's built a ten-foot wall around himself, topped it with barbed wire, a high-tech security system and two Rottweilers to guard it.

The health club has not been one of my favourite places since I got locked in the steam room by an over-protective mother some months back. Steam burns are painful and leave sore memories.

It was as I parked in the yard of the health club that the penny dropped with a clang. This was Luton Road where Sonia Spiller lived. I sent up an instant prayer that number eight might be in view from the car park and not obscured by the West Sussex pebble-faced wall. It was in sight. Cover: iron-pumping fanatic. It would not attract her attention. I could use my ladybird, park at the health club, all hours of the day and night. I just had to make sure I got one of the three parking spaces that had an unrestricted view.

The car park had once been the playground of the old school. The health club was the inspired conversion of a nineteenth-century charity school building. Its walls were hung with sepia photographs of rows of children in long skirts, pinnies and bonnets. A ramrod teacher in black bombazine stood like a sentinel over her brood. The yard had, a century ago, been filled with the laughter of children playing hopscotch, skipping, bowling hoops – a window on childhood. Nowadays, it was filled with BMWs, Hondas, MGs and Jags. Grunts and groans leaked from the windows, drowning the echos of long-gone laughter.

Despite the law of averages, I checked the door of the steam room at least four times as I sat on a wooden bench, inhaling the warm wet steam. More strategic planning: 9–12 am watch number eight Luton Road; 12–2 pm open shop to catch lunch-time shoppers; 2–6 pm number eight again; 6–7 pm catch late-night shoppers; 7–12 pm number eight and any follow-ons. It sounded a barrel of fun. Twelve hours surveillance as per contract. I was going to have some late nights. Goodbye social life. What social life? All those Christmas parties DI James was not going to take me to. Christmas was on the way and my party diary was void.

As the toxins oozed out of my skin, my brain listed gear: several hats, aviator specs, half-specs, old raincoat, unfashionable winter tweed coat, shopping bags to carry video camera. To stave off boredom and insanity: books, puzzles, fruit, water. Shopping list: cheap flask from Woolworths. Rating of first visit to steam room after last death-imminent episode: partial success.

Number eight was at the end of a row of fishermens' cottages, gutted and modernised by successive owners, but the outside untampered as it was built around 1840 and protected. The walls were a pale apricot wash, front door flanked by hanging baskets of last summer's flowers, a paved front yard for the family car. The car was a modest white Toyota. The cottage was a narrow two-up, two-down, both front windows being angular bays. The stable-style front door had heavy black hinges. It was the kind of place I'd like to live in. Mr Spiller was probably something in computers.

It seemed a good time to start my surveillance. I checked my watch. I would keep a log, date/time/type of activity. My first hour was zero. I decided to polish the ladybird with J-cloth. Second hour: zero. Ladybird now had cleanest wheels in Latching and immaculate carpet picked at with spare toothbrush. Third hour: just about to pen in zero when woman emerged. My first sighting.

Sonia Spiller was in her late thirties, about 5 ft 4 in tall, slimmish build with long flowing black (dyed?) hair, parted centrally so that it fell either side of her face. She had a wide, down-turned mouth. Petulant. She was wearing cord trousers and a smart grey sheepskin jacket and trying to get a demented black and white puppy into the back of the car. Puppy thought this was game of the day and bounded around everywhere except into the back seat. He preferred to drive.

'Jasper! Please, really! Bad dog!' I heard a sharp, penetrating voice. Nothing sweet here.

Jasper tried licking her face.

'No! God! Get down. Sit, SIT!' Jasper needed to go to classes. Sonia Spiller was losing her patience. Any second now and Jasper wouldn't get his ride and walk. But, suddenly he tired and lay down on the back seat. I noted he wasn't wearing a seat belt. Oliver had been right. Handling that dog took some doing.

She reversed carefully into Luton Road before turning

13

seawards. I started my car and followed at a distance. Perhaps I was going to get lucky and catch her gambolling on the beach with Jasper, flinging a ball on a rope high into the air with dislocated shoulder. Except I didn't have the camera with me. Blot on hitherto spotless report. But dogs need daily walking and there was always tomorrow.

After half an hour of watching Sonia Spiller walking listlessly along the beach with Jasper rushing in and out of the waves chasing seagulls, I was rigid and cross-eyed. Normally I love walking the beach. My kind of walking. There are a hundred different things to look at and observe: the mood of the sea, the changing colours, the vast arc of the sky. But this was work and I could not take my eyes off the woman for a second. Her hair blew blackly. She had a habit of constantly flicking it back, completely useless whatever the force. It was a childhood habit. She'd been one of those teenagers, forever flicking.

'How much longer?' I asked a passing seagull. He squawked and flapped his wings in disgust.

Her hands were dug deeply into her pockets. I was cold, having forgotten my WI pattern gloves. I tried brisk arm swinging to keep the circulation going. Eventually she decided Jasper had had enough. I'd had enough. She climbed the slippery shingle slope and bundled damp dog back into the car. He was tired, too, and ready for food. I found some broken polos in my pocket. They had no taste. Did mint evaporate? Perhaps it was time to graduate to a stronger version.

Back at my shop, I flung myself into work, rejoicing in activity, music, noise, bustle, coffee, freedom to take my eyes off one boring, slow-moving object. This surveillance was going to be excruciating. I had to liven it up. I could dig up, sweep or patrol roads (traffic warden gear); do market research (clipboard); double-glazing salesperson; lost old lady; researcher writing book on nineteenth-century cottages. Still, I had the cleanest car in the whole of West Sussex and been paid whilst doing it.

The shop door opened and DI James came in. He immediately filled all available space. His heavy trench coat was buttoned up. He felt the cold. His ocean blue eyes were frost hard.

'I thought I could smell coffee,' he said. 'Black please, Jordan.'

I recovered quickly. 'Is this a social call or official?'

'Half and half. An official social call,' he said enigmatically, following me through to my office, leaning on my desk. He noticed its lack of clutter. 'Business slow?'

'Seasonal. It's Christmas. Hadn't you heard? Ding, dong merrily on high and all that. No one wants anything done over Christmas. It might spoil the season of goodwill.'

'Then you have time to do me a favour?'

Do him a favour? I'd do anything for him. Didn't he know? Lay down in front of a bus, cut off my hair, shift shingle. I was taking in the dark crew cut, tinged with grey around the ears. My fingers did not know how it felt. I had never run my fingers through his hair. Those penetrating blue eyes, scanning me now like laser beams. There was always this fear that I might never see him again. He might get mown down by ram-raiders, shot in a hostage situation, promoted and moved north to a different patch.

'Do I get paid?' I asked, pouring coffee steadily.

'No. You owe me a favour. Several actually.'

'Name one.'

'Rescuing you from hermit hole.'

'That wasn't a favour. You were working on a call out. What a nerve, calling that a favour.'

'We could have left you there.'

'Then you'd have had another corpse on your hands. Starved and suffocated. Very unpleasant. Plenty of ID. Found in the middle of the next service when they went to fetch the hymn books. So, OK, tell me. What is this favour?'

'You may have seen the story in the papers. Some kids took a JCB and wrecked Latching bowling green. They did two laps of the green, churning up the grass and leaving deep tyre marks, an expensive wrecking spree. We've nothing to go on except a gaping hole. We do have the JCB which they left half in and half out of the pavilion, though. The trail of destruction began when they drove through the wire fencing and then the park before getting onto the bowling green. There are huge seven-inch tyre marks.'

'So it's a bad day for bowlers. What do you want me to do?'

'The vandals fled when the JCB got wedged in the debris. They got away. I don't have the resources to tour the clubs, the pubs etc. It's Christmas. I thought you could do it, cruise the clubs, more your scene. They're bound to drink too much and start boasting. The cost of the damage is £140,000. That could go to any thick head.'

'What about my alcohol units? You could be damaging my health.'

DI James smiled. It was the sweetest sight, lit up his stern face, enough to melt any woman. He used it rarely. 'I know you'll switch to juice, Jordan. You can't become an alcoholic in a few days.'

'Try me.'

'And it's Christmas and what you drink over Christmas doesn't count.'

'So you do know it's Christmas. Are you going to send me a card?' Or give me a present, kiss me under the mistletoe?

'Doubt it. No time for cards. Archaic custom.'

'Now about this favour, firstly, it's not "more my scene". The Bear and Bait is my only pub and that's for the jazz. Secondly, I'm busy. I do have a case. A big time-consuming case. Nothing that I'm going to tell you about.'

He looked genuinely disappointed. 'Jordan . . . what can I say? I thought we had some kind of give and take going? All I want is the gossip. Nothing dangerous. Just mooch around and listen. Is that too much to ask?'

I couldn't deny him anything. Except he did not ask for the right things, like can I stay with you tonight? Will you rub my back? Can I sleep on your shoulder?

'Oh, all right,' I said, tired of fighting him off. 'I'm a fool. I know it. Don't bother to tell me.'

'Thank you, Jordan.' He put down the empty coffee mug and started to move. He laid a tenner on the counter. 'Have the first couple of rounds on me.'

It wasn't fair. He wasn't to know that I would never spend it. I'd used the note to mark a page in a book of old Scottish love poems and put the book in the top drawer of my desk. Only the direst emergency would force me to part with it.

Tatters of rain ran down my shop windows. My £6 price labels were switching between items at an astonishing rate. Half of Latching was doing their Christmas shopping at First Class Junk. I sold a couple of old maps of Sussex, a massive silver candlestick (tarnished) and a pair of his and hers embroidered hot-water bottle covers. Weird . . . I mean, if you were a his and hers type item, you wouldn't need a hot-water bottle.

A middle-aged woman came in. She was drenched, tinted brown hair dripping, beige trouser suit with matching waist-coat. No umbrella or raincoat. She was a ripe case for arthritis or rheumatism.

'Have you got a soup tureen?' she gasped.

'A soup tureen?' I knew what a soup tureen was, but my mind was racing through the boxes of china stacked out the back.

'I need it for serving punch. I'm having a party and they drink like fishes, all of them. Damned club. My turn, of course. So, it's going to be hot punch, pints of cheap red wine and orange juice with a few cloves stuck in an orange thrown in.'

'Sounds lovely,' I said.

'Well . . . have you? Have you got a soup tureen?'

I took a deep breath. 'I do have something much better. I have a Victorian washstand set. A deep washbowl, jug for the hot water and small soap dish. All matching. Probably white earthenware, maybe ironstone Mason, blue and red pagodas. Very colourful.'

'May I see it?'

It took some rifling through my stock. I'd forgotten that I'd bought it in a mixed box of china oddments from a local house auction. £10 the lot, I'd paid, and I hadn't even unpacked it.

'Yes, the washbowl is perfect,' she said instantly. 'I'll have it.'

'I'm afraid I can't split the set. The price is £20 for the three items. Quite a bargain and you could use the jug for topping up glasses or serving juice.'

The woman was doing calculations in her head. She was planning to serve cheap punch but my pagoda washbowl was steep at £20.

'OK,' she said at last. 'Perhaps my guests will be too busy admiring the bowl to worry about the strength of the punch.'

'Style is always more important,' I said.

I wrapped the items carefully in tissue paper and then packed them into a recycled carrier bag. She handed over the £20. Diamond solitaires sparkled on her fingers. She could afford it.

It was still chucking it down. She looked outside the shop apprehensively, her unsuitable suit clung like cling film.

'Would you like to borrow an umbrella?' I offered. 'Just drop it back anytime you're passing.'

She spun round, her face a wreath of smiles. A bit like the Queen. 'How kind,' she said. 'Thank you. I don't drive, you see.'

I lent her a decent umbrella from my props box. It didn't matter if it came back or not. But it did come back, the next day, and attached to it was an invitation to the party. My first. Christmas was looking up. She was Mrs Brenda Hamilton, secretary of Latching Bowls Club . . . now that was interesting. They were having a party despite the demolition of their clubhouse. Bowlers had stamina.

Three

S onia Spiller was starting to invade my dreams. It was weird. I saw her everywhere, long black hair blowing in the wind like a Hallowe'en witch. I spent all the next day watching her to no avail. She did nothing to arouse suspicion, nothing worth filming. Guilberts Department Store might have to pay out compensation.

Nor did she act as if she was in agony. No ouches.

I was developing sympathy vibes for her puppy. Sonia was not the right person to own a dog. Shouting doesn't earn respect, love, affection or obedience. I could have told her. Jasper the puppy wanted a playmate. She didn't play with him. As yet I had not seen Sonia's husband. He commuted to London at times outside my surveillance and had not appeared.

The long afternoon of nothing, watching number eight, was boring me rigid. What did this woman do? Nothing much. Watch soap after soap? Knit, crochet, cruise the internet? Or was I watching the wrong place? This thought kept pricking my brain. Perhaps she was not inside.

Had she slipped out the back? Her back garden was narrow and led onto a fisherman's alley, a twitten – an escape route for smugglers and short cut to the sea. There was a gate in the wall, but it was overgrown with weeds. I stood for an hour at the end of the alley, immersed in a free newspaper till my eyes glazed over. I ate two Twix bars, but forgot to taste.

In sheer desperation for entertainment that evening, I coasted bars as asked by DI James, clutching glasses of St Clements (orange juice topped with bitter lemon), deafened and jaded by inaudible conversations and the inane ringing of mobiles. This was another purgatory.

But in the din some overheard words shone out. They'd seen an old geyser driving a JCB, a man laughed. I edged towards the group. Then I pin-pointed the man talking, a security guard. Talk about luck. He was still being treated to drinks on the story.

'My goodness,' I said, all girly-eyed. 'So you're the security guard at the building site where the JCB was, I mean, from where it was stolen. Wow, is that right? Were you there at the time? Do tell me what happened.'

He was only too willing. He was drinking bitter shandy. I nodded to the barman for another. The guard was sweating with all the attention and all the drink. His glasses were slipping off his nose. He did not look tough enough to guard a garden fork, let alone a massive JCB on a building site.

'I heard all this crashing noise and ran out outside and saw the lights.'

'What lights?'

'The JCB's lights. This guy had switched them on and they were moving around like crazy in the dark.'

'So what did you do?'

'I went back inside and called the police! They came in no time with sniffer dogs, but although they tracked the machine, he got away.'

'He got away on a JCB?' I had to laugh. No wonder DI James did not want to put any of his men on this one.

'Apparently he drove through fencing and across a field before slicing up the bowling green. It was like a tank. I suppose I ought to have stopped him, being the guard and everything.'

He sipped the fresh shandy reflectively. Perhaps his employers were cutting up a stink.

'Well, I think you were very brave,' I consoled. 'After all, you could have got mown down, flattened. A JCB shouldn't be argued with. Did you catch sight of the kids?'

'It weren't kids. This guy had a lean, older look. He was

wearing a baseball cap, but that doesn't mean anything these days.'

'I wonder if I could have your autograph?' I gushed, sliding a beer mat towards him. 'You're nearly famous, in the newspapers and all that.'

It cheered him up to be asked. He scrawled Jeff Hopkins and added his phone number. Just what I wanted.

'I know a Fred Hopkins,' I said without thinking.

'My brother,' he said.

It was time to move on before he discovered I was a PI. The greengrocer Hopkins knew what I did for a living and often slipped me a bargain of cut-price fruit or salad stuff.

I folded myself into sleep that night, stomach gassed up with bitter lemon and hair full of cigarette smoke. I'd wash it in the morning before phoning Oliver Guilbert with my report. He'd be regretting his payments to me soon. I had to find something dubious about Sonia's behaviour.

'I'm not surprised,' said Oliver Guilbert the next morning after hearing my report. 'I'm sure she's being extra careful not to arouse suspicion. Maybe she'll slip up. Just keep watching her, please, Miss Lacey. It's early days.'

I wondered how I was going to get through the day and thought darkly of escape. The brisk settlement of winter on Latching did not help. Me and my two vests were inseparable. My bones were cold. I'd forgotten summer. Had it ever existed? Had I ever walked the beach, barefooted and in shorts, splashing in the shallows, singing unrestrained choruses of songs with memorable words? Gershwin, Porter, Madonna.

Damp air clambered up my ankles as I walked to my shop. The ladybird was parked in the backyard. I could only park near my bedsits at the weekends when the double yellow lines did not herald catastrophic fines. So much for my parking permit. £20 down the drain.

I opened up the shop briefly. This was going to be a five minute wonder, just to reassure my friend Doris, of the next-door but one grocery shop, that I had not been abducted again. But in seconds the door swung open and a wino lurched in. I reached for the air freshner.

'Do you buy things, missus?' he croaked.

He was half-past windward already at nine thirty in the morning. Poor soul. What was he drinking? Cleaning fluid? He smelled awful. My stomach contracted. Sometimes I thought I must be incubating an ulcer.

'No, sorry,' I said. 'I don't buy anything. I sell things instead.'

'I've got this box,' he went on, ignoring me. 'I don't want a box of stuff. Gotta sell it. I can't carry a box around, not with all this glass stuff in it.'

He was indeed carrying a cardboard box, supermarket size. It looked heavy. It tinkled, glass-like.

I wanted him out of my shop. His presence might give me a bad name. The box was probably full of empty beer bottles.

'Won't the pubs give you a few pence for the empties?' I suggested.

'I need the money now,' he said. His eyes were already clouded and dead. Strands of greasy hair were caught in his mouth.

'OK,' I said. Anything to get rid of him. I was feeling rich with my current daily pay rate. 'I'll give you a pound.'

'God bless you, miss. God bless you . . .' He shambled up to the counter, put the box on it and held out a grimy hand. I couldn't even look at him as I dropped a pound coin into his palm. His face was etched with squalor and wretchedness and I didn't want a print of it on my memory. He hovered, breathing beery fumes over me. I added fifty pence to hasten his exit.

As soon as he was out of the door, I flew around with lavender air spray, opened windows and doors despite the outside air temperature. The box could go out in the bin for collection by the council. I could not even be bothered to take it to the bottle bank collection point.

But then the badly fastened lid opened, all by itself. Dust rose. These weren't beer bottles. They were old medicine bottles, blue, brown, green, all shapes and sizes, some rarities still with stoppers or corks. There was a bottle with a glass seal and family crest. Several old ginger beer and Codd bottles, scarce now because of time and breakages. Where had he got this lot?

Some of the Codd bottles still had the marble stopper which returned to the top and kept the fizz in the drink. A wooden cap and plunger supplied with the bottle released the marble each time a drink was drunk. Hiram Codd had thought up this ingenious idea. No one remembered him now, 125 years on.

I supposed I ought to run after the wino and give him a couple of tenners. But he'd only drink it all, probably kill himself in the process.

So, where had the wino found these treasures? On a skip? Had they fallen off the back of a lorry? They'd probably come from a house clearance and had been dumped by the clearance men who didn't recognise their worth. I didn't want to know. I put the bottles away. No washing or cleaning. People paid more if the dust was intact.

I was late for number eight Luton Road. And there was no parking space with unrestricted view. I put the ladybird in another slot, jammed on a hat and a tweed coat and ambled out with the video camera in a plastic Safeways carrier bag.

At exactly the same moment, Sonia Spiller came out of her cottage swinging a squash bag. Ten seconds later and I would have missed her. I scrambled back into my car and did a racing exit. She drove straight to an out of town leisure centre where there were indoor courts. I had never been there before, being the kind of person who could not see any point in bashing a ball around a confined space.

It was an unlovely grey concrete building, planned on a bad day, built unimaginatively on corner wasteland that some farmer had given up on. It had acres of car parking space so I was able to put my ladybird out of sight of the white Toyota. The entrance was automatic glass doors so that the athletes did not tire themselves out having to open a heavy door. A colourless foyer processed members to courts, changing rooms, showers, the cafeteria. I had to buy a ticket to watch from the gallery.

The cashier gave me a funny look. I suppose an ancient tweed coat and felt pork pie hat did not have the right sports ambience.

'My niece,' I explained. 'I'd like to watch her play.'

'Oh. Right.'

Such a syncopated conversationalist. I couldn't get a word in edgeways. I left the girl pressing the till and wandered upstairs. By the time I spotted Sonia Spiller, she was thrashing a small rubber ball on court four, legs and arms flying. There was one other player in the enclosed court below. It seemed they had to hit the facing wall above the horizontal line. Fascinating. I got out the video camera and filmed her for several minutes. The dislocated shoulder was giving her no trouble.

'My niece,' I said again to the person standing next to me in the gallery. Perhaps it was not so unusual to film family these days.

'She plays well. Nice returns.'

Her shoulder seemed to be working normally, but then how could I judge? I knew nothing about shoulder injuries. An expert would have to look at the film. I was doing what I was paid for.

But she did not play for long. She stopped abruptly, mopping her face with a towel. Something was wrong. She thanked her partner, left the court and disappeared into the depths of the concrete. I hung around but could not find her, gave up and went outside to my car. The Toyota had gone. I'd lost the woman.

I cruised around, hoping to catch sight of her white car but that was doomed. It was nothing like a chase in the movies. There were white cars everywhere. I didn't know which way to go and I had forgotten to note the number plate. Mega-size blot on A4 copybook. At least the log was going to be a few degrees more interesting than usual.

Sonia Spiller had not gone home. The front yard was empty except for weeds in the paving cracks. I had lost track of her. She could be anywhere, doing anything and probably was.

There was no point in hanging around now. I'd blown it. The shop was my haven, a place to hide and lick my wounds. How could I have forgotten something so basic and necessary as the number plate? I made myself clean and clean and clean as a punishment.

Doris put her head round the door. 'I could hear you doing that floor mopping two doors down,' she said. 'What's the matter? Got an infestation of bugs?'

'Don't worry, it's nothing Health and Safety need know about,' I said. 'Self-inflicted discipline. Cleanliness is next to godliness.'

'You a Methodist?' Doris asked suspiciously.

'Heavens, no. Why?'

'John Wesley said that. Founder of Methodism.'

'Doris, you amaze me.'

Doris inspected her long crimson nails and grinned. 'I amaze myself sometimes. Come and clean my place if you want some more discipline.'

The collection of old medicine bottles looked good on my newly acquired Ikea shelf. They were not worth a £6 price ticket on each. I had a conscience and did not want to disturb the dust. Perhaps a collector would make me an offer.

But the ginger beer and Codd bottles went in the front window with rural items of interest – a few dried flowers and a book on the Sussex countryside. It was easy to imagine those 1875 farm workers taking their lunch break under a shady hedge in a field, swigging ginger beer and getting their mouths round huge chunks of bread and cheese. No burgers or elitist smoked salmon and rocket sandwiches delivered by bike.

I stood back to admire the arrangement at the same time as a familiar shape appeared in the shop doorway. DI James had arrived for the latest gossip on the JCB cock-up.

'They think it was an old geyser wearing a baseball cap,' I

25

said without turning round from the window. I was denying myself that moment of yearning bliss when I could look at him, drink in his unsmiling face, drown in those brilliant blue eyes.

'I beg your pardon?' said a voice with a university edge. For a moment I was disorientated. Had DI James had a personality change? His own voice was deep, world-weary, a touch of accent from somewhere up north.

'James?' I said uncertainly without moving.

'Sorry?'

This was one ridiculous conversation. Time to remove misery, disappointment, fear. Fear? Fear that DI James had been revamped overnight and removed himself from my sphere.

It was the same bulky shape with subtle differences. Less authority, more clothes sense, younger by about ten years. The hair was dark, but longer, eyes unfathomable behind Clark Kent heavy-rimmed specs, a face without lines, edges or jutting chin. Nice though, pleasant and approachable.

'Hello,' I said. 'I thought you were someone else.'

'This is my anonymous look,' he said. 'I can pass in any crowd. DS Ben Evans, local CID. Have you a minute to spare? I'm making enquiries about a hold-up at the Mexican restaurant, four doors down, sometime last night.'

'Oh, I'm sorry. That's awful. What did they take? A ton of tortillas?'

'Something like that.'

'No one has been flogging Mexican.'

'Did you notice anything unusual yesterday, youths loitering, people not usually in this area?'

In this area? This was a backwater of Latching, the last of the shops that petered out into a residential area where the Edwardian terraces were split into flats. But even so, DS Evans needn't make it sound like downtown.

'There was a wino in here this morning,' I offered, upping my blinking average for the day. DS Evans obviously did not know I was a PI and I wasn't going to tell him. 'He wanted cash before making his daily purchases at Threshers.'

'Cheaper at a supermarket.'

'He'd have trouble getting into one. They'd smell him a mile off and escort him out.'

'Can you remember anything else? A van parked nearby, or a group of youths hanging about?'

'I'm really sorry but I can't remember anything special about yesterday.' Except that I'd been glued to Sonia Spiller's uneventful activities. 'I'm not much help.'

'Never mind. You obviously know what you're selling,' said DS Ben Evans, looking round at the meagre stock. 'Selective and imaginative.'

'Sure,' I agreed. 'No point in housing a load of rubbish. This is all first class stuff.'

'I'll leave you to your . . . er . . . window dressing.' He did not seem to want to leave. 'It's a nice shop.'

'Thank you. Are you new here?'

'Just arrived. Bit difficult settling in after the Metropolitan. Slower, quieter.'

I nodded agreeably. 'We still get a lot of crime.'

'So it seems. Mexican etc . . .'

'If I think of anything I'll phone you,' I said, feeding him his exit line. His eyes thanked me. He gave me his phone number, which I knew by heart. I could have dialled it in my sleep. Probably did.

'You've been very helpful.'

'I hope you'll catch them. Nothing is safe these days. What actually happened?' He was not supposed to tell me, but he had relaxed.

'These two men came in, ordered a meal, ate it, stayed on, then they threatened the owner, and got away with the day's takings just as he was closing. Nasty business. No one seems to have seen anything.'

He was so like DI James and yet not like him at all. What was the matter with me? I was seeing DI James everywhere. I'd be embracing lamp posts next.

I needed a sweet treat. I swanned into Superdrug and bought

myself a strawberry-tasting lipstick. The colour was OK, too. I'm not into a lot of make-up, merely smearing my lower lip, pressing them together and hoping the result looked natural. Actually defining the top lip seems excessively vain.

I decided that the Spiller surveillance was not progressing swiftly enough to justify the generous fee. I felt I should be producing the goods faster. Conscience pricking again. Perhaps I should give Oliver a discount on bad days. Or better still, he could give me a store discount in place of a percentage of the money and I could stock up on his fancy bags.

My feet dragged me back to number eight. The house was empty, windows dark and hollow. No dog, no woman, no husband, in that order of interest. Somehow I had missed them. My confidence bruised easily. It was time to think seriously of a career change.

Four

The next day I stepped up the pace. I arrived at the health club car park, already in character gear, stonewashed jeans, navy jersey, anorak and careless scarf and earrings. Careless scarf and earrings being the cover.

Trusty clipboard in hand, I pressed the polished brass bell of number eight. I had decided to throw caution to whatever force was gusting, and face the woman herself.

Sonia Spiller opened the door. She was a little older than I had first thought. Approaching forty with coarsened skin and deep lines from nose to mouth. She needed to exfoliate. The mass of black hair hung lankly, straggling on her shoulders. Obviously not a shampoo day.

'Mrs Spiller?' I asked pleasantly.

'Yes.'

'I wonder if I might have a few moments of your time?'

'I don't want to buy anything.'

'Heavens no,' I said, with a little nervous laugh. 'And I'm not selling anything. I'm not one of those people. I'm a member of the Latching Historical Houses Association and we want to include number eight Luton Road in our examples of perfect fishermen's cottages of the nineteenth-century.'

I don't know how I think up these things. It was all on the spur of the moment. But it worked. Sonia Spiller relaxed visibly.

'Well, that's very nice,' she said. 'Of course, number eight is one of the best in this row. Some of these people have really spoilt their houses, no imagination at all, and without the proper building consent half the time.'

'I'm afraid I can't go into the legality of individual alter-
ations,' I said primly. 'But I would like to know what improvements you have done to preserve the authenticity and whether
you did the work yourself.'

'Come in then. It's freezing on the doorstep. Would you like
to have some coffee while you look around?'

'Lovely.'

'You didn't say your name.'

'Lucy Locket.' I was a quick thinker.

'Come in, Miss Locket. What an unusual name. It's nice and
warm in the kitchen. We've just had a new Aga put in.'

I could have swooned in the heat. Instead I was busy making
notes about all the improvements and restoration work that she
and husband Colin had done. I gathered that Sonia did most of
the work herself. The solicitor's letter had said she had had to
give up teaching but she did not seem to have another job.

'This pretty stencilled frieze around the ceiling, most attractive and in keeping with the period. When did you do all this?' I
asked, sipping my coffee. Instant, not bad. Cold milk.

'The frieze is a new innovation. I did it about two weeks ago.
I made the stencils myself, the grapes and trellis work, got the
design from a book in the library. It took me a whole day to
paint.'

'My goodness. I couldn't do that,' I burbled on. 'I've no head
for heights. Can hardly change a light bulb.' I know lots of
jokes about changing light bulbs, like how many politicians
does it take to change a light bulb? Six. One up the ladder and
five to kick it away.

'Oh, a step ladder doesn't bother me. The trick is not using
too much paint.' Sonia rambled on about the technicalities of
stencil work while I roughly calculated the height of the kitchen
walls and the mileage of grapes hanging on the trellis.

'I've done our bedroom as well,' she added with enthusiasm.
'Different design, roses and trailing clematis. It's very effective.
Would you like to see it?'

'Lovely.'

The bedroom was feminine. Where did Colin fit into all this? A crowd of family photographs cluttered the top of a white chest of drawers. Her matching dressing table was a witness to her fight against time.

I thought I had got her now, in my mind. No woman with a dislocated shoulder could have wielded a paint brush on intricate work at that height, for several days, without getting severe rigor mortis. But there was no proof. If challenged, she would say her husband did the work; that I had misheard her. Time to leave while I was still ahead.

'You've been very helpful,' I said, putting the notebook away. 'May I come back if I think of something else I need to ask you?'

'Of course, Miss Locket. I've got to take my dog for a walk. I've got a new puppy and he's a handful.'

I could hear Jasper barking and whining and scratching at a door. She had shut him into the utility room, and when she opened the door, he came rushing out, overjoyed at the scent of freedom.

I went down on one knee. 'Hello, Jasper,' I said, fondling his handsome head. He was ecstatic with all the new smells of my coat and my jeans. He tried licking my face. 'No,' I said firmly, pushing his head away. 'Down. Sit.'

Jasper did nothing of the kind, not knowing the meaning of the words, bounded about, tail wagging dangerously.

'Jasper. How did you know his name?' She looked puzzled.

'You called him Jasper,' I said, face straight. Red card. 'Surely I got it from you?'

'Oh, did I? Well, I suppose I must have.'

Sonia Spiller collected a coat, car keys and a lead. I don't know why she didn't walk down to the sea front. It was no distance.

'I just hope that damned car doesn't follow me today,' she said, showing me out. The cold hit my face as well as her words.

'What?' I pretended indifference but my heart did a nasty jerk. I stared at the front door step, seeing the cracks, hoping for inspiration from some good angel.

'I keep seeing this stupid red car with black spots,' said Sonia, putting the dog's collar on with unnecessary force. 'I think it's following me. Everywhere I go, this damned car goes, too.'

'Heavens,' I said. 'How strange. Probably just a coincidence. After all Latching is a small place. I'm always meeting the same people.'

'I can't see the driver so I don't know who the hell it is that's following me. I'm only seeing the car. It was even parked at the leisure centre where I play squash the other day.'

'Heavens, however do you find time to play squash?' I laughed, trying to distract her. 'All this DIY work in the house . . .'

'I like to keep fit. I've always been very fit.'

'Thank you, Mrs Spiller. You've been very helpful. Bye, Jasper. Have a lovely walk.'

I had to walk away from where my car was parked, go in a northwards direction, abandon it. I'd retrieve it at a safer time. She'd spotted my car. Not funny. I wondered how I could get round still using the ladybird. I felt sick that she'd seen me. It was a blow. It had been too damned convenient. I couldn't go back to the car park until it was dark.

There was no way I was going to creep around Latching till nightfall. Sonia Spiller might be keeping her own vigilance behind the curtains. Hell, hell. Still, the owner could be a health fanatic, pumping iron daily, flabby-arm syndrome. Better, surely, to let Sonia think that. If the car disappeared from the car park now, it would only confirm her suspicions and she might attach those suspicions to Lucy Locket.

Plan: continue parking car in health club till Sonia was reassured that ladybird was not following her. Whip into health club, heavily disguised, then follow Sonia on foot or on trusty bike.

The Latching Bowling Club had grounds at the back of the town, behind the gasometer. They were green and peaceful with designer flower beds and shrubbed hedges now lying in winter fallow. The flowers always looked spectacular in the summer, bedded out at great expense, colour co-ordinated and making intricate patterns. Last year, one flower bed had been a clock face and another an anchor riding the waves, Latching's town emblem.

Now it looked as if an enraged dinosaur had gone on the rampage over the lawns – obviously the creature had been denied membership. The JCB was abandoned, wedged into the debris of the veranda and porch of the pavilion. I suppose if they removed it there was a danger that the whole building would collapse. I wandered around, hoping to spot something that CID had missed, i.e. a baseball cap with name and address inside.

The huge mud-caked yellow machine had certainly done a lot of damage. It was a gruesome sight, the caterpillar wheels halfway into the veranda, the scoop about to shovel down half a wall. Seriously, it might be the revenge of some middle-aged bowls fanatic who had been denied membership. Who else would want to wreck such havoc apart from mindless youths high on beer and vodka?

I ought to speak to Brenda Hamilton, the club secretary, but hey, hold on! I caught myself up sharp. This wasn't my case. I wasn't being paid money for this. DI James might treat me to an occasional plate of chips, but he'd never even taken me out for a meal.

This reminded me that I hadn't eaten. My feet went on autopilot to Maeve's Cafe, a slightly run-down place, one street back from the sea front. Mavis, the owner, cooked the best fish in Latching, caught overnight by one of her brown-faced fishermen. She was crazy about fishermen, their muscles, the danger they faced nightly, the taste of salt on their skin. I don't know how they found time to woo our Mavis since they were out fishing all night and slept all day. Maybe they made up for it when the weather was bad.

She looked contented enough on her diet of fish and fishermen. It was impossible to put an age on her. She could have been fourteen or forty. The eyes were mature but the body girlish. She had got over her nasty dose of Not Talking to Jordan, relating to one of my past cases a while ago, and actually smiled at me across the counter.

'Hi,' I said. 'I'll have anything that'll warm me up.'

'Is this breakfast, lunch or supper?'

'I can't actually remember.'

'You need someone to look after you,' she clucked.

'Have you got a spare fisherman?'

'All taken, sorry.'

A big mug of tea appeared at my window table, as I liked it, very hot, weak and sweetened with honey.

'That'll keep you going. Where did you get that scarf? It's pretty.'

'I don't remember, but you can have it, if you like it. Change of neck. It would suit you.'

'Thanks, Jordan. Nice of you. I never have time to shop.'

Mavis grilled an enormous plaice for me. It hung over the edge of the plate like a ballerina's skirts. With it came a side dish of mushrooms, peas and shallots. Not a scrap of crisp batter in sight.

'Where's my chips?' I asked.

'Not good for you,' said Mavis, who served chips with everything, even chips with chips.

'If you say so,' I sighed.

Eating healthy was my lifestyle so I could hardly complain. Not so, DI James. I'd never seen a man put so much grease down his throat, yet his tanned skin was clear, frame lean and firm, eyes unclouded. I hadn't measured his cholesterol count. I couldn't get near enough to measure anything.

As I paid for the meal, I warned Mavis about the Mexican hold up. 'Be careful, locking up, late at night,' I added.

'I'd like to see them try anything on me,' she said. 'That's why I keep this under the counter.' She produced a heavy old black frying pan, battered and corroded with rust, but as solid as hell.

I shuddered. 'You need an alarm. A panic button fixed somewhere.'

'I don't panic, girl,' said Mavis complacently. 'But thanks for the warning and the scarf. I'll wear it now.'

The collection of medicine bottles were snapped up immediately I opened the shop that evening. A retired Latching doctor, taking a stroll, was jubilant. I vaguely remembered him from my WPC days, stitching up someone's cracked head.

'These are really excellent,' he said, looking but not touching. He stooped a bit now, iron grey hair, pale blue eyes behind half-moon specs. 'What do you want for them? I collect old medical curios.'

'To be honest,' I said. 'I don't know. I haven't put a price on them. They're not going separately, only as a collection. There's ten bottles, some still with stoppers, one is slightly chipped. Would you like to make me an offer?'

'These are definitely Victorian. Forty pounds for the lot,' he came back instantly.

'Done,' I said. So what. Maybe they were worth more but I liked to keep stock moving. 'How would you like them packed? We don't want to disturb the dust.'

'Just put them in a box, laid flat.'

The old medicine bottles went out in the same box they'd arrived in. I hoped the good doctor was not fussy about germs.

'Hey, what's this? You've missed something at the bottom.' His eyes were keen despite the specs. His long fingers groped around the newspaper packing.

It was a very small item of glass. A perfect mermaid, barely two inches long, her scaled tail shot with blue and silver dye. The doctor took it out and looked at it closely.

'Venetian, I should say. You ought to take it to a dealer, though it would look nice in your window.'

The mermaid was enchanting, her face a vision of sweetness. I knew I'd have no trouble selling it if I could even bear to let it go. And I'd given the wino £1.50 for the lot to get rid of him.

Where had he got it all from? No clues on the cardboard box. Standard supermarket recycled.

The doctor carried the box carefully while I held open the door. I wondered if I should remind him of my beat days but thought not. The less people who knew the better.

'Thank you. I never thought the hat suited you,' he added with an attempt at an elderly wink.

'Nor did I,' I smiled. I might need a retired doctor one day.

'Why did you leave?'

'Ah. A long story. A disagreement with a superior over letting a rapist go scot-free.'

He shook his head. 'One of life's injustices?'

'Something like that.'

'I know all about injustice,' he added.

But it wasn't me who needed a doctor. It was Mavis. Doris came rushing in the next day, pale faced, clutching her chest and hardly able to speak.

'The cafe's been robbed . . . Maeve's Cafe, late last night, and Mavis has been beaten up. They hit her . . . oh my God, with her own frying pan.'

'Come in, come in. Slow down, Doris . . . tell me about it.'

'She was just locking up when they came in and threatened her. They took all her takings, the whole lot and the float. It came to quite a tidy sum,' she sobbed. 'Just like the Mexican restaurant next door, the night before. Latching isn't safe any more, not for the likes of us ordinary folk.'

I sat Doris down and gave her a glass of my medicinal brandy. 'Is Mavis going to be all right? Is she in hospital?'

Doris coughed on the fire-water. 'Her face is a bit of a mess, she says, bruised and cut up. She managed to stop the bleeding with a scarf before the ambulance people came. They kept her in overnight, but she's gone back home now. I'm going to close my shop and spend the day with her, cheer her up a bit.'

'You do that,' I said soberly. 'Give her my love. Tell her I'm so very sorry and I'll see her soon.'

Doris finished the brandy valiantly, still talking, and hurried out to visit her best mate, her best friend. I think they'd been to the same school together. They'd known each other a long time.

Now I might not be getting paid a cent for it but this was, from this moment on, definitely my case. No one was going to bash up my friend and get away with it.

Five

O liver Guilbert was pleased with my report. I phoned him as soon as Doris had gone. It had as many details as I could pile in without giving away the guise I had taken on.

'This is really excellent news,' he enthused. 'Just what we want, playing squash and up ladders. Well done, Miss Lacey. But how can we prove all this home decorating?'

'I don't really know. It's a tricky one. I can hardly set up CCTV.'

'And she hasn't spotted you?'

The phrase was unfortunate. It was beyond a joke now.

'Not that I know. If her claim is fraudulent, then she will continue to be cautious. There's enough in the newspapers about social security claimants in wheelchairs seen carrying wardrobes and going to disco parties. She's being very careful. By the way, Mr Guilbert, I am going to reduce my daily charge to you as I am no longer able to do a complete twelve hours surveillance every day.'

'Why is that?'

I didn't tell him that the ladybird had been sighted by Mrs Spiller and my mobility curtailed. 'I have taken on another case.'

'Is that ethical?'

'In this instance, yes. It's for a friend. She's been beaten up, rather badly. They held her up in her restaurant. I have to find the mindless thugs who did it.'

I had upgraded Maeve's Cafe. He did not need to know everything.

'You mean Mavis, don't you? Yes, bad news travels fast. I've heard all about it. Nasty business.'

'You know Mavis?' I was surprised.

'Of course, best chips in Latching. Except that I mustn't be seen going in there. We have a restaurant on the top floor of Guilberts and it would look disloyal. Our chef would have an emotional breakdown.'

'That's sad,' I grinned to myself. 'To be denied one of life's pleasures because of store loyalty.'

'It's the price of running a store with a well known name.' I got the feeling he was laughing too. I hoped Leroy thought he was worth a late-night coffee. I might have cultivated him myself if my affections had not been totally engaged elsewhere.

I spent the rest of the morning starting files on Mavis and the Bowling Club. Mavis was my case from now onwards. Pay was not important although I did need to eat, occasionally.

Sonia Spiller was walking the seafront with Jasper on a lead. The tide was in, lashing the shingle with relentless surges of power. Yet the sea did not seem to have its heart in the exercise, acting more like a circus lion going through an old routine. It had grown tired of winter, yearned for frolicking summer visitors and sunlight on splashing waves. Even the seagulls were walking. They had given up aerial displays for Christmas, conserving their strength for Boxing Day largesse. Chunks of dry Christmas cake, cold roast potatoes, lumpy bread sauce and mince pies. They were not choosy.

I was wrapped up to my nose with a woolly scarf, hair crammed under a felt brimmed hat, thick glasses, anorak zipped to the neck. My mother would have had trouble re-cognizing me. Only my eyes showed.

Jasper was dejected. His tail hung down, brushing the promenade. Perhaps Sonia was breaking his spirit. He barely took any interest in his surroundings, ignoring doggy smells, not investigating any interesting bags of garbage piled against the bins.

There was nothing to video, nothing that was out of the ordinary. I hoped she'd shift a rock, drag driftwood out of the sea, help pull a laden fishing boat up the shingle. But she only meandered, hands in pockets, thoughts locked away.

I kept my distance, consulting a street map occasionally like a lost tourist. The video camera stayed in a carrier bag, knocking against my hips. At least I was getting a walk, short but bracing. I reached out for the tip of the wind with my nose, but it had gone.

The object of my affections phoned after lunch, his voice cutting into my brain, activating neglected sex cells. My heart leaped and settled into a different pattern. I was adding up my shop takings: zero, nil, nought.

'I've had a complaint,' he said, coming straight to the point. 'A woman phoned the station a while ago, very annoyed. She said she is being stalked. By a man in a woolly hat who drives a red and black spotted car.'

'Is this a joke?' I said.

'You are the only person in Latching with a car that meets that description.'

'So? I don't look like a man or haven't you noticed that much recently?'

'Perhaps one of your many disguises?'

'I am not completely stupid. I would not use my car to follow anyone. The ladybird's too distinctive. Unique. Not made for surveillance.'

'But this woman is convinced that she is being stalked by a spotted car. And you do admit you are following someone?'

'Yes, I am on a surveillance operation for a client, but not in my car, and definitely not stalking. That's a fabrication. Have you checked whether she is a trustworthy citizen of Latching?'

'She?'

'You said a woman phoned. Obvious gender connection.'

'She has lots of evidence. Times, dates etc.'

'Oh, come off it, DI James. Anyone can come up with times

and dates. Fact and fiction. Anyway, who is this stalked person?' I asked, putting righteous indignation into my voice.

'Mrs Sonia Spiller, number eight Luton Road, opposite the health centre where you were locked into the steam room a few months ago.'

'I'm touched that you remember.'

'I remember the scalds on your skin.'

I went weak with the thought of DI James remembering anything about me. My new skin melted without being touched. My brain was seriously out of control.

'OK, occasionally I still go to the health club, for my asthma. In fact, more frequently of late, as my courage is returning.'

'So do you know anything about this stalking?' he went on. 'Mrs Spiller says she's seen someone peering into a downstairs window of her house.'

'There! That proves it's not me. I never peer into windows. Not my style and you know that.'

Nor had I, at number eight, ever peered into a window. Far too risky. Perhaps Sonia did have a stalker or perhaps Oliver was employing two PIs. It was known in the profession. I didn't like the idea of a back-up but it made sense.

'She says this stalker was filming her when she was playing squash. She caught sight of the flash of a lens. She's also getting a lot of dead phone calls, probably someone checking to see if she's in. They can't be traced as the caller dials 141.'

'Husband checking if she's taken a lover,' I said flippantly. Caught sight of the lens . . . she was supposed to keep her eye on the ball. 'What else has she dreamed up?'

'This spotted car keeps driving past her house.'

'Oh, come off it, James. If I'm going to the health club, then, of course I drive past her house. She lives opposite. The woman is paranoid.'

'How do you know she lives opposite?'

Ah. Quick thinking required. 'I can count. Hey now, bright idea! How about you employing me to keep tabs on this stalker? My rates are reasonable. I could slot it into my current case and reassure this lady that no one is going to bother her. I might even find out who it is.'

'Ingenious idea,' said DI James with more patience than he usually showed. 'But you know I am not allowed to employ civilians.'

'Are you going to give her protection?' I hoped not.

'I don't have the resources. Nothing has actually happened, nothing threatening, that is. I don't have the manpower and she hasn't actually asked. So you can't help me with this one?'

'Sure, I'll keep an eye open every time I drive past her house. If I do see a man in a woolly hat peering in a window, you'll be the first to know. By the way, the driver of the runaway JCB was an old geyser wearing a baseball cap.'

'An old geyser. How old? Is that the best you can do? I should have thought your beat days would have trained you for a more detailed description.'

'This is a secondhand description. Remember, I wasn't there and it wasn't me that the JCB got away from. It was a couple of your flashy new patrol cars. And who thinks up those colour schemes? Red and yellow stripes, green and yellow squares, flashing blue lights . . . at least my car is colour co-ordinated.'

'Let me know if you get any more information.'

'Not if you accuse me of being a stalker.'

'I didn't accuse you.'

'And give my regards to that new DS Evans,' I said sweetly. 'He has such lovely manners.'

The phone was replaced swiftly, but I had the satisfaction of knowing I had stumped him. It was not often I got the opportunity. But if Sonia Spiller did have a stalker, what on earth was going on? Did Oliver Guilbert know? I decided to keep my eyes wide open. Perhaps I was the one being followed. Now that was not a pleasant option. Creepy. It had happened once before, when Derek had stalked me and I had been thoroughly frightened. I knew the feeling. He had even thrown a stone through my shop window.

I went along to the Mexican restaurant, three doors down

from my shop. It was not a place that I ate at although I love Mexican food, enchiladas, tortillas, hot and spicy. The price list in the window put me off. I couldn't fork out for one dish, not even a starter. The price of a meal would keep me in food for a whole week.

The restaurant was dimly lit as it was before opening time. But a lot of cleaning was going on. The small tables were topped with ethnic oilcloths, nothing flashy. Plants hung everywhere; travel posters and mirrors decorated the walls. They were putting fresh flowers in bright red vases and laying the tables for the evening's customers, folding red linen napkins. The recent hold-up had not defeated them.

'Can I speak to your manager or owner?' I asked. I handed over one of my new business cards. They were understated, professional. The waiter was small and dark skinned, lithe. He flashed a smile at me.

'Of course. Please wait. Please sit. A glass of wine, *señorita*?'

Heavens, this was the treatment. Why had I never come here before? They were my neighbours in the row of shops.

'Thank you,' I said. Who cared what the time was? 'A house red would be fine.'

'Chilean special for you. Only the best.'

In seconds the young man placed a statuesque glass of wine before me. It was not a normal sized wine glass. It was enormous. The wine glistened like dewed rubies. I was speechless and could only thank him with a Goldie Hawn smile.

'Boss not long,' said the waiter.

For a few estatic minutes I forgot all about being unloved, unpaid and unbelieved. The wine ran through my veins, healing the hurt. I almost forgot why I was there. The air broke into an alcoholic fragrance. This was supposed to be working.

Then the owner/manager arrived. He was a clone of Omar Sharif, only a decade younger. Even the same sultry, dipped-in-treacle voice. Half of Latching's female population must be swooning at his feet, especially the newly divorced and widowed. No wonder they paid his prices. He was a man and a half,

43

Maya, Toltec, Aztec, all the Spanish conquests. I could see ancient civilisations spinning in his blood. I hoped he had a name I could pronounce.

'Miguel Cortes,' he said, holding out his hand. It was brown, strong fingered, capable, wrists sprinkled with dark hairs. He was wearing a crisp white shirt, jeans and a chef's striped apron. The man cooked for a living. He liked food.

'I'm Jordan Lacey,' I said, hoping my tongue could get round the wine. 'I'm a private investigator. My office is on the corner, behind the First Class Junk shop.'

'I know,' he said, his dark brown eyes drinking in my face, my casual clothes, my tawny red hair. I don't know what he thought of them. His clientele were probably smart dressers. 'I have seen you many times. You are the brave lady who tackled the thugs on the pier. I nearly sent you a bottle of wine only I forgot. Forgive me?'

'It was nothing,' I said. 'I just happened to be there. Would you mind telling me about the hold-up on Sunday night? I know you have already told the police all that you know. DS Evans was at my shop the next day.' I threw in Ben Evans' name for authenticity. 'And it does link with another case I am working on.'

Miguel threw up his hands, almost rocking my wine. I took a quick drink. 'It was like on the films. These two men. They came in, ordered the lot, good meal, no expense spared. Wine, my best. They waited until everyone had gone, heads talking close together. The place was empty, my staff gone, then they held me up. Guns to my head. Beat me with the butt of the guns. I am no fool. I give them everything. Hundreds of pounds. It had been a good night. Still I am here and I am alive.' His face was full of emotion, reliving every moment.

'It must have been awful,' I sympathised. 'Can you describe these men?'

'Sure. Stupid. Mean. Greedy.'

My hopes fell. 'What did they look like? You know, face, height, appearance? Did anyone use a name?'

'Sure. One was called Chuck. I know that. He had a thin moustache. The other man was mean looking.'

Miguel Cortes was not being very helpful but he had been in the kitchen, cooking and cleaning, before he had been held up. His eyes soothed me with kindliness. I knew what it meant now to drown in a man's eyes. It was the wine seeping deep into my veins.

I got out my notebook, hoping I could see the lines. 'Let's go into details. Man One – named Chuck with thin moustache? What else can you remember?'

It was painful but I dragged out some sort of description from the charming Miguel. Chuck: short, thin, dark hair, moustache. Man Two, the mean-eyed one, took on a more recognisable form: heavy, tall, thinning hair, greasy. I would run these by Mavis and see if the hold-up pair were the same.

I was on my second large glass of Chilean when I ran out of things to ask. It was a long time since I had felt so comfortable with a man, sitting in his restaurant, three doors down from my shop. Resolution: I should cultivate my neighbours.

'You never come here,' said Miguel, with regret in his voice. 'I never seen you eat here.'

'I can't afford your restaurant.' I couldn't afford any restaurant.

'Ah . . .' He nodded knowingly. 'My prices are high, on purpose. I only want special clientele. The credit card, the expenses, the big spenders. If you want to impress someone, you come to eat Mexican; casual decor but the food is from heaven.'

'I can believe that.'

'So what do you eat, Miss Jordan Lacey who is a very private detective?' This man was laughing at me, but I did not mind. I could forgive his brown eyes anything.

'Soup, salads, sandwiches. Occasionally fish at Maeve's Cafe.'

'Please eat here, one night. Be my guest. We will sit together, no hurry, have a bottle of good wine and talk about nice things, not hold-ups and beatings.'

'But don't you have to cook . . . ?'

'I have a deputy. That is what I am training him for.'

It was hard to leave, to extract myself from the calming surroundings. I didn't even know the name of the restaurant. I looked at the menu. It was called Miguel's. Some detective.

Miguel Cortes stood outside on the step of his restaurant, a big dark man full of confidence, not defeated by the hold-up or the gun to his head. Why was he here in Latching? I could not understand his purpose in cooking in a small restaurant in this seaside town. He should be in some big, cosmopolitan capital of the world, cooking for diplomats, politicians, millionaires.

'Thank you for the wine,' I said. 'And the information. It will all help. I'm sure we'll find these thugs.'

'*Gracias. Adios.*'

I turned slowly with a new thought. 'If they took everything, then they will have taken all the credit card counterfoils as well?'

'Yes, sure, but that money I do not lose. It is credited to my account instantly.'

I went back to my shop and drank two glasses of cold water to dilute the wine. It was a long time since any man had been so pleasant to me. I could not count Jack on the pier with his awful coffee. Miguel had style and made me feel cherished and cared for. Fool. He probably had a Page Three sex-bomb at home, panting for his return every night.

Doris put her head round the door. She'd been discount shopping again, arms full of bags. She smiled knowingly.

'Dishy, isn't he?'

'I don't know what you mean.'

'Miguel. It's taken you long enough to meet him. I could have told you.'

'I didn't need telling.'

'Jordan Lacey, you should have therapy. Miguel Cortes is the most gorgeous man in Latching, apart from several fishermen, and you have only just noticed him. There are queues of women from here to Brighton who will pay anything for a smile with their meal. And you've just had time for free.'

'I was working.'

'Pull the other one. I can smell the wine.'

'How's Mavis?'

'Poorly. It's been quite a shock.'

I spent a pointless evening standing near number eight Luton Road, an address I was beginning to dislike, which was not fair to listed fishermen's cottages. I pretended I was waiting to meet someone, preferably tall and crew cut, consulting my watch (imaginary). Walking up and down, I had only the valley of my intimate thoughts to keep me warm.

Where was this husband of hers? Colin Spiller. Surely he came home sometimes? The last train from London would have arrived by now.

The cavalier eyes of Miguel intruded. If only DI James would look at me with a quarter of Miguel's directness and warmth, I would be a happy woman. My one-man reticence was holding me back. Why didn't I just throw myself into a gloriously mad, ecstatic Central American love affair and forget the cold, critical detective whose one diversion in life was pulling me to pieces?

'Clear off,' someone shouted from an upstairs window. 'You've been hanging about long enough. He's not coming. Go home or the police'll get you for loitering.'

It was so humiliating.

Six

M avis lived somewhere down at East Latching, the stretch of beach that is almost desolate, *sans* boats, *sans* buildings, only a narrow gravel path at the top of the shingle. I got the address from Doris. On my way, I stopped at Mr Hopkins, my friend the greengrocer, and bought three bunches of his best spray carnations and some clementines.

'I don't want bargains,' I said. 'These are for a friend who's had a rough time.'

'That's nice. Going to see Mavis, are you?'

I contained a sigh. 'Does Latching know everything I do?'

Fred Hopkins grinned. 'Take her this nice melon from me. If she's not eating, it might tempt her. Sweet and ripe, easy on the teeth.'

'Thank you,' I said. I had forgotten about teeth hurting, though I'd been beaten up several times.

I parked the ladybird outside the small terrace of Edwardian villas where Mavis had a flat. Doris said Mavis lived upstairs at the end, number five B. It overlooked a pond where there were ducks and geese and clusters of thick reeds for nesting. The water was a deep green, very Monet, and as still as glass.

'You can't miss it,' Doris said. 'It's the one with weeds growing in the window boxes. She only plants her boxes once a year. Half an hour's work and she's done all her gardening.'

It was a terrace of small, sturdy houses, built to last, with bay windows upstairs and downstairs, identical porches, ornate lintels over the front doors. They looked as if they had been built for the staff of a much bigger house. If they had, then the mansion had long since been pulled down for an estate of identical semis.

It was easy to spot the prolific weeds. Grass and dandelions hung down in a tangle from the two upstairs windowsills, a wisp of cow parsley. I pressed the bell under a label saying No. 5b. Footsteps came down the stairs and somone peered through the peephole.

'Who is it?'

'It's Jordan, Mavis. Jordan Lacey. It's quite safe to open the door. It's only me, no one else is here.'

'Oh, Jordan, thank goodness. Just a minute. I'll let you in.'

I heard bolts being drawn back and a chain rattle. Mavis had turned her home into a fortress and I didn't blame her. She opened the door cautiously and it was a shock to see her. I tried not to stare, but her face was a mess. One eye was half closed and an ugly bruise spread down her cheek, a gross purple and yellow stain. Her chin was swollen and butterfly strips held together random cuts on her other cheek.

'Wow,' I said, heart contracting. I put my arms round her gently and gave her a light hug. She smelt of Radox muscle soak and was still in her dressing gown. 'Oh Mavis, I'm so sorry.'

'You did warn me.' She tried a smile, but her face was too stiff. 'Let's go upstairs.'

She went through all the locking and bolting again. I presumed the tenant of the downstairs flat had agreed. I followed her up narrow, carpeted stairs and into her kitchen. It was small and odd-shaped, with the air of once having been the smallest bedroom which had changed its purpose in life and was still trying to get used to it. I don't think Mavis did much cooking at home for there was only a kettle jug and a microwave oven. She took the flowers from me.

'They're lovely,' she said, trying to find a vase. 'Thank you.' She seemed to have no idea where she kept her vases and opened several doors before finding a simple white china jug. Her hands shook as she took scissors from a drawer to trim the stems. She was still in shock. I didn't help her.

'The melon is from Fred Hopkins. He thought you might have lost your appetite.'

'I have. It hurts too much to eat. All I can do is drink. Tea and soup, that is,' she hastened to add. 'I get my spuds from Fred Hopkins. Only the best, of course. He gets them in special for me. Would you like some tea?'

'I'll make it,' I said, worried that she would scald herself. I didn't want to talk about the hold-up, but I had to if I was going to catch these mindless thugs. I filled the kettle and switched it on, got out two mugs. They were brightly coloured flower mugs. She had plates to match. I wondered if her fishermen liked them.

'I've spoken to Miguel Cortes about the men that held up his place. He's given me some descriptions but they're pretty vague. I know it must be painful for you to talk about it, but are you able to describe the men?'

'I'll never forget them,' said Mavis grimly, staring out of the window at the duck pond as if she had never seen it before. 'Their faces will haunt me for the rest of my life.'

I had never heard such misery in her voice. Mavis had always seemed such a cheerful, down-to-earth person, with her basic cooking and basic fishermen lovers. She had some dogmatic ideas at times, but they were all part of her personality.

'But why you? Maeve's Cafe, of all places. You do good business, but hardly in the same income bracket as the Mexican restaurant. How much did they take?'

'I don't know. I hadn't counted the takings. It could have been about a hundred pounds or thereabouts. It hadn't been a good day, too cold and too wet. Your policeman friend hadn't been in, that dishy DI James. You're a bit slow there, Jordan. Or some of my other regulars. Christmas and all that.'

'Ah, Christmas. What will you do for Christmas? You won't be alone will you?'

'Oh no. There's Doris. She's a brick. She's staying overnight with me for a bit. Till I feel better. And I'm not going out until my face is back to normal.'

She meant she would not be seeing any of her male friends until her face was back to normal. It was sad. I didn't think they bothered to go fishing over the holiday, no sales, too much turkey being consumed.

'What about the cafe?'

'It's closed for the time being. I'll re-open it when I feel better.'

'Let's sit down and I'll read you the descriptions of the two men who did the Mexican, if you feel like it, that is.'

'Let's get it over with.'

'Man One: short, dark hair, skinny, small black moustache. Man Two: heavier, bit taller, thinning hair, mean-looking eyes. Not much is it?'

'That's them.' Mavis put down the mug of tea and dabbed her face with a handkerchief. 'I'd know them anywhere.'

'Are you sure? You aren't just saying this because you want the two cases to be linked? Sometimes people do agree with whatever is suggested to them.'

'You know me. I don't agree with anything I don't agree with.'

I did know what she meant. Mavis was not the most amenable of people if she was in a certain mood. Several times I had borne the brunt of her sharp tongue.

'Can you add anything, give a more detailed description?'

'I didn't have time to look, Jordan. They came up to the till and demanded the money. They were wearing Mickey Mouse masks but in the tussle, they slipped down. I got out my frying pan but the larger man grabbed it out of my hand and started hitting me with it. What could I see? I was trying to protect my face. Look at the back of my fingers, all black and blue.'

They were badly bruised and swollen. It was a wonder she didn't have broken bones.

'Mickey Mouse masks?'

'Those plastic things from fancy dress shops.'

'What happened next?'

'They pushed me down on the floor and then one of them

said, "Get the money, Chuck," and I heard them opening the
till and tipping out the money.'

'Are you sure the name was Chuck?'

'Oh yes, I remember that all right. Clear as a bell. Then they
ran out of the door and I called 999 pretty quick. There was
blood splashed everywhere. The edge of the frying pan must
have been damned sharp.'

'Thank you, Mavis. I expect CID will want you to look at
photographs of known villains, in case you can identify them.'

'I'll do that, anytime. But I'm not going out till the bruising is
gone,' she sniffed.

'They'll probably send a car for you.'

I left soon after. Mavis was tearful and I can't cope with
tears. I'm a pathetic friend. Before I left I put the little glass
mermaid into her hand.

'Pressie,' I said. 'To cheer you up.'

Mavis looked quite astonished with her one open eye. The
mermaid was exquisite, her scales sparkling. 'Ain't she lovely,'
she said, looking closer. 'Thanks, Jordan.'

I had no idea how I was going to track down these two thugs.
They must be the same pair. Chuck is not exactly a universal
name in these parts. If I could get sketches made, I could trawl
the town, shops and restaurants where they handled money, in
case the two were seen again. But the men could be anywhere by
now; Brighton, Manchester, even Belfast if they could stand the
weather.

It was hard to understand the thinking behind the second
hold-up. The price board in Maeve's Cafe should have told
them that the till was not exactly floating in cash. Or was there a
different motive, something more sinister? Mavis had a lot of
men friends, the kind with small sexy bottoms. That always
causes trouble.

Number eight Luton Road looked shut up and unoccupied.
The car had gone. There was no eager doggy face peering out at
a window. I cruised Latching looking for the white Toyota,

registration now memorized, but Sonia was not out shopping. She was not walking the beach. I drove in and along the lanes of cars parked at the supermarket. I drove to the leisure centre on the outskirts. Sonia was nowhere. She'd escaped me again. At this rate I should be biting my nails and grinding my teeth. Shopping list: aromatherapy oils and meditation mat.

And no Maeve's Cafe open where I could down my sorrows in chips. Where was I going to eat now? Where was DI James going to eat? This was serious decision time.

There seemed to be activity at the Latching Bowling Club. Several police cars were parked outside and I could see figures moving about. Something was happening. It wouldn't hurt to have a look around. I parked the ladybird alongside a patrol car and strolled towards the group of men talking.

Oh dear. Something had definitely happened. They were getting out the scene of crime tape.

'Go away, Jordan.' DI James strode over to me, inches taller, shoulders squared and in bristling Detective Inspector mode. 'This one is ours. We found him, not you. So go away.'

'I'm a spectator. A member of the public. You can't boss me around. Found who. Found a him? Who have you found?'

My eyesight is pretty good. The damaged pavilion was not that far away and the JCB was still impacted on the pavilion, but even at that distance I could see something very disturbing. In the shovel, bucket, whatever it was called, a stiff white thing was protruding.

It was a human arm.

I had never really got over finding the nun in Trenchers Hotel. Death is never pleasant. Now this and the rest of the body must have been there, under the debris when I had wandered round the damage the other day. Zero marks for not noticing. The arm looked like a slim branch, skinned of bark and bleached by the sun.

'Do you know who it is?' I asked.

'No, not yet. But we have found a baseball cap.'

'Good heavens, the driver. The person who drove the JCB off

in the first place. But how did he end up in the shovel? If it is him. I mean, he was last seen in the driving seat, rampaging across parks. It doesn't follow.'

'Jordan, I don't have time for this now. I'm too busy.' DI James dug his hands into his pockets and swung away. 'A nasty business.'

'But you did ask me to cruise the pubs, which I did, at great expense to my weekly units. You did ask me to listen to the gossip, which I did, endlessly, and I got stuff from the security guard. You can't cut me out now, simply because the crime has moved on from building site theft and damage to murder.'

'How do you know it's murder?'

'You don't put yourself in a bucket and let tons of debris fall on you. If you want to commit suicide there are easier ways. Say, an overdose of Valium, cannabis and a bottle of brandy.'

A fleeting glance crossed DI James' face. He looked concerned. And that was a one-off. His brain was teetering between work and some tenuous link with normal human relationships. 'You're not thinking . . . Jordan?'

'Heavens, no,' I said brightly, storing that momentary feeling of concern. 'I've everything to live for. Work. Shop. Several panting admirers beating a path to my door. Life is immense fun. Except that I don't know where to eat. Mavis is staying out of circulation till her face heals. And by the way, it's the same pair of thugs that held up the Mexican. One of them is called Chuck. Tell your nice DS Evans. He'll be interested.

'There's Macaris, McDonalds or the Pizza Hut.'

I shook my head. 'No, thank you. Let's find a small pub with music and a secluded garden.'

It was an outrageous suggestion. But he did not seem to mind. His eyes softened and mellowed for a fleeting second before he went back to the grisly discovery. Was there more than an arm, or just a single arm? It made me feel so sick that eating was the last thing on my mind.

'Sorry, James. I have to go. You know how it is. I'm following a dog called Jasper.'

'See you around, Jordan. Don't overdo it. You look stressed.'

'I'm not stressed,' I said indignantly. 'I'm just ignored and lonely. When did you last come round for a coffee?'

But he had gone. He was striding away, looking chilled and just as lonely. He was a man, work-obsessed. He had no time for anything else. Not even me.

Jasper was in the car. Sonia had left him locked inside. He looked miserable. He was cold and it was way past his lunch time. I did not know what to do. I could hardly knock on her door and say I was representing the RSPCA now. I didn't think Mrs Spiller would believe me. But why had she left the puppy in the car? Had she had enough of him? People threw unwanted pets out of car windows onto the motorway.

I walked down to the end of the road and back again. The sky was leaden, dark clouds gathering in fistfuls. The temperature was falling. My hands were frozen. I ate a yawn. I'd forgotten my WI gloves again. I ought to have them sewn to the sleeves like a toddler.

I went into a phone box. At least it was working and not vandalised. This was not a mobile type call. I put in some coins and phoned the local animal rescue branch.

'There's a puppy been left in a car in Luton Road,' I said. 'It's a bit cold for a puppy to be left outside, isn't it?'

'How long has it been there?'

'About twenty minutes, maybe a lot longer. I don't know.'

'We'll send one of our inspectors round. It won't hurt to have a word with the owner. We could offer a training programme if the owner is having trouble.'

'Good idea.'

'And what's your name, please?'

I put the receiver down and cut off the call. Sneaky, but I did not want to be traced. Nor did I want Sonia Spiller to catch sight of me and report that her stalker was about again.

The answer was right in front of me. I went into the health

centre, signed on and went upstairs, passed the changing rooms, the steam and sauna, into the gymnasium suite. It was not full. A few members glanced at me. I was not dressed for a workout.

One of the high windows faced number eight. I climbed onto an exercise bicycle, set a programme, level six, and began pedalling. The extra height was just enough for me to see over the wall and into the front paving area of number eight. The car was still there with Jasper looking forlornly out of the back window.

It was some time before a man in a fawn raincoat turned into the house. He stopped by the car and said something encouraging to Jasper. Jasper responded with violent tail wagging.

He rang the bell and after a pause, the door opened. It was Sonia Spiller wearing a tracksuit, her black hair tumbled over her shoulders. A man stood behind her in the dimly lit hallway, one hand casually on the door.

Was this the elusive Colin Spiller, the husband I had never seen? I leaned forward on the bike, perilously balanced on the pedals. My foot slipped and I almost fell, nearly catching my toes on the spinning pedals.

I knew the man in the doorway. It was a shock. And it was not Colin Spiller. Oh no, it was a man I knew quite well. A man I liked. A man I trusted.

Seven

T he bike went into a slight wobble as I hung onto the handlebars, my feet still slipping off the pedals. They spun round and caught my ankles on their next circuit. I leaned over to see what was happening on the doorstep.

Sonia Spiller stormed out of the house, obviously annoyed, and unlocked the car door. Jasper bounded out, delighted at his release, all forgiving, poor doggy fool. The inspector was saying things which Sonia clearly did not like and she turned on him, giving him a piece of her mind.

The man standing in the doorway made some comment, calling her back indoors perhaps. Jasper jumped around, getting in the way, adding to the confusion. The inspector gave Sonia some leaflets which she barely glanced at. Anyone could see she was going to throw them away as soon as he had gone.

I drew back in case they saw me.

The confrontation was coming to an end and the inspector was losing. He shrugged his shoulders and walked away. He was used to awkward people and knew when to retreat.

Sonia and the man went back inside number eight, Jasper scampering after them, and closed the door.

I slipped off the bike, wishing I had not caught sight of the man in the doorway. I was not prepared to change all my opinions about him without further evidence. There might be a perfectly good reason for his presence. Though just what that was I could not think. I needed a walk or a good night's sleep. If I could sleep. My brain was bruised and I did not like the feeling. I was lost in a maze of fast-growing prickles.

It was getting dark. Rows of Christmas lights were glowing along the front and strung across the shopping arcades. Cascades of tiny silver lights twinkled prettily through the trees in the clock square, as if Tinkerbell had suddenly multiplied in their branches. Santa drove his reindeer from one store shopfront to another; a seal balanced a ball on his nose; Charlie Chaplin raised his bowler hat, then his walking stick. Latching council had gone to town with their decorations.

The Christmas fair people were arriving, rumbling lorries with trailers and caravans, littering the seafront with food packaging and empty Coke cans. The young love the scary excitement of the funfair attractions, screaming their heads off as they pay to be spun around in the air at dangerous speeds.

The tide was out, stretching blackly into the distance, the sand cold and dark. The pier tracked out to sea on grim stalks, dominant and forbidding. A loose shuttle of rain was peppering the deck. I avoided walking under the pier in the dark, keeping to the hard sand not far from the shingle. This was no time for going further out. My leather boots were not made for the shallows and pools.

It was bitterly cold, but I welcomed the numbing. My brain did not want to think. *Non compos mentis* was more comfortable. I had to put a gate on my feelings and stop sitting on it. Emotion doesn't travel in a straight line. The darkness was like a shield. I was hidden within it, scarf wrapped round my neck, hat down to my ears, hands thrust into pockets. The sand was a murky grey carpet, barely visible, rocks hard and sharp to catch my unaware feet. All my thoughts concentrated on walking safely in the dark, the sound of the waves lulling my ears, the wind low and mocking.

I could not understand why we, as a nation, are so keen to scare ourselves silly. It was something to do with facing death but knowing that you are going to walk away afterwards, a bit shaken maybe, but unscathed. It was the thrill of acceleration, the spinning, the suspension, hanging upside-down, the sudden lurching towards the earth, chests flung hard against a harness or bar, the sickening drop. Errck!

Every year the fair had some new attraction. Something higher, faster, steeper, more devilishly cunning. One day, some skinny thirteen-year-old blonde with butterfly clips in her hair was going to die of fright, strapped in mid-air.

I'd once paid a pound to go on a rotor drum amusement ride. The Cage, I think it was called. All the kids were smaller and younger than me. It was my way of ridding myself of this absurd fear of funfairs. We stood against the inside curved wall, not talking. It revolved at a gentle pace. OK, I thought, I can cope with this.

But all at once the floor dropped several feet and the drum gathered speed. Centrifugal force, fierce and unrelenting, pinned us against the wall. The kids turned themselves sideways, spread-eagled, upside-down. I closed my eyes and prayed for the ride to end. It was the most terrifying thing I'd ever experienced. I thought my inside was going to fall out or be flattened to a pancake. Something sharp stabbed into my thigh. I found out later it was my pen.

It took me a while to get over it.

The long walk along the beach helped my suspicions settle down and make some kind of sense. But the man in the doorway of Sonia Spiller's house was another male to be struck off my meagre list of upper bracket guys. It was shrinking rapidly. I knew the sea was dangerous in the dark, but I was beyond caring.

Stars shone through the inky blackness of the sky putting on their own Christmas show. I climbed the shingle and found a gap between caravans parked on the front. Some of the caravans were bigger than my two bedsits.

More lorries and forty-foot trailers were crawling along the promenade as a clutter of amusements arrived. They parked in alloted spaces and unfolded their contents like a magician's box. The sides of the trailers let down to become the floor of a sideshow; central hydraulic hubs arose to support the wheels;

cars and capsules and swings were slotted into place with the ease of fifty venues a year. Bolts were slammed in, structures braced, motors run.

The shingle disappeared, the sea retreated. The seafront became one enormous pleasure park. Win a giant stuffed lion, leopard, bear, dog on the Black Jack stall. Get it home somehow. There, what do you do with it? Sit on it? Give it to the hamster?

Then I saw Sonia Spiller. She had hurried right into my line of vision. No Jasper tugging on a lead. She was obviously going somewhere and I had the perfect opportunity in these crowds to follow her. She had a heavy zipped holdall with her which she was swapping continually from hand to hand.

It was easy to keep her long black hair in sight. Her sheepskin collar was hunched round her ears, crunching her hair untidily. I wondered where she was going with such purpose. Twice I almost bumped into her as she stopped abruptly. She was looking for someone, or watching out for someone. Someone who said they would meet her along the front, forgetting the crowds and the funfair perhaps?

The milling crowd had become a blur, a noisy disjointed blur, but I kept seeing another figure. It was a man in a belted navy raincoat, quite smart and upright, wearing a sort of uniform. He had a dark cap on, but I could not make out what it was. Again, I got the impression of a uniform. I could not see his face, shut in shadows.

Something was not quite right. I couldn't pin it down. A feeling chilled my spine. A thin, driving spike of fear. Then the truth dawned.

We were both following Sonia Spiller. He paused at the same time as me, half turning his face away; he hurried at the same time, not wanting to let her out of his sight. She was right. She did have a stalker. This man was definitely stalking the woman. Her instinct had been right.

Sonia made a sudden dart across the road and into Macaris, the Italian cafe and ice cream parlour. She stood at the counter, ordering, and moments later took a tall, frothy coffee in a glass over to a bench seat. She cupped her hands round the warmth, her face a mixture of agitation and anxiety. She was clearly worried.

Now I wondered what the raincoated man would do. He went into a bus shelter opposite and lit a cigarette. He leaned against the wall. But he wasn't waiting for a bus. He let two Stagecoaches to Arundel go by before he even changed his weight.

She was sitting so still, letting her coffee grow cold. I was dawdling by a burger stand, the hot, greasy odour of old frying fat in my nostrils, keeping both of them in sight.

'Want anything?' the woman behind the counter asked. She was tossing sizzling onions, turning burgers, rolling sausages with easy familiarity.

I shook my head. 'Haven't made up my mind, thank you.'

Nothing was happening. My legs were turning to stone. Any moment now my tear ducts would freeze over. I really wanted to go home. But I couldn't move. This was what I was being paid for.

'Coming on the bumper cars with me, Jordan?' It was DI James beside me. I hadn't seen him coming. He was also staring across the road as if trying to work out who was holding my attention. He was in casual dark clothes, face pinched with cold, eyes glittering with frost.

'No way, I've sampled your driving.'

'I'll keep to the speed limit.'

'Go find some other sucker.'

I don't know what makes me say these things. I would have followed him to the moon, trod burning coals, climbed Mount Everest in bare feet. I tried to soften my words with a smile but it was a long time coming.

'I'll let you drive,' he offered.

It was probably the second or third nicest thing he'd ever said to me. How I treasured these morsels of normal human behaviour between us. But I was working, had to stay anchored, earning my crust. How could I tell him without telling him?

In that moment of inattention, Sonia Spiller disappeared. The bench seat was empty. She had gone. So had the man at the bus stop. Together, separately or whatever, but they had both gone. I'd blown it again.

I turned to James, failure in my eyes. There was no reason to refuse him now. He was daring me to take him on, though a bumper car was hardly gladiatorial.

'Still wanna go on the cars?' I drawled, hoping he'd changed his mind. 'I'll drive.'

'Yes.'

'I'm not paying,' I shivered.

'Did I say anything about you paying? I always treat a lady.'

We walked back to the bumper cars, not touching, with the steady, even stride of coppers. They had set up early and were already doing a good trade. We climbed into a dingy blue bumper car. There was hardly room for two tall people. We sat knee to knee, hip to hip, shoulder to shoulder, material rasping.

'Strap yourself in,' he said.

'I know the rules,' I said, gritting my teeth. Dilemma: did I drive carefully, soberly, avoiding all collisions, impress him with skilled manoeuvring and steering? Or should I drive hell for leather and bump the guts out of him?

Five minutes of hell later – it was a long five minutes – and we slowed down to a stop as the power was cut off. I was still clutching the steering wheel as if I'd just won the German Grand Prix. James had a fixed grin on his face, but I could see from his brow that I had generated some heat. He climbed out stiffly.

'Thank you, Jordan. That was an extraordinary experience. I'm trying to find the right word. Electrifying. We'll hire you to drive when we want some witness scared witless in the back of a patrol car.'

'Gee, you said all that without moving your lips.'

I felt exhilarated and smug. I'd shown him I could drive.

Even the attendant looked shaken. He wouldn't let me on again in a hurry.

The exhilaration had worn off by the time I got back to my bed-sits. I'd behaved like a scabby teenager with a turnip for a head. No excuses. Grow up, Jordan. No wonder James never took my work seriously.

I comforted myself with some burning hot home-made watercress and Stilton soup and French bread. *Très bien. Je suis une belle cook.* I wrote up my notes for the day and realised that I had barely stopped working. Lunch had been less then a memory. I'd existed on air since that coffee with Mavis. Then I remembered that I hadn't told DI James about my conversation with Mavis.

And Sonia Spiller in the Italian cafe, all alone. What could that tell me? I threw on my anorak, grabbed scarf and WI pattern gloves and flew out. They wouldn't have shut yet, not with all the funfair crowd still strolling about, gasping for coffee and hot chocolate.

The cafe was packed to the walls. I could hardly find anyone to talk to. Perhaps I would come here while Maeve's Cafe was closed. They sold twenty different kinds of ice cream. Hardly staple diet.

'Sure, I remember the lady,' said the dark-haired young owner between serving and taking money. 'She sit there for a long time. I ask her if she is ill. And suddenly she runs out, forgetting her bag.'

'Forgetting her bag?' I remembered the heavy holdall and the way she kept changing hands. Excitement gripped me. 'Have you still got it?'

This was a forlorn hope but sometimes my luck changed.

'No, the lady come back for it, only moments ago. You have just missed her.'

I thanked the young man, promised to come back for an ice cream, amaretto flavour. An ice cream in this weather? Serious malfunction.

'Ver' nice,' he promised.

I hurried out, scanning the crowds with laser eyes, hopping and skipping through the clusters of people like someone with urgent business to attend to. Then I saw her. She was going on the pier. No one goes on the pier at this time of night. It was ridiculous. I tried to catch her up, remembering the look in her eyes. She was walking fast, the bag now clutched in her arms.

But no. Sonia Spiller was not going to throw herself off the pier. Instead she threw the bag over the end of the pier, using the strength of desperation to send it as far as possible. I heard it splash into the dark sea. She turned away and went landwards, using the other side of the pier, so she did not pass me.

I leaned over the rail, looking down into the murky depths, but the bag had sunk or already drifted out of sight. There was no way I could retrieve it. It might be washed up on some shore with the next tide, or be taken by the current halfway to Brighton.

I wandered back. We'd never know what was in that bag or why Sonia had to get rid of it. Training weights? For one crazy, horrific moment, I thought it might be Jasper.

Hell's Revenge was revolving at full speed, lights flashing, heavy metal rock pounding the air. It was a large spinning disc with a dozen four-seater capsules bolted round the edges. These capsules spun loosely and erratically in the opposite direction to the base disc. The youngsters were screaming, hair flying, legs and arms waving. Red devils leered from the hoarding.

The ride was over, slowing down and coming back to earth, disjoined legs and hair settling. One capsule held a single male occupant. He looked awkward as if he had slipped although there was a protective bar and brace which held customers in place.

A skinny orange-haired young man in a duffle coat sauntered around, approaching each capsule as it reached ground level, opening the safety catches of the bars and turfing people out.

Suddenly he stopped and ran back to the woman in the cashier's booth. She followed him to the last capsule, annoyance written all over her worn face.

Then she began screaming, a rough primeval sound. It pierced the cold night air. People stopped, alarmed. I moved towards Hell's Revenge, dreading what I might find, knowing what I had already suspected. The flashing lights brought the scene into sharp focus. Beams strobed his face.

The man in the capsule was dead. He wasn't going to get out and stroll to the nearest burger stand for a quarter pounder. He'd been spun to death.

And I knew who it was. My heart nearly came into my throat. His handsome features were distorted, hair ruffled, head lolling from a broken neck. It was Oliver Guilbert, my present employer, now no longer my employer.

He was the man I'd seen earlier in the doorway. The man who had seemed very much at home with Sonia Spiller at number eight Luton Road.

Eight

T he shock rooted me to the spot. Part of my brain told me
   to move. It would not do to be found on a crime scene
again. Being seen (or loitering, as DI James so uncharitably put
it) near the Fenwick fire had caused me enough trouble. And I
had found the poor dead nun myself. No, Lacey, this was
retreat time, and fast.

I shut down my face and turned away. There was enough
commotion going on without another gawping sightseer in the
crowd. More gasps and screaming above the pounding rock
music. People running about. Other fair folk converging,
mobiles at the ready.

Oliver Guilbert. That fit and good-looking young man and I
had liked him so much. I could barely believe it. He was just not
the funfair type. Those smart suits, expensive shirts and ties.
That car. It didn't go with riding Hell's Revenge.

Leroy Anderson came into mind and I hoped she was not
emotionally involved with Oliver. A third death in a year might
be too much for her. The death of her sister, Waz, and her
employer, Adrian Fenwick, had come as successive blows and
had been hard enough.

I could contact her but I did not want to be associated with
more bad news. She'd find out soon enough. News in Latching
travelled faster than light.

It wasn't easy to sleep that night with uneasy dreams. Next
morning I decided to phone the leisure centre. I unlocked my
shop, hoping the routine of opening up would calm my equi-
librium. I wrote out a hasty notice: LATE NIGHT SHOP-

PING SOON and hung it in the window. It might attract a few customers. Some Christmas. Then I remembered I had an invitation to Brenda Hamilton's party for members of the Latching Bowling Club next Friday. Perhaps I could go catch a few minutes of festive joy. It might cheer me up.

I looked up the number for the leisure centre and keyed the digits.

'Latching Leisure Centre. This is Tracy. Can I help you?'

'Hello, Tracy,' I said brightly. 'I'm sure you can. I want to give a friend of mine a year's subscription to the leisure centre for a Christmas present. Lovely idea, isn't it? He plays such a lot of squash. But I thought I'd better check first to see if he's already got a year's subscription.' Every word hurt. I should be using the past tense.

'What's your friend's name?'

'Oliver Guilbert.'

'One moment please. I'll look it up for you.'

'Thank you.'

I heard the silence of computer keying. Tracy coughed and spluttered.

'Yes, Mr Guilbert is already a member but his subscription runs out at the end of the year.'

'So I could give him a new one?'

'Sure.' She coughed again. 'Shall I send you a form?'

'That's not necessary. I'll call in for one. You've got a nasty cold.'

'Yes. I can't get rid of it. I've had it a week. I'd go to the doctor but it's always such a long wait.'

'There's a lot of it about. Hot lemon and honey with a generous dash of whisky,' I suggested. 'Knock it on the head.'

Tracy giggled. 'That'd knock me on the head all right.'

So Oliver Guilbert was also a member at the leisure centre. I wanted to run the film I'd taken of Sonia playing squash. Perhaps he'd been calling at number eight to arrange a match. Highly unlikely. And he'd not said a word about knowing Sonia Spiller at our first meeting. He'd given no indication that she was anything more than a customer, a customer suing for a hundred and fifty thousand.

Phew. It was a lot of money said like that. Nasty suspicions floated round my head. I do have this suspicious mind. On a piece of paper I made two lists. They were headed: Reasons for Paying Out and Reasons for Not Paying Out. I knew what I meant.

Reasons for Paying Out
1. Keep SS quiet.
2. Good name of store.
3. Maybe store gets back half as cut.
4. Or OG gets half as cut.
5. If OG gets more than half (blackmail).
6. Has OG pressing debts?

Insurance scams were not unknown. Get the insurance pay-out and then share it among themselves. Pay for a few nice holidays.

Reasons for Not Paying Out
1. Claim proved untrue.
2. Store going bankrupt.
3. No insurance cover.

My pen hovered over the last line. I was getting a headache. No insurance cover. Supposing the Guilberts did not have any valid up-to-date insurance? What if Oliver, for the last few years, had been using the insurance money for something else, say, his posh car, his suits, his subscription at the leisure centre?

How could I find out? But why should I bother? It wasn't my case anymore. I might not even get paid for these few long, boring days of surveillance.

I'd lost out again. No case, no money. Only a couple of writs to deliver. It was unlikely I'd get anything new before now and Christmas. I might as well turn shopkeeper.

There might be some domestics after Christmas. It was the season for family rows. More couples split up over Christmas than at any other time of the year. Perhaps it was the way she made the gravy.

The shop door opened and someone came in. I slipped out of my office. Shoplifters were rare in my neck of the woods, but there was a chronic shortage of cash.

It was a schoolboy, about fourteen years old, grubby, dishevelled, rumpled socks, tie undone, shoelaces trailing, Harry Potter shape. I checked his zipper.

'I want a present for my Mum for Christmas,' he said, coming straight to the point. 'Your shop's called First Class Junk. My Mum always says she wants everything first class.'

'A discerning lady. But this is not first class new. It's what it says, junk or second-hand, occasionally antique.'

He had freckles and clear hazel eyes. The eyes reminded me of Oliver Guilbert and my heart contracted. I wished I had not started suspecting the man of anything devious. And he wasn't even cold yet.

'*Antick* will do. My Mum likes old things. She likes my Dad,' he grinned.

This was obviously a family joke so I smiled and laughed, tried to think what I had that might be pocket-money size. My £6 label could easily come off.

I had an early Edwardian evening bag stored out the back, waiting for its turn in the window. It was beautifully embroidered and decorated with bugle beads and pearls with a silk lining. The clasp was tortoiseshell. I had thought I might use it myself if DI James ever asked me out to something special. It was well worth six pounds, but I felt the boy's mother might like it.

'How about this evening bag?' I said, going to fetch it and removing the price label with a swift flick as I returned.

The boy looked at it. 'OK. How much?'

'Two pounds,' I said.

'I'll have that. Can you gift wrap for me in Christmas paper?'

'I'm sorry. I'm right out of Christmas paper.' What a nerve. Kids these days expect everything done for them.

The boy was looking at a tray of old military cap badges that I'd put in the window that morning. I'd found them at the bottom of a box of junk I'd bought at a house clearance sale. Sad. The collection of badges had once been somebody's pride and joy. I had no idea of their value but put six pounds on each until I had time to check them out with a book from the library.

'I'll have the Liverpool Regiment Badge, the Officer's Cap Badge, the Rifle Brigade, and the Cameronians Glengarry Badge,' the boy said.

I shook my head ruefully. 'They are very expensive,' I said. 'Way beyond your means. They're six pounds each.'

'I can add up,' he said. He dug into his pocket and brought out a handful of crushed notes. He sorted out five dirty five pound notes and put them on the counter. 'Twenty-four pounds for the badges, two pounds for the bag. Twenty-six in all. Right? Make it twenty-five the lot.'

'Twenty-six,' I said faintly, breaking out into a sweat. He dug out a pound coin and put it on the counter with a surly glance. Served me right. You can't go by appearances. Probably ran three paper rounds. I'd get my money's worth out of him somehow. 'Have you been to the funfair on the front?'

'Yeah.'

'Been on Hell's Revenge?'

'Yeah. Tame stuff.'

'Didn't look tame to me. Pretty scary. Could you fall out of a seat?'

'Nargh. You've got shoulder straps and a bar in front of you. No way could you fall out.'

'Does it jerk your head around?'

'Nargh.' He was getting tired of the third degree and was edging to the door. 'Kids' stuff.'

He was gone. How he managed to walk without tripping over

those trailing laces, I'd no idea. I gathered up the money slowly. I'd practically given him the Edwardian bag. I hoped his mother appreciated it.

No one else was coming now. I didn't feel well so I shut up the shop and drove home. The car responded instantly. She had a nice little engine, nothing noisy or aggressive. I knew vaguely where Brenda Hamilton lived on Sea Avenue, one of the big houses passed the roundabout where Latching went up-market into West Latching.

I needed a hot bath to soak the smell of death out of me. I was stung by the thought of Oliver dying so young. I did not want to die yet. There was too much to do. And how could I leave my dearest James? Some other woman would get him. Though I suppose, in death, he would be always mine. I would be at his side every moment of the day (and night), protecting him.

My legs were aching, and my arms and my head. This was weird. The bath made me feel hotter than ever. Out of curiosity, I took my temperature. The thermometer was the digital kind so it couldn't make mistakes. My temperature was 102. I'd got the 'flu.

The acute symptoms took a couple of days to work through my system. Every few hours I crawled out of a tumbled, smelly bed for jugs of lemonade. My asthma didn't like the influenza virus and had a few arguments with it. My cough hacked.

The depression was bad, linked with Oliver's death no doubt. Nothing cheered me up. I couldn't even listen to smooth jazz. In time I staggered back to the world, weakened and several pounds lighter.

The phone rang as I washed. It had that feeble Joshua kind of ring. Sweet, apologetic, on the make.

'Hello, Jordan. How are you? Thought we ought to get together for a Christmas drink.'

'Hi, Joshua. That's a nice idea but I'm not very well. I'm getting over the 'flu. Fever, aches and pains.'

'Jordan! How awful. I'd better ring off.'

I could hear the panic in his voice. He was such a baby. 'It's not contagious by voice. You can't catch it down a phone line,' I reassured him.

'Look after yourself,' he said hurriedly. 'I'll ring again when you're better.'

I delivered the two writs that afternoon that were long overdue. The recipients looked surprised. They did not expect to see a half-ghost person doing legal legging. Perhaps that's why they took them without the usual hassle.

It was the evening of Brenda Hamilton's party already. Gloomy thoughts did not encourage party mood or party dressing so I switched on Jazz FM and let some soul and blues lift my spirits a few degrees.

Party dressing? That was a joke. Newest indigo jeans, embroidered blue cowboy shirt and usual boots. It was the best I could do. Black leather jacket, of course. Anyway, I was driving there, so wrapping up weather resistant was not essential.

My face was wan. I put on some mascara. I might meet the man of my dreams.

How can you go to a party when Oliver Guilbert has died, my conscience nagged, as I drove towards Sea Avenue. This is work, I argued. How come? The JCB is not your case. In fact, you are out of work at the moment. No cases, no work, no income. There's the two muggings. So who's paying you? Santa Claus?

I can't argue with my conscience. It wins every time. But I still went to the party.

Brenda Hamilton lived in one of those really nice houses that faced the green sward that ran along seawards after the road petered out. They were built just before the war, no particular style, but elegant and well proportioned. It had a classy blue tiled roof, a balcony along the upstairs, a spacious porch and an in-out circular drive. Lights were on in every room and I could see tasteful Christmas decorations. Every room was crowded, too. I nearly turned on my heels.

'Come in,' said Mrs Hamilton, seeing my hesitation on the doorstep. 'I've forgotten who you are but do come in.'

She was smartly dressed in black silky trousers and tunic top, lots of gold jewellery, bangles, beads and earrings. She jangled at every movement. My efforts were easily unnoticed.

'You did invite me,' I said. 'Jordan Lacey.'

'Of course.' She clearly didn't remember when she had invited me and I did not remind her. 'Come and have a drink. There's a lovely punch. We used a very good claret. You can taste the difference.'

I bet, I thought.

'Do you know the members of the Bowling Club? I'm sure you can introduce yourself. There's lots of people you'll know. Just make yourself at home, Jason.'

'Jordan.'

So I made myself at home. It was a big room with the kind of comfort I scarcely knew. The armchairs and two three-seater settees were deeply upholstered in pale blue silk damask and would be like sinking into a cloud. The toning carpet was inches thick. The wall lights were gold-fitted and mirrored so the light reflected. Floor length blue silk curtains hung with intricate pleats and swirls that looked like a stage set.

I couldn't think why she would have wanted to do the bowls party on the cheap. Mr Hamilton must be seriously wealthy.

There was plenty of hot wine punch, with floating fruit and mint leaves, and my Victorian wash bowl looked splendid on the long side table. She'd used a snowy white linen tablecloth and there were trays holding excellent cut glass. She was also using the jug for replacement punch. Even the soap dish held peanuts.

'One of my finds,' I heard her telling a guest. 'Victorian. Isn't it perfect?'

One of her finds indeed . . . she'd wanted a cheap old soup tureen.

Plenty to drink but very little to eat. A plate of reheated

sausage rolls from a supermarket bumper pack came round and disappeared in seconds. A few cheese and pineapple sticks appeared and vanished. I soon finished the nuts.

I wondered if I dare wander out into her kitchen and find something edible. The punch, even though it was cheap, had gone straight to my head. It needed soaking up with food. I ate some fruit out of the punch bowl.

I also did my duty networking the party. When anyone asked me, 'And what do you do?', I immediately brought up the subject of the JCB. They all had their theories, ranging from drunk yobbos to disgruntled ex-bowls champions.

'Disgruntled?' I asked. 'Why should this be? I thought bowls was the most civilised of games. It always looks so polite and slow paced.'

'They've just changed the club rules and everyone is up in arms about it,' said a thin woman, her rimmed eyes darting round the room as if daring anyone to contradict her.

'Does it make a difference?' I asked. 'After all, it's just a game.'

'It's not just a game,' she said indignantly, slaying me with crisp consonants. 'Mind what you say, young lady. Remarks like that could get you into trouble.'

Wow. I slid away, murmuring insincere words of apology. An unwise second glass of punch reminded me that I had a dependent car to drive home.

The room was getting very warm. I shed my leather jacket behind a chair. It was a potent punch. Cheap wine or not, it was lethal. Perhaps Mr Hamilton, knowing his wife's parsimonious ways, had emptied a bottle of his best brandy into the bowl. I wondered how many of the guests would be breathalised on their way home. The orange juice was hardly touched. I did not know which was Mr Hamilton. No one introduced me.

'Just as well I've arrived,' said DI James, coming straight over to me. 'You're going to need driving home. You're weaving.'

'I'm not weaving. This is circulating.'

'Call it what you like. Don't you know you can't drink and drive?'

He looked more than just normally gorgeous. DI James's stern look riveted me to the carpet. He was all dark and authoritative with glinting blue eyes that bored into my soul. The air broke into a fragrance of desire. The vaulting halls of my head filled with love for him. I wondered if he would ever know . . .

'And I thought it was just plain old red-tinted lemonade,' I said, enunciating carefully. 'Punch isn't usually so strong.'

'And you aren't eating . . .'

'There's nothing to eat. The food is rationed, half a sausage and six nuts each. Trust me, I've counted them. Find me something to eat and I'll eat it. Don't worry about me, I can easily walk home.'

'Not in that state, you don't.'

'What state? I'm not in any state. Go on, I dare you . . . walk me the line, go on. I can walk any straight line.'

'Stay there,' he commanded. He walked back into the hall-way and was gone several minutes. Someone refilled my glass. He returned with a tumbler of water and a banana. 'Drink this and eat this.'

'You're wonderful,' I said, all smiles and lashes fluttering. I was glad I'd worn mascara. 'What would I do without you?'

'End up in the slammer.'

'Why are you here?' I asked, mouth full of banana.

'I was invited. JCB, remember? Thought I might get a line.'

'They've just changed the club rules and some people are upset,' I offered.

'Really. But it's only a game.'

I grabbed his arm. 'Don't say that. You mustn't say that. It's enough to get you lynched here. It's seriously hostile.' I was even copying words.

'Jordan, I'm taking you home.'

I was still holding onto his arm. 'If you want to take me

75

home, then you have to do something for me first. Please, James.'

A flash of apprehension clouded the vivid blue of his eyes. He was obviously thinking mistletoe and other pagan rituals. 'So . . . ?'

'Don't look so worried. I only want to sit in a real armchair. You know what my upright moral chair is like. But these sofas are just so utterly decadent and look so comfortable. I want to feel what it feels like to sit in one.'

'I don't know what you're talking about . . .'

But I was leading him across the room to one of the three-seaters and I sank down into the soft cushions, pulling him with me. It was like wallowing in marshmallow. The party guests vanished into the haze of alcohol and cigarette smoke. There was only James and me. No one else existed. We were alone on a soft, blue cloud, a doorway to heaven. I could barely breathe. The closeness and intimacy was suffocating me. I hardly dared to look at him, but I could feel him and smell him.

For a few delicious minutes, maybe I slept. When I awoke I was stone cold and he had gone.

It was a unpalatable revelation. My muscles knotted with anguish. James did not care about me. I wondered if anyone, anytime, was ever going to love me. Perhaps I am so worthless, so unlovable, that life will be a stoney road, always alone, growing middle-aged and increasingly crotchety as desolation envelops all hope. It was a sobering thought.

'Miss Lacey?' A young male voice entered my ear. 'DI James had to go. They have found something washed up in the river estuary down at Shoreham. He's asked me to drive you home.'

The world tipped right again as DS Ben Evans' face came into view. He was smiling as if driving a scatty, only just sober, red-headed female home was his sole ambition in life.

'Terrific,' I said, hoping I could heave myself up off the drowning softness. 'I'm ready to go now. My car is outside. The red and black one.'

'I know. I've seen it,' he grinned. 'We call it the bumming bird.'

My brain was too befuddled to think up a smart answer. It would come to me in the middle of the night. But I did latch on to one fact.

'That something in the river,' I asked. 'Is it another arm?'

Nine

I t was a phone call that I never expected to get. The voice was achingly familiar. A voice that I had spoken to every morning for almost a week. It was unsettling. Yet I had seen the man, neck broken and very dead. It could not be Oliver Guilbert.

'Can I speak to Miss Jordan Lacey?'

'This is Jordan Lacey. How can I help you?'

'Am I interrupting you?'

'No, go ahead.'

'I wonder if you could come round and see me in my office this morning. It's not something I want to discuss on the phone.'

'Do I know you?'

'I'm sorry. This is Francis Guilbert of Guilberts Department Store. We haven't met but I feel I know you.'

I did not want to see Mr Guilbert. It was too close to Oliver's death, but he probably wanted to settle up the arrangement we'd had. Tidy things up.

'Would eleven a.m. be OK?'

'Yes. Take the lift to the fourth floor. My office is just beyond the restaurant.'

I was in my usual jeans and polo-necked jersey, not Guilbert gear. My props box was unhelpful, but a man's red brocade waistcoat might lift the outfit a notch. Unusual but distinctive. The anorak was creased from daily wear. Shopping list: second iron.

I locked up the shop and put CLOSED FOR LUNCH on the

door. A bit early for lunch, but then I was a hungry working girl. Breakfast had been a banana. It only took ten minutes to walk into the centre of town where the big department store dominated the High Street. The window displays were Christmasy with inches of fake snow and silver trees hung with baubles. The prices of the goods in the windows were way above my budget any day of the week. Given the one hundred percent mark up, Guilberts could well afford my daily charge for following Sonia Spiller. I hoped Mr Guilbert was not going to try and cut me down.

Judging by the crowds milling around inside, most carrying the distinctive mauve carrier bags, business was booming. I strolled through ground floor perfume and cosmetics, handbags, hats (fur) and accessories (leather), then took the lift to the restaurant. That was also packed with shoppers having reviving coffees and cakes. Why couldn't I have that relaxed lifestyle? Would I ever have time to sit and do nothing? The smell of coffee was stomach churning.

A discreet door at the end was labelled, Administration – Private. I knocked and opened it. An open-plan office was beyond, busy with clattering keyboards, phones ringing, and the murmur of voices. A fresh-faced receptionist smiled at me from her desk.

'Can I help you?'

'I have an appointment with Mr Guilbert. Miss Jordan Lacey.' I was about to flourish my card but changed my mind. Sometimes it paid to be discreet.

'Please go straight through to Mr Guilbert's office. It's the last door at the end. He's expecting you.'

The door had a plainly typed card saying, Francis Guilbert, Managing Director. He did not believe in throwing money away on fancy name plates. I knocked again, went in when he said, 'Come in,' found myself in an office, equally austere. But I glimpsed a high panoramic view over Latching from the windows, the sea, pier, hotels and shopping precincts. It was magnetic even on a frosty winter's day. I could have spent hours leaning on the windowsill, watching the world at the seaside.

But there was a man behind the plain oak desk and he stood to greet me.

'Miss Lacey. Thank you for coming to see me at such short notice. Please sit down.'

'Mr Guilbert,' I said, immediately. Get it over with. 'I can't find the right words to say how sorry I am about your son, Oliver. It was a terrible accident.'

'Thank you, Miss Lacey. We just don't understand what he was doing on the funfair ride. It was so unlike him. I'm trying not to think about it. He was such a fine young man and liked by everyone.'

'I know. It's always a shock. How is your wife taking it? She must be devastated.'

'My wife died two years ago, so she has been spared this tragic time, thank goodness. I expect you think it's strange that I am here, at work.'

I shook my head. 'No. Work can be therapeutic. It can anaesthetise the pain for a while.'

'And these three days running up to Christmas are our busiest time. We're open Sunday as well. No point in staying at home in an empty house.'

Francis Guilbert was an older version of Oliver with thick grey hair brushed back, the same hazel eyes and strong features, a lean figure with only the slightest thickening around the waist.

'You have wonderful views of Latching from your office,' I said, changing the subject deliberately. I was no good with death.

'That's why I chose this room as my office,' he said. 'I can see that you love Latching as much as I do.'

I smiled. 'My favourite seaside place. Now, I take it you wanted to see me about finalising (oh dear, wrong choice of word) the work I was doing for your son.'

'He did tell me you had made considerable progress, Miss Lacey, and I thank you for that, but I have actually asked you here on another matter. Guilberts is losing a lot of merchandise and it seems to have escalated in the last week. I believe there is a well-organised gang at work. It's not the usual type of shoplifter.'

'Tin openers,' I said.

His bushy eyebrows raised slightly. 'We are losing whole rackfuls of clothes, entire consignments of shoes, bags, suitcases, umbrellas. Yet we have received the goods in the normal way and signed for them. It's not your average shoplifter stuffing a jumper up her skirt, if you'll excuse my crudeness.'

'Doesn't sound like it,' I said, wondering where I came into this, and feeling decidedly guilty about my furtive squirts of Diorissimo.

'My son thought highly of your ability, Miss Lacey, and I should like you to work here undercover – I believe that's the term – here in the store. Starting as soon as possible.'

It was just as well I was sitting down. I can't take surprises like this. Work in the store! Percentage staff discounts came straight to mind although I had already bought the silk scarves for Cleo and Leroy. Downside: I'd have to shut my shop. What about my Christmas trade?

'I can start now,' I said before he changed his mind.

'Good. I was hoping you'd say that. We'd pay you the same rate as Oliver was paying you, plus lunch in the staff canteen. We take on a lot of extra staff at Christmas, so one more will hardly be noticed. We'll provide you with a black dress and black shoes. You can choose what you like from Ladies Dress on the first floor and charge it to my account.'

I was walking on air again. I was about to become a bona fide shop assistant, undercover, in a discreet black dress. I half hoped DI James would come in and be suitably impressed by my rise in status.

'Thank you. It will be necessary for me to check your various security systems and tagging devices.'

'Of course. My warehouse manager, Alan Preston, will explain everything to you, then I suggest you become a sort of roving assistant, going to departments that need help. This is quite normal with our seasonal extras. Alan Preston will be the only person to know that you have another role here.'

'The fewer people who know, the better.'

'I trust Alan Preston implicitly. He's worked for us since he started as a boy in the basement warehouse, stacking stock.'

'And the Sonia Spiller investigation?'

'I think that can take a rest for the time being but I will pay you any sum owing up to date.'

'I'll send you an invoice.' It was beyond me to work it out in my head especially with Oliver's death drawing a hasty line.

'And sometime I'd like to run the videos you took.'

'Sure. I'll drop them by.' After I'd checked that none of them showed Oliver Guilbert visiting number eight Luton Road. No point in muddying the water now.

We shook hands and said goodbye. I felt really sorry for Francis Guilbert coping with the frantic Christmas rush while his son resided in the Latching mortuary with a label on his big toe.

Since Mr Guilbert hadn't offered me a coffee, and particularly as I could now afford it, I had a pot of coffee in the fourth floor restaurant. It came in one of those fancy gilt cafetière contraptions where you press the coffee grounds down through boiling water, then strain it off. It was a generous size and I got two cups out of the pot, sitting in the restaurant pretending I was one of the idle rich.

In Ladies Dress on the first floor, I explained that as I had to start work straightaway, Mr Guilbert was being debited and then I would pay him back from my first week's wages. I didn't care if they believed me or not.

I chose a plain, straight, creaseless black jersey dress, with a scoop neckline and three-quarter-length sleeves. There was a tiny satin edge to the neckline. Very neat. It would do me for parties, weddings, funerals, dates with DI James or DS Evans, whoever asked me out first. The shoes were black suede pumps with the tiniest heel, a sensible choice as I was going to be standing on my feet all day.

'The black will look lovely with your hair,' said the assistant, who was quite a friendly soul. 'Here, how about this black velvet scrunchie to tie it back? It was in the autumn sale, only £1.50, but it didn't go.'

'Thanks. Perhaps I'd better pay for the scrunchie myself.'

'Don't you worry. I'll put black accessory on the bill. Could be anything.' She winked, then looked sorry that she had winked. 'Mr Guilbert won't check it. I mean, he's got a lot on his mind.'

'You mean, his son . . . ?'

'Sure. Isn't it awful? A funfair of all places. We just can't believe it. The last place . . .'

'Did you know him well?'

'He was very friendly. He visited all the departments regularly and stopped to listen to anyone. We could go to him with complaints, suggestions, problems. We shall all miss him.'

'Perhaps he did it for a dare. You know, Hell's Revenge.'

'Some dare. I don't believe it. Not like him at all.'

I put my own clothes in one of their mauve carrier bags and left it in my allocated locker in the staff cloakroom. It was like being back at school with a locker, only this time I got a key.

I tied my hair back with the scrunchie and tried to look dedicated and professional, when really I wanted to whoop around a bit. Mr Preston would not be impressed if I whooped around. My errant legs were on the verge of a tap dance along the corridor. At this rate I'd have to tie them together.

Alan Preston was not in his office. He was down in the basement talking earnestly to one of the female staff (black dress). It was easy to recognise him from the sober suit and plain tie, also from the worried expression on his face.

He was in his late forties with a thinnish face and pale brown hair combed neatly in place. He was wearing spectacles which seemed to be sliding down his nose and needed constant pushing up to the bridge.

'I simply don't understand it,' he was saying. 'We can't be out of luxury jug kettles. We had a delivery only yesterday. I saw it come in myself. Would you ask if the customer can come back tomorrow and we'll put one aside for her. I'll give the suppliers a ring.'

'Certainly, Mr Preston. She's got an account so she probably won't go elsewhere.'

'We don't want to risk that,' he rumbled.

As soon as he was on his own, I introduced myself. He'd been told of my purpose there. He launched immediately into a whole list of goods which had gone missing recently, including the consignment of luxury jug kettles.

'The stuff's disappearing under my very nose,' he said, pushing his specs up. 'I can't understand it and I can't explain it. Perhaps you'll be able to throw some light on the problem. It's got to stop. We're losing thousands.'

'Perhaps you'll take me through all aspects of your security system,' I said, as if I dealt with security systems every day of the week. My own shop security system was a front lock and a back bolt. Anyone could be rifling through the place at this very moment.

Mr Preston took me to the back of the warehouse area where there was a loading bay. He explained the electronic locks with codes on the double-bayed door. The codes were changed frequently.

'There's coded locks on all the doors to the store, customer, staff and goods entrances. Only three of us know the codes, Mr Frank, Mr Oliver and myself. Oh, I keep forgetting, so sad . . . only two of us now.'

'Very sad,' I murmured.

'There are magnetic tags on most of the clothes and accessories but, of course, not on electrical goods. There's a sophisticated alarm system with video cameras on all the walls near the ceiling. The tagging machine is over there. We tag everything before it goes upstairs in the service lift. Our store is well protected.'

Video cameras . . . automatically I looked up. Thank goodness the tap dance had been aborted.

'Yet they are stealing your merchandise.'

He sighed. 'And I wish I knew how.'

'Someone must have discovered the codes, knows how to disarm the security alarms, shuts off the videos and robs the store while it's closed.'

'Impossible. I think the goods are being smuggled out while the store is open. But how, I just don't know.'

'I know you're busy, Christmas and all that, but I really do need a list of your staff and a list of all the goods which have disappeared recently.'

'No problem. My secretary can print out a couple of lists for you. I'll leave them in a sealed brown envelope with Iris, the receptionist. You can pick them up in about an hour.'

'I appreciate that,' I said. 'Thank you for your help, Mr Preston. I'm sure you've got a lot to do, so I'll start my own surveillance now. I need to learn where everything is. Some pattern may emerge.'

I did not really know what I was talking about. I was out of my depth. Come back hate letters and trashed WI stands. This was going to be a serious failure but I kept a smile on my face and went into seasonal extra role. It could have been fun going round all the different departments, but I was too worried to take much pleasure from the tour. Perhaps the thieves had dug a tunnel under the store and were moving the stuff out onto the beach where it crossed the Channel in a fishing boat, hidden under a pile of smelly nets. Some hope.

A lateral thought nagged me like toothache. Supposing I tried a different tack? Instead of finding out how the goods were stolen from the store, supposing I went to the end of the trail and tracked the goods back to Guilberts?

An almost impossible task but there was a glimmer of hope. My smile began to look a degree more natural. A customer asked me the way to Linen and I was able to tell her; another wanted to know the closing time.

'We're staying open till seven o'clock tonight,' I told her.

'And we are open all day on Sunday.'

'Thank you, miss.'

A girl in torn jeans and windcheater passed me, swinging an ancient rucksack. She looked vaguely familiar. Where had I seen her bleached dreadlocks before? Then I remembered. I slid up to her side in my best shop assistant manner.

'Can I interest madam in a tin opener?' I asked.

Ten

Nine to seven was my inescapable routine from now on. It was as intimidating as the clang of prison gates. Start digging the tunnel. Shift work on my beat days was nothing compared to this relentless grind. At least I did not have to stand behind the same counter, but could move about the store as demand demanded.

But I was determined not to neglect First Class Junk. I made a new notice: VERY LATE, LATE NIGHT SHOPPING. I planned to stay open from seven thirty to nine each evening, including this Sunday, to catch the odd panic customer. To hell with my social life. What social life, Jordan? The highlight of my social life was clearly going to be the staff Christmas Eve party after the store closed. It was scheduled for the fourth floor restaurant. Perhaps we got to eat up the leftovers.

The list of staff duly arrived in a brown envelope plus details of the most recent losses. I did not recognise any of the names. Instant villain did not leap out. The stolen goods were all items which would disappear easily. Men's suits, trousers, leather jackets and handbags, electrical goods, perfume, CDs. I couldn't spread the net too wide. I didn't have the time or opportunity.

I decided to skip the canteen lunch, delicious though I'm sure it was, in order to see my friend and goldmine of local information. Jack, owner of the Pier Amusement Arcade, had the mentality of a magpie. I walked fast through the shoppers and onto the pier. The sea air was cool after the artificial temperature of the store. The tide was way out leaving

87

a long stretch of flat and grey sand. It was on the turn, that suspended moment. I knew the tide times by heart.

'Cor. Strewth. Jordan?' Jack swore, spotting me through the bulletproof windows of his kiosk inside the arcade. He keyed in the code to open the door. He kept a very old green steel safe for the money. 'What a corker. Whatcha doing tonight, Jordan?'

It was the black dress, the velvet scrunchie, sample lipstick given me by Estée Lauder beautician, free squirt etc. She'd offered me a make-over too but seasonal extras are not make-over material. Jack had never seen me before in anything but washed out jeans and anorak. My scruff gear as per normal.

'You look a million dollars,' he groaned, knowing he did not stand a chance. His furrowed face fell into degrees of gloom, then recovered as he put the kettle on for his revolting coffee.

'Don't exaggerate, Jack. Fifty dollars perhaps.'

'Would you come out with me if I paid yer?'

'Don't talk daft. I don't go out with anyone.'

'I know that,' he groaned further. 'It's not as if I'm being stood up for some classy fella. You're not one of them . . . yer know?'

'No, I'm not,' I said gently. 'Gosh, that coffee smells good. Can I have a mug? I've skipped lunch to come and see you.'

'Have a biscuit.' He offered an open pack of Garibaldi, the kind scattered with bits of raisins like dead flies. 'My favourite.'

'Mine too,' I lied.

'Really?' He brightened. 'Something else we got in common.'

'I've come to pick your superior brain,' I said. My lunch half-hour was ticking away. 'I'm trying to trace good-quality stolen leather goods, mens' and womens' jackets, windcheaters and handbags. Where do I start?'

'Wanna handbag for Christmas?' he asked hopefully. 'I can get you one cheap.'

'No, thank you, Jack. But I do want to know where you were going to get it from. I guess you don't shop at shops, do you?'

'Catch me going into one of those potsy places. I'd go to a midnight.'

Jack's coffee was thick with whitener and heavy on the sugar. He thought everyone liked it the way he did. I drank some knowing I needed the kick and the calories. 'A midnight?' I asked casually, but my spine was already tingling. 'Tell me, what's a midnight?'

'A midnight car boot, out Ford way. Ain't you heard of them? Thought you coppers knew everything. They get raided occasionally. Like yer regular car boot, only a bit special. In an old barn.'

'And a bit late. At midnight?'

'Course. When the pubs have closed. Not going to lose good drinking time.'

'When's the next one?'

'Termorrow night. Christmas shopping, like. Wanna come?'

'OK.' I must be mad. I'd let myself in for several hours of Jack's eager company and at the same time I'd be raising his hopes when he had no hope at all. But there was no way I could find this old barn place by myself. 'Strictly business, Jack. It's not a date.'

'Have it your way, dicky bird.'

At least I wouldn't have to fight him off like Derek, or be lending him money like Joshua. I knew that much about his character. But it was not going to be easy. He'd want to buy me everything in sight. I'd need to practise a dozen different ways of saying no firmly.

'Pick you up about quarter past eleven. Your place. You gotta be early to get the bargains.'

How did he know my place? But then Jack knew everything. Time was running out. Guilberts summoned the faithful. First call this afternoon was Ladies Dress. Pass me patience and a generous heart. These women spent more on one outfit than I do in an entire year.

Most of the afternoon passed helping ladies size sixteen into gowns size fourteen, agreeing with them that the manufacturers cut everything very small these days. I sold several outfits. I wondered if I got commission.

'Anybody ever walk off with things?' I asked casually to one of the other assistants. She was as skinny as a coat hanger with make-up a quarter-inch thick.

'You bet. You've got to watch some of them, usually the most unlikely of people. We caught a little old lady the other day trying to get a ball gown into her shopping basket.'

'I mean really serious theft.'

'Sure. There's regulars. They try to distract our attention while a mate slides outfits off the rails.'

'What about the electronic tags?'

'They go into the cloakroom and try to get them off. Or they make a run for it, out the front entrance and into a waiting car. Oh, it's all well planned.'

In a tea break, I took the opportunity to commit to heart the brand labels of the present stock of leather coats, jackets and windcheaters. I also memorised the current fashionable styles of handbags. I'd never spent so much time looking at clothes in my entire life. So many shapes and sizes and styles. It was a whole new scenario.

It was dark outside now and trade was intense as office workers called in on their way home. I barely had time to look out of a window. Everyone seemed to have gone shopping mad. I imagined all this stuff changing hands on Christmas Day, half of it unliked and unwanted and returned the week after. Still, it was the thought, as they say, and I still hadn't got anything for DI James. Shopping list: buy gun, shoot self. Slightly.

It was *Last Chance Saloon* time. I'd got two shopping days to Christmas and my beloved was presentless. Not even a stand-ard, slimline diary. I could always pretend that I didn't cele-brate Christmas on moral grounds. Coward.

'Could you help me, please, miss? I want a present for my mother. Something special.' His head was inclined towards me. I could see the merest sprinkling of silver in the cropped hair. If only I could touch it. I knew it would feel like velvet. DI James waited for an answer.

I did my best to come down to earth. I cleared my throat and tried to think of something cool and professional to say. Inspiration looked the other way.

'Certainly, sir. What kind of thing did you have in mind?'

'I've no ideas at all. I thought perhaps you might have.'

His mother. I didn't even know that he had a mother, a mother that was alive and well and about to receive a Christmas present.

'Well, sir. There are these beautiful leather handbags but they are extremely expensive and overpriced.'

'You're not supposed to say that, Jordan,' said DI James, leaning further towards me and dropping his voice low. 'What is this? Why are you here? Is this a career move?'

'Please don't act as if you know me,' I said. 'Pretend you've never seen me before.'

'I've never seen you in a black dress before.' He sniffed in the direction of my right ear. 'And wearing perfume.'

'A free squirt,' I admitted. 'Now about this present . . . is this a genuine purchase or are you just trying to disconcert me?'

'I have a genuine mother and I do want to give her a present. But not necessarily an expensive handbag. I don't think she would appreciate that. She's a practical lady and lives on a farm.'

'Electric jug kettle?'

He shook his head. 'She's got one.'

'Tights, bath foam, scarf.'

'No. Too ordinary.'

'How about a personal CD player so she could walk round the farm listening to music all the time, or around the house, or driving a tractor. Very cool. There's some neat ones downstairs, pretty colours and well designed. She could get CDs of all her favourite tunes.'

'Now you've sold me one of those, Jordan. She enjoys music. Lead the way.'

I took him downstairs to the basement and left him buying a pale mauve Matsui CD player for his mother. Perhaps he might buy two. If pigs could talk. I'd be happy if he bought me a box of After Eights. Perhaps he might return and thank me for my brilliant idea, but he didn't. I scanned the crowds for his dark cropped head but he had gone. As always.

By seven p.m. I was exhausted, ready to drop. The last customers drifted out of the doors and the security men locked up. I changed back into my own clothes and left the black dress in the locker. I actually hung it up. My jeans slipped on like old friends, a warmth I needed round my legs. The plan was to open up my shop, but I was tired and needed a break. My brain buzzed with facts and ideas, spinning in my head as bright as fireworks. My feet took me automatically towards the sea. The tide was in now, crashing against the shingle, the waves dark and mysterious. Its power was awesome.

Sometimes the sea took my breath away. I didn't want to move. I was lost to its magnetism, my breathing synchronised with the pulse of the waves. Lights winked back to me from the distant horizon, enticing me towards it. Tankers in the Channel. How simple it would be just to walk into the sea and not have anything more to worry about.

A lot of people were milling around me, arriving and greeting friends. The funfair was in full swing, music rocking. Some sort of function was beginning on the pier. The clothes were strange. I'd got clothes on the brain, granted, but these were from another world . . . the sixties and earlier. Then the ten pence dropped. It was the much publicised Swinging Forties Ball with a popular band playing the music of the era, unquote. Teddy boys, US Army uniforms, thick khaki battledress, zoot suits, black tie and tails, British service uniforms and service caps and that was only the men.

The women were wearing the fashions of the forties, fifties and sixties. Anything went. Short utility skirts, the New Look, turbans, flowers in their hair, service uniforms, a nurse, long stain evening dresses, some carrying gas masks.

I blinked. I had strayed into another time and it was unnerving. It was as if it was wartime. Some girls had even managed a strange sausage-roll style with their hair. Did women really wear flowers in their hair in wartime?

I didn't buy a ticket. I wasn't staying. This was curiosity time. There was a stage door entrance round the back manned by a boy practising with drum brushes.

'I'm with the band,' I said, trying to look singer/sound technician/page turner.

'In there,' he said, jerking his head.

The Swing Ball had already started. The band was playing forties jive and all the old wartime tunes, 'Opus One', 'The Donkey Serenade'. The dancers were hopping and spinning and throwing themselves about. It looked fun except that I couldn't jive. No one had taught me. I wondered if James could dance, apart from party social-moving. It would be heaven. 'Strangers in the Night', 'I'm Getting Sentimental Over You', some slow tune like that. The mood, the closeness, the inner bliss of being held by the one you love.

The dress code at the ball was out of space. There were braces, a tatty brown squirrel fur coat, bovver boots, co-respondent shoes, flying jackets. I went for those. Very sexy. It's the element of danger. A man with casual courage.

I blinked. I had strayed into another decade, before I was born. It was wartime. Any minute a bomb might explode, filling the pavilion with dust and debris. I knew the Germans had targetted the Latching gasometer and the London railway line but missed both, destroying small houses in their bombing raids. There's a cobbled wall round a park, now rebuilt, where a plane had crashed, but the difference in stone texture is visible.

The forces uniforms transformed the men. They grew into the mould, loved the status aura, preened, became tough men. Some men could even dance. They had spinning feet and writhing bodies, all arms and legs, spine distorted.

The music was fabulous. I had forgotten these old tunes. Tunes with real melodies and lyrics that said something. I sank onto a seat at the back and let the rhythms invade my body. I nearly twitched.

There were older couples, reliving their first romances, jiving in slow remembrance, the husband still fitting his uniform (almost) even if he could not button up the jacket. Silver heads still loving. I envied them. I'd never had time to dance, to meet anyone on the dance floor. I could never look so pretty, so small, so feminine.

The tide of people at the edges of the dance floor grew till I could hardly see the dancers. Moving spots of light from the mirrored ball flew round the walls, darting like silver moths. I was in danger of starting to dance by myself, on my own, making a fool of myself.

Then I saw her. She was wearing a red taffeta skirt with frou-frou petticoats, a tight bodice, cummerbund, flat shoes and bobby socks. It was the socks that threw me. But there was no doubt it was Sonia Spiller, dancing her head off. Her black hair flew. Her face was alight, glowing with perspiration. Her partner was an anonymous sergeant in khaki with the required stripes on his arm.

Out came my notebook. Date, time, place. This could count. Surveillance in operation. Jordan Lacey never stops. Payment time, no question. No one could dance like that with a painful shoulder.

Ethical dilemma. Was I still working for the unfortunately accident-prone Oliver Guilbert or was that contract suspended? It was not an easy answer. It was as I put my notes in order that I realised that DI James and DS Evans had sauntered into the pavilion, both looking completely out of place, and were scanning the crowds. Sometimes you could spot a policeman a mile off, even in civvies. What on earth were they doing here? I tried to shrivel into my seat, hide behind the heavy velvet curtains at the pier end. But DS Ben Evans had seen me and came over.

'I didn't know you liked dancing,' he said.

'Not normally my scene. I'm actually working.' Only a slight exaggeration. 'So why are you here?'

'Two boyos in Mickey Mouse masks held up the cinema.

Took the whole day's takings. They were seen running in this direction. Have you seen anyone wearing a mask?'

'Come off it. The first thing they would do would be to take off the masks and mingle with the crowd. You know that. They could be anyone on the dance floor. It's the perfect place to hide.'

We looked on the dance floor for tell-tale sweat. But everyone was sweating, even the women. A land-army girl in leggings and shirt bobbed by, armpits stained.

'It could be her,' I said. 'Are you sure that it's two men.'

'You're right there. I'll mention that to the DI.'

'Ask him to come and talk to me. I've something to tell him,' I said. This was news to me. I could not bear being ignored. The music filled me with artificial boldness. I might even ask him to dance.

But he was there before me, measuring the distance between us. This was three foot six time. 'I don't dance, Jordan, especially this stuff,' he said. 'So don't even ask.'

'Heaven forbid,' I scoffed. 'Last thing on my mind. I wanted to ask you about Oliver Guilbert. You've got to tell me how he died. I was working for him. It's relevant to my case.'

He looked at me keenly. 'You tell me and I'll tell you.'

'I was on surveillance for Oliver Guilbert. They were being sued by a woman customer for a substantial amount for injuries sustained when she slipped on a plastic bag in their store. They believed that the claim was fraudulent. And that's the woman, Sonia Spiller, the lady in red, gyrating all over the floor.'

He looked at the spinning figure and then at me. 'So you're her stalker after all.'

'No way,' I said, hardening my heart to his closeness. 'Her stalker is a tall man wearing a sort of smart uniform, very upright. I've seen him. She has got a stalker, but it's not me. And it wasn't Oliver because I saw the stalker following her moments before poor Oliver was found on Hell's Revenge.'

'Can you describe him?'

Dear me, was the man dim? 'I have just described him.

95

There's nothing more I can add. It's the uniform I can't describe because I didn't see it properly, but he did seem to be wearing some kind of official suit and coat. Darkish. There's nothing else. I never saw his face.'

'Traffic warden, policeman, army, navy, airforce?'

'I tell you, I don't know.'

'Salvation Army?'

'Don't be daft. I thought this was a serious enquiry.'

He gave a heavy sigh and lowered himself into the seat beside me. I could see the tiredness etched into the lines on his face. 'This is serious,' he added. He stretched out his long legs into the aisle. 'Buy me a drink, Jordan. Pineapple juice. A double.'

I didn't ask why he didn't get it himself. I threaded my way through the spectators and waited in the bar queue. Everyone was thirsty. They were doing a roaring trade. It was surprising that I had enough money. A double pineapple was not cheap. I could have bought a litre carton for the same sum.

When I went back, balancing the full glass, his eyes were nearly closed. 'What's the matter?' I asked.

'Thank you.' He smiled his thanks, jerking himself awake. 'Jordan, I'm sick and I'm tired. Do you know of a nice hospital? Do A & E departments find beds for stressed and overworked CID? I've five off sick, two on leave, one about to retire who couldn't file a report marked A.'

'I know a very nice convalescent home,' I said. 'It's small, privately run. Superb attention. Home-made soup, soft music, sleep all you want, no one would disturb you. No phone calls, no newspapers, no television. Just care and comfort.'

'Sounds bliss,' he said, yawning. 'I wish I could say lead me there, Jordan. But you know how it is.'

'I know how it is. So how did Oliver Guilbert die?'

'Broken neck. Maybe a counter jerk of the car against the spin direction of the wheel and his head was thrown back against the headrest. We shall have to wait for the full forensic.'

'But what was he doing on Hell's Revenge in the first place? It's so unlikely. He was not a funfair type person.'

'Now that's the real mystery, Jordan. Solve that and maybe we'd get a lot of answers.'

I caught something then. Shorthand for not a straightforward accident and DI James wasn't telling me.

'What about the second arm?' I said, hating to change the subject, but horribly curious.

'Matched,' he said. 'I suppose bits are going to turn up all over Sussex, spoiling my Christmas.'

'What are you doing for Christmas?' I couldn't help asking. Ask him round, an inner voice urged. Spoil him with goodies.

'I'm on duty. I'm the only one without any family ties.'

'You're a saint,' I said brightly. 'I'm working, too. PIs never stop.'

'Thanks for the drink, Jordan,' he said, getting up. 'I owe you one. See you around. Let me know if you remember anything about the stalker.'

Owe me one? He owed me a hundred plus.

At that moment, Sonia Spiller swanned by with a military escort who was very red in the face and wiping his forehead with a khaki handkerchief. She stopped and looked at me.

'Don't I know you?' she asked. 'Historial cottages, wasn't it?'

I nodded. 'Fascinating,' I said. 'I thought the friezes were delightful.'

'Are you sure you don't play squash, too?' She narrowed her eyes. All sorts of suspicions were bobbing about in her over-stimulated brain cells.

'This lady wouldn't know a squash ball from an orange,' said DI James, pausing. 'Believe me, she's no athlete.'

I was grateful but not flattered.

'Why do you ask?'

'Something funny is going on.' Sonia turned to DI James. 'I told you that I've got a stalker and it's not my imagination. I keep seeing this person. And this car. It can't be a coincidence.'

'Has this person approached you yet?'

'No. I don't think so . . .'

'Stalkers usually start phoning or sending letters,' I said helpfully. 'They are not content with just following you.'

'Know all about it, do you, Miss Whatever your name is?'

DI James was just about to supply my name when I pinched his rear. It was unforgivable but stopped him in his tracks. He was astonished. So was I. The band started playing Glenn Miller's 'Bugle Call Rag'. Sonia Spiller's feet began to twitch.

'Come on, baby, let's hit the floor,' said her partner.

'Did you know,' said DI James in a quiet voice, 'that could be classed as an offence? Molesting a police officer.'

I smiled sweetly. 'Arrest me, then, officer. You nearly blew my cover.'

Eleven

Sunday shoppers are a relaxed bunch. They have all day to wander. A carnival atmosphere had been generated at Guilberts with silver balloons outside the entrance doors, a live choir singing carols in the foyer and free coffee and mince pies being served at various points throughout the store. Pastry crumbs began to assemble.

Francis Guilbert was functioning on autopilot, determined that the store should not be rudderless during the lead up to Christmas. Most of the organisation had been done weeks earlier so he could rely on his arrangements working.

The creases in the black dress had hung out overnight. It was good quality. I poured myself into it and I knew when to say when. The beautician gave me a sample sachet of super hydrating 24-hour anti-aging cream. And did I need it.

'You should let me do your face,' she urged. 'You don't make the best of your features.'

'I know, I neglect my ears,' I said.

I took up my station in Linens. The display stands were a rainbow of colours. Piles of thick luxury towels, packets of matching sheets, pillowcases, valances and duvet covers, mountains of varied tog grades of feathers and foam to fill the covers. My modest pink and white floral duvet cover was a limp poor cousin compared to these glorious creations; my towels a hodge-podge collection garnered over the years, many threadbare.

'Everything matching, that's what I should aim for,' I told myself. 'Get with it, girl.' I fancied a pair of fashionable pillowcases, splashed with poppies. Then I saw the price ticket and did a quick retreat. Even with the staff discount, I'd never get my head to sleep on them.

People stole the odd face cloth or hand towel from Linens. The goods were too bulky to stuff under a jumper and you could hardly leave the store wearing a minimum-iron sheet. They were not magnetically tagged but there was less shop-lifting in this department than anywhere else. The beautician told me that the cosmetic testers disappeared all the time.

I had made a lot of enquiries but was no nearer finding the black hole through which the goods were slipping. The head of Linens, an upright, smoothly grey-haired woman in an im-maculate black suit and designer specs, sent me down to the basement warehouse to check if a range of unisex luxury towelling bathrobes had arrived yet.

'They're selling like hot cakes,' she said. 'We need a dozen up immediately. They are the ones with an embroidered pocket. Very classy.'

'Very classy, Miss Kent,' I agreed. I always wore a big towel sarong-wise, in and out of the bath, no embroidery, no pocket. 'A perfect gift.'

'Sure,' said Alan Preston, who remembered me. 'They ar-rived first thing this morning. Signed for them myself. Wait, here's the delivery note. Two dozen bathrobes, white and pastel. I'll get a boy to bring them up.'

'I'll just check if they are the ones with an embroidered pocket,' I said. 'Miss Kent might be annoyed if they've sent the wrong ones.'

'OK, they're over there.' Mr Preston directed me to the area where linen goods were stored. I hunted around the shelves and racks but I couldn't find one, let alone two dozen bathrobes. Yet they had only arrived that morning. I'd glanced at the delivery note, duly signed and dated. They must be here some-where.

'I can't find them anywhere,' I said. 'Please send them up to Linens as soon as you can.'

'Sure,' he nodded. 'How are you getting on?'

I didn't know how to answer. I really had nothing to go on, but I did not want to look too incompetent.

'Slowly,' I said. 'Nothing definite.'

'It's a puzzle,' he agreed.

I took the service lift back upstairs. Shop work was tiring. Support stockings loomed. It was all that standing, trying to look both helpful, but inconspicuous. Difficult at my height.

'I want a present for my daughter-in-law,' said a cow-faced woman in a fur hat marching up to me. 'She's completely impractical. She needs guidance. My son just isn't used to living in such chaos. Please show me some towel sets.'

'Is this a Christmas present?' I asked carefully.

'Of course,' she snapped. 'I'm trying to sort out her household arrangements. She simply has no idea how to run a house.'

'Are there any children?' I asked, putting out a selection of our prettiest matching towel sets on the counter. I couldn't make up my mind which I liked the best, the apricot or the lilac. They were all gorgeous.

'Twins. Eighteen months old.'

'Perhaps that's why her household is chaotic,' I murmured. 'She has her hands full. Not much spare time for chaos-sorting.'

'Nonsense,' the woman snorted, her hat bobbing. 'It just requires organisation. I'll take these plain white ones. My son isn't used to coloured towels.'

'We have a special gift-wrapping service,' I said smoothly. 'Would you like them gift-wrapped? There's no charge.'

This was not strictly true, but I reckoned she was not the sort to pay extra. I'd do it for nothing. It worked.

'Thank you, miss,' she said, momentarily gracious.

I turned away and busied myself with a large sheet of festive paper covered in holly and mistletoe. Did DI James know what mistletoe was for? He probably thought it was a churchyard weed. I tied the ribbon and expertly frilled the ends with scissors. Very professional.

I took the money, keyed in the code and rang up the amount, then handed over the parcel, receipt and change with a smile.

'A pleasure to serve you,' I said. What a liar. 'I do hope your daughter-in-law likes her present.'

'It doesn't matter whether she likes it or not,' said the hatted dragon. 'It's what she's getting.'

I thought she would like them. I'd switched the sets. The ones I'd gift-wrapped were blue, edged with navy and embroidered with yachts and seagulls on rolling waves. Very nautical. The twins would love them. Mother-in-law would be thanked with flattery for her excellent taste. She could hardly come back and complain.

Marriage note: always meet mother-in-law before committing self. Urgent reminder: present for DI James. Extra note: don't panic even if falling apart.

I did not exactly have to get him a present. It was not as if we were mates, great buddies or even close friends. But he had come to my rescue, twice. The wing walking and the hermit's hole. Both episodes still made me shudder, could bring me out in a cold sweat. I wanted to give him the moon but I thought it would have to be a slimline diary.

Would I survive till the midnight car boot at this rate? If I fell asleep in Jack's car I might end up at Gretna Green. A sobering thought. Was I fit enough to walk back?

My boredom threshold is abysmally low. I had to play games to keep my brain active. How long could I make a Polo Mint last? Record: three and a half minutes. Could I sell a customer something they obviously did not want? I sold a thirteen tog duvet to a man who was emigrating to South America. Criminal. Could I introduce the topic of ferrets into the conversation? One woman actually bred the creatures and showed me photos of her babies. They were piled into hammocks, all arms and legs and tails intermingled.

'How sweet,' I said.

The day wore on. I will never, ever, again be short with a shop assistant. They are angels, martyrs, heroines of the first order. Ask after their corns.

Did I have lunch? A bland cottage cheese and shredded salad passed in a haze. If the luxury towelling robes ever arrived, then it was all water under the bridge to me, for I was transferred to Electrical and spent a rivetting afternoon discussing the merits of steam irons and jug kettles. I only wanted one that played a tune.

At closing time I rushed round to Stationery. 'Can I buy a slimline diary?' I gasped.

'Too late, sorry. We've just closed the till. Come tomorrow. There's plenty left.'

I staggered home, glad to have air-filled trainers on my sore feet. Yet I had to open my shop. Another couple of hours lay ahead, selling first-class junk. But it was buy anything time. Trade was blooming. People were still shopping. They bought surprising things. So much so that I opened a bottle of Doris' special offer cooking sherry and gave everyone a glass. If Guilberts could dispense coffee, I'd go one better with sherry. No one commented on the quality. It was the concept that counted.

Sixty-nine pounds in two hours. I don't quite know how it came to that odd sum when all my goods have six pound price labels. Maybe some books got sold. I couldn't remember. I didn't care. It was money, not maths.

I needed sleep. I went home, set the alarm, curled up in bed and tried to get a couple of hours before the midnight boot. It was going to be a late night or early morning, whichever way the clock ticked.

When Jack arrived for me, I was as fresh as a newly opened daisy. Indigo jeans, black polo, black leather jacket, usual look. It was becoming a uniform. I made sure he would not be buying me anything by looking one hundred per cent confident and independent. My wallet was in my back pocket. The video camera hidden in a cheap, canvas shoulder bag.

'A million dollars!' he said again.

'You're right there,' I said. 'And all my own gear.'

'Get in, Jordan, and I'll take you for a spin.'

I nearly had a heart attack. Outside on the road was a gleaming top of the range Jaguar sports car. It was low slung, metallic blue, gleaming headlamps and grill. The amusement arcade business was a runaway money maker.

'Is this new?' I asked, wondering if he had bought it specially for this evening. It was the kind of crazy thing he might do to impress me.

'I buy a new one every year. Always the best, Jordan. My little hobby. I like cars.'

And other people's hobbies was the rate at which they lost their money on the machines, creating windfall-sized profits.

Jack had cleaned himself up, marginally. He was wearing a cleanish, untorn T-shirt, nondescript jeans, and a baggy anorak. He had even combed his hair. It lay on his head like a slick of tar. He'd almost shaved. Shown it the razor.

'And can this baby move,' he said. 'Fasten your belt and we'll burn up a few miles.'

Burn up a few tyres, a few roads. I held my breath. Jack was a good driver, deft and in control, but dear God, he broke every speed limit in existence. OK, there was little traffic on the road at that time of night, but at every clear stretch he upped the gear and the speedometer needle swung over a hundred. I stopped looking at it.

He glanced at me. 'Like it?' he shouted. 'Isn't she grand?'

I nodded. Keep your eyes on the road, Jack.

'What a baby! She can do a hundred and twenty. Wanna try it?'

'No, thanks,' I shouted back. 'This is fast enough for me.'

The thought of my ladybird crawling along at twenty-five on a good day was a comfort. I didn't have to prove anything. I just had to get where I wanted to go, without getting wet.

He swerved suddenly. I was thrown against the seat belt. But he straightened up almost immediately.

'Sorry,' he said. 'Fox in the headlights. We missed it.'

I sighed. 'Could we slow down a bit?'

'Anything you say, lady.'

The speedometer dropped to eighty. I suppose that was cruising to Jack. We were nearing Ford. I recognised the bridge over the river Arun. There were eleventh-century farmhouses in the village but we barely slowed down enough to look at them.

Jack knew the way. He turned down a narrow lane, bumping over a badly made road at thirty. Low foliage hung like a canopy, shutting out the night sky. I gripped my bag tightly. A frisson of fear touched my spine, yet there was nothing to be frightened of. Or was there? And Jack? Was I leading him into danger, into something that was not his concern? He sensed my worry.

'Don't worry, baby. I'll take care of you. I won't leave you behind.'

I tried a smile. 'I'm not worried, just apprehensive.'

A beam lanced through the trees. A lorry was following us. Shadows passed through the beam. Ahead loomed a big slate barn and round it were a dozen cars and Land Rovers parked haphazardly in the yard, bonnets darkly red, gleaming grills. Jack turned in the gate and parked at a distance among some bushes.

'Don't want nobody scratching my baby,' he said. He had a sophisticated security system, more alarms than Buckingham Palace. It took a minute to code it in. 'Ain't taking no chances. Come on, girl. Let's buy you a present.'

He took my arm and lead me through the open barn doors. Spotlights had been rigged up on the beams. Round the walls were casual stalls set up and selling areas, like a Middle Eastern marketplace. A pile of rugs here, a heaped mixture of tools, loads of batteries, shavers, cigarettes, lighters and mobile phones on trestle tables. A lot of dealers were milling about. A CD player was blaring heavy rock.

'See anything you fancy? Don't pay what they ask. Bargain first. I always do.'

Two racks of clothes stood at the far end, heaps of handbags tangled in cardboard boxes. Some dark-faced men hung around. Even at this distance, I could see the goods were leather, not imitation. It was the smell. Real leather has that unmistakable smell.

'Let's look at the jackets,' I said.

'Wanna jacket? I'll get you one.'

'Jack, please.' I slowed him down. 'Look, I've got a leather jacket. I'm wearing it, see? My parents gave it to me for my 21st. It's special. I don't want another.'

He looked disappointed. 'OK. Whatever you say. You're the boss.'

Dear man, whatever could I do with him? He was like a puppy, yapping at my heels, adoring, pleading for a pat on the head.

'Believe me, whoever drives that shiny monster is the boss.'

He cheered up instantly. 'Yeah . . . she's a monster, a beautiful monster. C'mon. Let's see what they've got.'

I'd cut a hole in the canvas bag just big enough for the lens of the video. I switched on the camera, hoping the contraption would work, holding it steady against my hip. Pretty cool.

I recognised the labels, the styles, the manufacturers. I bet my entire fee that this was part of the consignment delivered to Guilberts. I moved the hangers along the rail, making inane comments.

'This is nice. Classy. Oh, I like this one. Not my size. Pity. Belt's a bit tight. Don't like the buckle.'

'Real leather, lady,' said a man, strolling up. 'Surplus stock. Nothing shady. You won't get better value in the whole of the UK. I'm letting them go cheap because it's Christmas.'

'How much is this one?' I asked, turning so that the camera would get a view of him.

'Four hundred quid. Cost a thousand. Tell yer what, how about three hundred and fifty to a nice lady like you?'

I gave him a totally false smile. 'I'll think about it. It is a lovely jacket.'

'Wanna handbag?' said Jack. 'This one you're carrying is a bit naff.' He nearly shook the video camera. I clutched it to me. It was filming a great view of my right hip.

'No, thank you, Jack. No bag.'

I deliberately moved, making a mental description of the man. He was joined by another. They rolled cigarettes and blew smoke in my direction. I coughed. The atmosphere was heavy with smoke, worse than any pub.

Then I spotted the luxury towelling robes, each still in clear plastic packing, folded so that the embroidered pockets showed. Miss Kent's pride and joy.

'Forty quid,' said the stallholder, seeing my interest. 'Any colour you like, miss.'

'No, thank you,' I said, making sure I got a shot, then moving on. There were a lot of people now and I was being jostled from all sides. I'd lost Jack somewhere along the way. He was not particularly tall so it wasn't easy to find him. Still, he could not have gone far. Probably looking at car accessories.

'Whatcher got, Chuck?' I heard someone say. I stood still, trying to pin down the direction of the voice. The din was distracting. 'Heard you'd gone Mexican,' came a chuckle.

My throat hardened like I'd swallowed a pebble. I thought of Mavis and her poor face. I looked carefully, pretending to be scanning the goods, but making a survey of all the nearby faces, one at a time, trying to fit her description to someone. Nothing. Short, dark, skinny; the other – taller, heavier, mean eyes. Those descriptions fitted half the men in the barn.

Then I heard the chuckle again. It was a rotund little man in a flapping raincoat that wouldn't fasten. He was greedily stuffing crisps into his mouth and swigging from a beer bottle. 'Got any whiskey?' he was asking a stallholder.

I didn't wait to think. 'Hey,' I said, a bit rough. 'Have you seen Chuck? I said I'd meet him. What's he got tonight?'

He peered at me through the fog. 'Dunno. Bits and pieces.'

'Come on, you can do better than that. He's always got something special.'

'Mobiles. But nobody's buying. They all got them. Market's down the drain. Even my granddaughter's got one and she's not out of her pram.' He chuckled again.

But I'd gone before he could elaborate. Mobile phones. I'd seen them somewhere. But where? People were packing up. The midnight boot did not hang about. Then I saw him. Short, dark, skinny, packing mobile phones into boxes, a cigarette hanging from the side of his mouth. Surely I'd seen him before somewhere, but I couldn't think where.

'Hi,' I said. 'Hold on, don't put them all away. I need a new facia for mine. Something bright and cheerful.'

'Take your choice,' he said morosely. Bright and cheerful he was not. 'But don't take your time. I gotta be somewhere else.'

I was drawing his face in my head. Long thin nose, slitty eyes, colour impossible to see, pointed chin, earring in one ear, heavy gold ring on wedding finger. Clean nails, bitten down. Height, weight, all recorded. Clothes: black trousers, white shirt, jacket . . . not the usual jeans brigade.

'How much?' I asked, pointing out a particularly lurid purple and yellow one.

'A fiver.'

What a nerve. They were only £4.99 in the shops. 'Three quid,' I came back.

'Four, take it or leave it.'

He was some salesman. He hadn't been to a charm school. 'OK. Gotta a bag?'

Chuck picked up the purple and yellow monstrosity. Nice prints. He put it in a brown paper bag. I gave him a fiver from my wallet, from my hard-earned day's takings.

He stuffed it in his pocket and turned away.

'Change please,' I said promptly, holding out my hand.

He reluctantly fished out a coin and put it into my open palm.

'Thank you.' I moved on swiftly and dropped the coin into the paper bag. There might be a print on it too. This was turning out to be a good night.

Jack appeared behind me and plonked something onto my head. He was grinning broadly. 'I said I'd get you a pressie. Perfick.'

I took it off and looked down at what was in my hand. It was a baker's boy cap in soft black leather. Just my style, my kind of gear. I slapped it back on my head dead straight and gave him a radiant smile.

'Perfick,' I said.

He grinned back. I'd just made his night.

'Cor. I ought to be buying champagne and stuff.'

Champagne. The word broke my slender recognition thread. The Latching Bowling Club party at the Hamilton's house. Chuck had been one of the waiters. He was in the casual catering trade.

Twelve

J ack turned out to be a real gentleman, rough cast, and left me at my door at ten to one, with a brief, almost apologetic hug and revved away in his metallic blue into the rest of the lonely night. I had expected a struggle and hassle. It was a relief. I liked him too much for any disagreement.

I went into the store early next morning for a wander around the basement. There was no sign of the towelling robes. No arrival upstairs either. Another consignment which had disappeared and I was one hundred percent sure that I had seen them at the midnight boot.

So how had they been removed from the warehouse? The answer struck me with simple logic. Perhaps they had never come in. OK, Mr Preston signed for the delivery, but had he checked the actual unloading and storing of the goods? He was busy. Perhaps the robes had never even left the van but were driven out again, on their way to Ford.

I would have to ask the poor man. And on Christmas Eve, too. It was enough to ruin his Christmas.

I also switched on a television set in Electrical and played my videotapes. It was a strange feeling in the empty department. I felt an intruder, which I suppose I was, although I had been told the necessary security codes in order to come and go as I liked. Apart from shots of my jeans, boots, hip and inside of bag, the midnight boot film was brilliant. DI James would be over the moon, give me a medal, buy me a drink.

Suspect number one for the Mexican and Maeve's Cafe

robbery was clearly in the picture and so were the racks of leather jackets, handbags, robes, and a variety of other goods.

The videotape of Sonia Spiller was less successful. Jasper leaping about on the beach and back views of Sonia walking were not conclusive. Nor were the shots of her playing squash because she played . . . left-handed. I had not noticed. Black mark, Jordan. The other significant person I had missed was her squash partner. It was Oliver Guilbert. From my bird's eye view, he had looked like any other man in shorts and white T-shirt.

So they had known each other, sort of. Muddier and muddier became the plot. But it was too late to ask Oliver. I hoped there was an innocent solution because Oliver was another man I had liked. I squinted hard at the film, hoping to spot her stalker in the background, the man in a kind of uniform. But apart from that one occasion, he stalked at a different time to when I followed. No wonder the woman was paranoid.

Guilberts was a madhouse on Christmas Eve. Shoppers scrambled to buy anything. And I was appalled at the behaviour. The season of goodwill had been replaced by irritability and sheer bad manners. Men elbowed old ladies, trod on toddlers, pushed pushchairs out of the way. They were far worse than the women. Clear cases of last-minute panic.

'Only just noticed that it's Christmas?' I said to one business-man, who rudely pushed to the head of the queue at the till. 'It's been around since last year.'

He flung his credit card at me. He was buying four identical boxes of lace handkerchieves. One for each mistress? I served him to get rid of him and I did not want a mouthful of abuse.

'I do apologise,' I said to the rest of the queue. 'For this gentleman's appalling bad manners. And thank you for waiting so patiently.'

He heard me and snatched the carrier bag off the counter. He could not get away fast enough.

At lunch time I threw myself into the ladybird and delivered my few presents to friends. I did not have time to talk to anyone. Fortunately I had had the sense to post Cleo's silk scarf to her in Chichester. There was still DI James to buy for. The situation was getting worse. Memo: start earlier next year, like on Boxing Day. I existed on black coffee. All that caffeine was not good for me. I was on a permanent high.

As I drove passed First Class Junk I saw a figure I recognised waiting on the doorstep. It was the retired doctor who had bought all the old medicine bottles. I stopped, parking illegally, and ran over to him, keys in hand.

'I'm not really open,' I said breathlessly. 'But can I help you?'

'It's those two biographies in the window, the Jonas Salk and Archibald MacIndoe. I'd really like to buy them for a present,' he said. 'MacIndoe was one of our greatest plastic surgeons, operating on badly burned airmen at East Grinstead, and Salk was the pioneer who produced the first vaccine against polio.'

'I didn't know, I'm so ignorant,' I said, unlocking the door. 'They're just books to me. I've only put them in the window because I'm short of stock. Hardbacks are £1 each.'

'That's not nearly enough,' said the doctor. 'Let me give you a fiver. Regard it as a Christmas bonus. You were very kind, packing those bottles so carefully. They are all displayed in a cabinet.'

I took the money. There wasn't time to argue. As the doctor went out of the door, books safely in a Guilberts carrier bag – it was the least I could do, he paused and looked back.

'Actually, I lied to you. The books are a present but they are a present from me to me. You see, I don't think I shall get any presents and I must have something to unwrap.'

My heart missed a beat. Join the club.

He didn't think he would get any presents. It was horribly sobering. How many other people in Latching would be spending Christmas alone? I was alone in a stern white way but going to make myself rush round, checking on friends, eating numerous mince pies and pulling crackers, when all I really wanted to do was to put my head down and sleep.

The afternoon at Guilberts was ratchety, only a kind of

despair had set in. People didn't care any longer. It was all too much. You could see the weariness in their shoulders and in their glazed eyes. Too much to do and too little time to do it in. The modern curse. The Christmas curse.

My enquiries narrowed down. In one break, I hovered near the delivery entrance. A van arrived and a cheeky soul got out of the driver's seat and waved a pro forma at me.

'I've got a load of CDs here. Will you sign for them, miss? I'm in a bit of a hurry. Got four more deliveries to do before six.'

Why me? It must have been the black dress.

'Sure,' I said. 'My signature is as good as any. And Mr Preston doesn't seem to be around.'

The driver did some bustling, acting busy, checked his lights, moved the van to a better position. I did not sign the delivery note, but stood there waiting.

'Thanks a lot, mate,' said the driver. 'Sign, please, and I'll be on my way.'

'Hold on,' I said. 'I need to check the goods.'

'You've got them. I gave them to you. First thing I did.'

'No way,' I said, shaking my head. 'You must have forgotten. Take a look in the van.'

He did not like it but reluctantly went round and reopened the doors to the van. 'Strike me,' he said. 'I must have forgotten. Here they are, miss.'

'Thank you,' I said. 'Now I'll sign the delivery note.'

It was not the loyal Mr Preston, I felt sure. It was someone down the line, accepting goods, signing for them, but not checking delivery. Or worse still, knowing the goods were not being taken into the warehouse. Perhaps he got a cut.

I wandered round the warehouse. They all looked the average kind of staff that dealt with deliveries, brown overalls, ordinary faces. All ages, all degrees of boredom and resignation in a dead end job. Which one was I going to shop? It was not pleasant. They were not your normal villains. They were men fed up with their jobs, mortgages, debts, wanting to make an extra buck.

The day ended. I was poleaxed. Heavens, now there was the staff party but I had to speak to DI James first. I went into the staff cloakroom and tested my newly acquired mobile.

'DI James, please. And it's urgent,' I said from the privacy of a white-tiled loo. The loo paper had run out. Nothing to blow my nose on.

'DI James.' It was his voice. It cut through me.

'It's Jordan. Jordan Lacey. Can you hear me?'

'Of course I can hear you. Where are you?'

'I wish I could say on the train. But actually I'm in the loo. The ladies' loo at Guilberts.'

'I thought so. I can hear lots of flushing noises.'

'This is the only place I can talk to you,' I said, holding the phone close to my ear. 'I think I have a videotape of one of the men who robbed the Mexican and Maeve's Cafe. Not one hundred percent sure, but it's someone called Chuck who fits both descriptions. I'll drop them by the station. Also shots of lots of possibly stolen goods. It's big stuff, except I don't want to be involved. Can we do a deal? You know, you can use the videos but you must not say where you got them.'

'You know me, Jordan. Anything you say.' He sounded so smooth I did not know whether to trust him. 'Where are you going now?'

'Just making a token appearance at the Christmas Eve staff party at Guilberts. I reckon I've earned it. I'm practically dead on my feet. A mince pie might keep me standing.'

'Party on, girl. I may join you.'

He cut off the call and I was left, mid-air, swinging halfway between heaven and paradise. He might join me. Promises, promises. I reassessed the black dress. It was too late for a make-over. I went upstairs to the restaurant. The beautician lady was halfway through a glass of ruby-red punch. Miss Kent was dipping her sausage on a stick into a glass of sherry. Wow, it was really swinging.

Francis Guilbert made an appearance. He had aged. I felt

really sorry for him. But he was doing his best, founder of the firm and all that. He was doing the rounds, talking to old and new. The staff gathered in groups and did not know what to say. Happy Christmas or sorry about your son?

'Mr Guilbert,' I said, rescuing him from tearful ladies in Hosiery. 'Can I talk to you?'

'Yes, Miss Lacey. I hoped we might have a moment.'

I came straight to the point. He was holding a glass but not drinking. 'I think I have pin-pointed the black hole in your system. I may know how the goods are disappearing and I'm half sure where they are being sold off. It just needs names and who is organising the racket.'

His tired face brightened for an instant. The lines were etched in pain. 'Well done, Miss Lacey. When do you think you will have the rest of this information?'

'It may not be up to me. It may now be a police job.'

'Ah, the police. But I had hoped we could do it without police intervention.'

'It's not that easy, Mr Guilbert. After all, stealing is a criminal offence.'

'But I don't want any of my staff prosecuted.' He looked quite distressed. 'I thought by employing you we could keep the police out of it.'

'Let me think about it,' I said. 'You're making it tricky. But I will do my best.'

'Do more than your best, Miss Lacey,' he said, suddenly very much the Managing Director, some of his old spirit returning. 'I don't want any of my staff charged. It's got to be settled within the firm. Do you understand?'

I slid away, trying to look understanding. Time to leave. I'd had enough of salty crisps and wine from a box. I hardly knew these people and my social skills were nil. I could turn on a smile, but small talk was beyond me. It was on the way to the staff exit that I saw the man of my dreams.

DI James was coming towards me, dark-coated and crew-cut and stern-faced. I stopped in my tracks, unlit embers of sex stirring. If he saw me, well and good, but if he did not, I would keep going, out of sight. The shadows merged with me.

'Enjoying the party?' he asked.

'I was just leaving.'

'Don't go. Not yet.'

The words hung in the air, waiting to be stored. Don't go. I waited, in my black dress and black pumps, wondering if he would notice a female form hidden inside. He was all man, me all woman. Surely something would surface in this little valley, this of all nights? Didn't he know he was supposed to kiss me under the mistletoe?

But all he did was turn me towards the main crowd of jostling party-goers. 'Now tell me everything, from the word go. Have another glass of festive wine. I don't want anything left out. I've no leads on those two robbers and anything you have is important.'

I let him fetch me another glass of red plonk. He did not touch it, but grabbed a handful of peanuts. I could not believe he was standing beside me. Dream angel, you have answered my prayer.

'I'm working on several cases at once,' I began.

'Usual scenario. You take on far more than you can cope with.'

I ignored the remark. 'Case One for Oliver: Sonia Spiller suing Guilberts because of shoulder injury sustained in basement, slipping on a plastic bag.'

'So?'

'Genuine injury, no dispute there. But she has recovered, I believe. She maintains that it is a permanent disability, loss of earnings etc.'

'Next?' He grabbed another handful of nuts. I knew the feeling. It was the salt. He was missing Mavis's chips.

'The sadists who bashed up Mavis's face. Have you seen her?' He nodded. 'Well, I've taken on this case, but, of course, no fee and Mavis doesn't have to know,' I said.

He shook his head now. 'Jordan, you need to go on a business course. You don't take on any case without a fee.'

'Mavis is my friend,' I said indignantly. 'And excuse me, Detective Inspector James, I'll do exactly what I please.'

For a moment, he looked amused. The sternness actually melted a nanometre. There was a glimmer in his ocean blue eyes. He refilled my glass from the wine box. I was losing count.

'Your hair seems to flash lights when you get angry,' he said. 'Did you know that? Like a lighthouse. How can you drink this stuff?'

'You're pouring it down me.'

It took me several moments to resume normal transmission. This interrogation was difficult in the middle of a party. People kept bumping into us and saying hello. I smiled back, nodded like a doll, making bland comments.

'Is this hunky guy your regular boyfriend?' asked the beautician who was passed drawing eyeliner even on an elephant.

'No,' I said. 'Just a friend.'

'Work on it, sister,' she advised, with a mascara'd wink. 'Come and see me. I'll give you a few tips.'

James came to the rescue. 'I am just a friend,' he said. 'But I'm working on it, too.'

His charm salvaged the situation and she weaved away, not knowing quite where she was going.

'Case number three,' he prompted.

'After Oliver's accident – and by the way, you have got to tell me what forensic have come up with – Mr Francis Guilbert took me on to solve the mysterious disappearance of goods from the basement warehouse. Really expensive stuff is going walkies.'

'And you think you have solved this?'

'No names yet. But I think I know how the scam is being worked and I've seen similar goods on sale.'

'Where?'

'Look, I don't really like this wine. Do I have to drink anymore?'

He took the plastic glass from me. 'I'm sorry, Jordan. It was unfair of me. This stuff is lethal. Great for removing paint. Go drink some water. I'll buy you a really nice wine somewhere else. Where did you see the stolen stuff on sale?'

'It's on the videotape. A midnight boot, somewhere near Ford. I don't know the exact place because I didn't see where I was going.'

'Blind drunk, I suppose.'

That almost blew it. There were only so many insults I could take, even from the man I cared for most in the whole world.

'No. I was in a car that was breaking all speed limits. And I'm not going to tell you who was driving because I like him. Not in a special way,' I hastened to add. 'Just as a friend, an informant actually.'

'One of your fans?'

'You could say so.'

'Blue metallic Jag?'

'I'm not saying.'

'We know it.'

He steered me towards the back exit of the store. I fetched my anorak, did not bother to change. No work tomorrow. The store was shut. I could have the whole day off apart from calling on friends. The creases could fall out at home.

Could James be classed as a lonely friend? Sometimes he looked very lonely. He rarely mentioned his marriage or the circumstances of his divorce. Just sometimes a clue dropped, like a window opening.

There was more of the festive atmosphere outside in the street. People were milling about, either going into pubs or coming out of pubs, or leaving staff parties. The strings of lights along the promenade twinkled. The lights in the trees flashed on and off. Santa rode his reindeer across the street. Christmas was the weirdest thing.

'So what are you doing tomorrow?' I asked, very casual.

'I told you – on duty, both shifts, the two till ten and the ten till six. I've volunteered. Everyone has families except me. I'm the obvious choice.'

'Oh.' So I couldn't ask him round. I couldn't even rustle up a turkey sandwich. I hadn't done any Christmas shopping for myself and even Safeways was closed now. Still, who wanted to eat? There was far too much eating done in this world already. Guzzle, guzzle. Remember the starving millions.

James took me to some nightclub that had a late licence. It was upstairs rather than downstairs and called the Skyliner Club. We went up and up, flight after flight, in some elegantly narrow Georgian terraced house that was rented off, floor by floor. The top floor was dimly lit, soft music, thick smoke. It was packed, but miraculously a table in a corner became vacant. James seemed to know the owner. How come he was accepted in this place?

'A bottle of red,' James ordered. 'But I want your best, the very best. Serve us rubbish and I will revoke your licence. And we haven't eaten. What have you got?

'The kitchen has closed but I expect we can rustle up a couple of sandwiches.'

It was an out of this world fantasy. I wondered if I was indeed dreaming, that I had fallen asleep upright, leaning on a counter. James buying the best wine in the house. A secluded table in a corner, seductive music breaking the air. Sandwiches on their way and the only man that I wanted was by my side. When the sandwiches arrived they were made of granary bread, thick with salad and pickle and Stilton, flanked with sliced tomatoes and green pepper. My mouth could not wait.

'Got the videotapes with you?' James asked. 'I'll take them now.'

Thirteen

The potent wine ebbed and flowed undeclared through my veins and I told James almost everything. I also told him again that I had spotted Sonia's stalker, in case he had not been listening.

'Describe the uniform.'

'Er . . . dark, quite smart.'

'Surely you can do better than that . . . was it military?'

'No, not a proper sort of uniform. It was only an impression, after all. We've been through this before.'

He nodded instead of sighing with exasperation. He had mellowed. It might be seasonal. 'Go on.'

I told him that I'd seen Oliver at Sonia's house and filmed him playing squash with her. James did not seem to attach too much importance to the fact.

'He could have been trying to talk her out of the claim. Perhaps he offered a few incentives. Discount on purchases for life? Free lunch on Saturdays in the restaurant?'

'Sure. We should not always think the worst.'

'Our records show he was a respectable citizen, worked hard, paid his taxes.'

'A sweetie. Rather boyish yet very serious. I liked him immensely. I can't understand what he was doing on Hell's Revenge. It seems completely out of character. How did he die?'

I threw the question at him. I was determined to get an answer. Surely it was not classified? It looked like an accident, a stupid, unexpected accident.

'He broke his neck. It could have been the force of the car

suddenly changing direction at speed while the wheel base was actually spinning in the opposite direction. Yet he was correctly strapped in and his head was supported by the brace. A freak accident.'

'Is that the final pathologist's report?'

'No, there are other routine tests they're making. As you say, we can't understand what he was doing on the wheel. Nor can his father. There's some bruising which can't be accounted for and residue of a sticky substance.'

James let it slip. Whoops. I could see from the slight tightening of his mouth that he had not intended to say that much. I did not pursue the comment. He would just clam up. Usual DI James reaction.

'Bruising where?'

'You know better than to ask me that.'

They were starting to sing round the bar, carols with dubious words that I couldn't quite hear, and some couples were dancing. If you could call it dancing. Hugging with movement. Would he ask me to dance? But my dream angel had gone off duty and James made a move to leave.

'It's getting noisy,' he said. 'Shall we go?'

I nodded. 'Thank you for a lovely end to the evening. The staff party was a bit awkward and I didn't really feel in the mood.'

'In the mood? In the mood for what?' He was teasing now, helping me on with my anorak, finishing his wine. 'I never associate moodiness with you.'

'In the mood for Christmas.'

'Is it Christmas? Oh, those lights everywhere? And I thought the council were trying to use up a bulk purchase of cheap bulbs.'

No present in the offing, obviously. He was not into Christmas unless one was related maternally. So I could stop wondering if he was going to give me anything. Shopping list: buy own diary.

It was as he was walking me home along the seafront that it

happened. There was a commotion near the pay kiosk of Hell's Revenge, people shouting and feet running. The crowd was thrashing around, distraught, arms waving, pushing and more shouting. Someone got shouldered out of the way and fell on the flower beds. Some kids started screaming. All hell let loose; revenge indeed.

'Come on,' I said. 'Something's happening.'

'Jordan,' said James. 'Stay out of it. It could be nasty.' He was talking on his mobile at the same time as running. 'DI James. Back-up required on the front. At the funfair. I'm investigating now.' He turned to me. 'Go home, Jordan. I don't want you here in case it gets rough.'

I ignored him. It was easy to do since he was already several metres ahead of me. It was almost as if he had forgotten that I was there. The crowds parted as DI James strode forward, waving his ID. It was only a few steps to the kiosk where a woman was sobbing.

The lights on the sideshows and the flashing lights on the neighbouring funfair novelty rides lit the gaudy night-time scene. Two men were jostling a path through the sightseers, pushing them roughly out of the way. It was difficult to see what had happened, but putting two and two together came up with robbery.

Then I caught sight of the escaping couple. Their faces were grotesque. The light caught them full face. They were wearing Mickey Mouse masks, red and shiny nosed. One was thin and short, wearing black jeans and a black T-shirt. He wove in and out of the crowd like an eel. It was a good performance.

He was clutching a leather pouch. The takings. At £1.50 a ride and forty available seats, it didn't take a maths genius to work out that Hell's Revenge was raking in a lot of money. And all of it in cash. The pouch looked full and heavy.

A flashing patrol car came screaming along the front. People scattered or gathered depending on whether they were frightened or curious.

DI James shouted back at me. 'Stay with the woman. I'll go after them.'

I took no notice. I can really run, even in a black dress, hitched up in my pants' elastic, and since I was further away I could dodge round the edge of the crowd and cut through to where I could see two masked bobbing heads emerging. They had gone on the pier, hoping to throw us off the track. At some point they would tear off their masks, mingle with the crowds in the dark. The pier was not as well lit as the seafront.

The pier was like a second home to me. I knew every route, bench seat, litter bin, kiosk, railing and step. I ran on to it, keeping my eyes firmly on the two ahead. They had slowed down, masks off now. They stuffed the masks into a litter bin. I noted which bin, caught a gloss of red paint.

Now they were going down the iron steps to the lower level walkway round the end of the pier where the anglers congregate. No hopeful fishing tonight. It was deserted except for a few courting couples who barely surfaced in time to look at the men.

I could almost see them. They were not youths at all. The shorter one was perhaps in his early thirties, but the heavier build was definitely late forties. It was time they were put away. They were causing enough trouble in Latching. If they were the same pair that had robbed the Mexican and Mavis. Perhaps the cinema robbery, too.

I suddenly thought of the owner of the Mexican and what a dish he was. Miguel Cortes. Probably too old for me, but hey, who cares these days? Age is not that important. It's character and personality that count and he had plenty of both. Perhaps I'd treat myself to a Mexican supper on Christmas Day. He'd buy me a bottle of wine, sit at my table. I had a black dress and a velvet scrunchie.

It was a mind-blowing idea. In that moment of inattention, the two men disappeared. This is always happening to me. Loss of concentration. Where could they have gone? I ran round the railings, peering over to the lower level. No sign of them.

Lights were bobbing on the water. I knew those lights. They were from a small fishing boat, going under the pier through the allotted span, where a notice said, 'No fishing between these posts'. I ran to the other side of the pier, just in time to see the fishing boat re-emerge, with extra crew I could swear. These small boats are usually a one-man affair, but I could see three people aboard. All men.

'Chuck,' I yelled down. 'Chuck!' An old trick.

It was automatic. He looked up. Bingo! But I could not make out the registration number of the boat, nor the colour it was painted. Brownish red, maybe. Too dark for any identification. Even the sea was almost black, only reflecting the lights.

I drew back instantly. Chuck could not see me and was confused. He was talking to the older man. They both looked up.

Now, where had they stashed the money pouch? I walked back along the pier slowly, unhitching the black dress, looking in all the bins, actually enjoying the night air. A few strollers looked at me with disgust. Bag lady, they thought.

Then I found the pouch. A few chips stuck to the leather, but I was not fussy. I shook them off. The woman in the pay kiosk would be pleased. It weighed a ton.

Substitute lover. The phrase came into my mind as I walked back towards the pier entrance. I was still thinking of Miguel. DI James caught sight of me. He came over immediately, his face dark with fury.

'You didn't obey me! I said, stay with the woman. Don't pursue them.'

'I don't work for you. Remember? I've left the force.'

'You are the most irritating woman.'

'Here's the money. I've got it back but I'll let you hand it to the woman who was robbed. One of the robbers is called Chuck, I think. You can take all the credit. I'm not mean-minded like some.'

It was a moment of glory. I gave him the pouch bulging with money. Our hands almost touched. He looked at me but I don't know what his eyes were saying. I was tired. I was almost passed caring. James, James . . . save me, stay with me, don't let me swop you for a hunky Mexican.

'They climbed down under the pier and a fishing boat picked them up. I couldn't make out which one. They've probably transferred to a motor launch out at sea or gone ashore by now.'

He took the pouch. 'Thank you, Jordan. Well done. Now stay here, and don't you dare move a single inch. I'm taking you home.' He went back on his mobile and passed on the fishing boat information. The coast guard could take over now.

He saw me home, both of us beyond talking, another gentleman who did not hassle me. But he could have hassled me from here to Littlehampton and I would not have whispered a word of protest.

It was Christmas Day. I lay in bed and for a moment thought of my parents and so many Christmases as a child. Christmas trees, crackers, presents in a stocking at the end of my bed, a proper lunch with all the trimmings after morning church. Not a good idea, all this thinking. Too weepy and nostalgic. I got up and made myself a mug of tea. I drew the curtains and Latching was bleak and rainswept. Rivulets trickled down the glass. Branches swayed.

I normally love the rain. It's so cleansing. Especially if you are dressed for it, not if you get soaked. A walk along the seafront would be wonderful before the kids invaded it with their presents, bikes, scooters, skateboards, roller skates, anything with wheels. It might blow away the cobwebs.

Breakfast was muesli with a sliced banana and some dried apricots for brainpower. I thought of the good doctor opening his presents to himself. I did not remember having supper, except for the sandwich at Skyliners. There was nothing in my fridge for Christmas lunch. A few pots of yogurt past their sell-by.

There were five Christmasy wrapped gifts for me to open,

125

delivered to the shop during the week. Expensive bath foam, another pair of knitted gloves, notelets of Old Latching and a box of Belgian chocolates. And a tin of herbal teabags from Doris. I had not given her anything. She had not been on my list.

The sea was inhospitable and un-Christmasy. It was in a bad mood. I could see anger in the waves pounding the shore. Pebbles slid into the froth. It looked as if a storm was brewing. The sky was scurrying fast with dark cloud formations looming like beasts of prey. Sometimes I loved it, sometimes I was plain scared.

We know nothing about the sky or sea, or what really controls it or makes it stay in place. Why doesn't the sea fall off? We are tiny humans, strutting about our planet like we own it, thinking we know everything when we know absolutely nothing. The planet is not even ours. We are here by accident. Email me if you think you know better.

I walked all the way to the Sea Lane cafe, open, bless them, eight days a week, and I had a glorious hot chocolate, creamily frothed with decadence, worth every penny of £1.65. Happy Christmas me.

Then I walked back, listening to the sea lashing the pebbles, hair blowing across my face. It was a south-westerly, the wind behind me, pushing me along, so I made it in good time. The rain had eased off while I was in the Sea Lane cafe. I was only a bit wet.

Back in my flat there was a message on my answer phone.

'Will you come and have lunch with me, Miss Lacey? I am feeling lonely and bereft. I will pay for your time, if that's necessary. Please phone Francis Guilbert.'

The message stunned me. He was offering to pay for company. I rang him back immediately. I'd be delighted. Just give me half an hour to change and get dry. I put on my best indigo jeans, black jersey, tied my hair back with a clashing red silk scarf which I'd borrowed from my shop. It was the only festive touch.

Just as I was leaving, the phone rang. 'Hi Jordan. Are you feeling better? What are we doing for Christmas? Something nice, eh?' It was Joshua, fishing for an invite.

'Hello, Joshua. Happy Christmas.' I wasn't rising to the bait.

'Shall I come over to your place? I'll bring the nuts.'

I hurt myself trying not to laugh. I knew Joshua so well. He'd bring a 500-gram packet of unsalted peanuts in their shells.

'I'm sorry I won't be able to see you,' I said, all sweetness and light. 'I've got an invitation.'

'How about I come along, too?' he said amiably. 'One more won't make any difference.'

'Two's company, three's an imposition,' I said. 'You won't starve. I'm sure you can get tinned turkey and oven-ready roast potatoes.'

'That's not fair,' Joshua whined. 'Making fun of me.'

'Bye, Joshua. Gotta go.' I put the phone down and went out.

The rain had eased, Latching style, and I decided to walk. My hands slipped into the silky sea of the pocket linings. The pockets of my black leather jacket were kept empty on purpose. The last gift of my parents was too special to be cluttered with crushed tissues, receipts, pencil stubs and old Polos. An anorak was different. The contents of my anorak pockets would have kept me alive on a survival course.

Francis Guilbert lived in an old house at the back of Latching, one of the imposing double-fronted Victorian villas, a few streets from the town. It was the size they now turned into solicitors' offices or doctors' surgeries. Not quite big enough to convert into a residential home for the aged, but ideal for a coastal office. I wondered if he lived alone.

The house was built of white stone and stucco, the wide-angled bays extending to the first floor. The entrance had fluted columns and carved stonework, the rooftops crested with ironwork. As soon as I walked up the drive, I knew that it was the kind of house that I would have loved to live in. Francis Guilbert opened the decorative stained glass, panelled front door.

'There's no charge,' I said immediately. 'I'm very happy to be eating with you, Mr Guilbert. I'm on my own, too. I won't say Happy Christmas because I know it isn't one.'

'Call me Francis,' he said, smiling. 'Come in.'

We went inside. The hall was marble and cool but so welcoming. Flowers and seascape pictures everywhere. Who looked after him now?

'I have a housekeeper,' he said. 'But she has gone home early. Her daughter is not well. We shall have to serve ourselves.'

'Lovely,' I said. 'I am always a bit intimidated by staff.'

'To tell the truth, so am I,' he said. 'Let's help ourselves and hope it's still hot. It's all standing on hot plates.'

The dining room table was far too long for two people. I moved my place right next to his. There was red and white wine on the table, more than I could ever drink, even at Christmas. I would have to watch it.

'Let me serve you,' I said. 'Dab hand at serving, but you will have to carve the turkey. Chopping up birds, I cannot do.'

So, somehow, between us, with a lot of harmless laughter and bantering, we managed to serve each other with overflowing plates of Christmas fare. I found I was quite hungry. It must have been that walk along the seafront. We had lots to talk about which was surprising considering the age and status difference. Francis was genuinely interested in my PI work, my shop and my former police work. I even told him about the rape case that precipitated my departure from the force.

He shook his head. 'You acted exactly as I would have expected. Totally right in the circumstances. But, of course, it's a disgrace that both of them got off. The detective and the rapist.'

'No more of that,' I said, waving the subject away. 'Water under the flyover. I don't think about it any more. Let's hope he's got caught for something else. So tell me how Guilberts got started and became one of the most expensive stores in Latching.'

'Ah . . . you find it expensive?'

'Yes, but I did buy two presents for friends at Guilberts. The quality was what I wanted and I wasn't disappointed.'

'That's it, Jordan. I offer quality. There's lots of cheap shops in Latching, you know, seconds and special offers. It's what many people can only afford. I understand that. But I offer quality for the other range of shoppers. Even if, like you, they only shop in my store occasionally. I see you are wearing one of our scarves. It's an old range. They last forever.'

'In the normal run of things, I can't afford you.'

'Understandable,' he said. We'd reached the Christmas pudding and whipped brandy cream stage. It was all delicious. I was full to the brim but just had room for a few mouthfuls of the lovely fruity pud. Could I take home a doggy bag?

'I have to stock designer clothes. There are many rich women living along the Sussex coast, and a lot of widows. I don't want them to go to London to buy clothes. They come to see what's the latest from Frank Usher and buy a new toaster on the way out. Please don't think I'm talking through the wine, but I'd be happy to give you a permanent, no strings attached, discount on all our goods.'

'Thank you,' I said. 'I may never use the privilege but I appreciate the thought.'

Francis did not pursue the subject. The man had tact. I wondered who I could introduce him to for company. He was such a catch. Mrs Fenwick came immediately to mind. A sweet woman. They had seascapes in common.

About mid-afternoon I left. I was full to the gills. I'd eaten enough for days. Francis was ready to sleep off the bottle or two of his good wine. He was not openly sorrowing, but I knew he was feeling the loss of his son, even if he did not show it.

'Thank you,' I said. My composure was unravelling. I wanted to see James but he was doing double shifts. 'I've enjoyed sharing your Christmas lunch. Thank you for thinking of me. There was only yogurt in my fridge.'

'And thank you,' he said. 'For your company. For helping me through a Christmas that was quite unacceptable.'

'I do understand. See you on Thursday, that is if you want me to carry on with the investigation.'

'I do indeed. But there's tomorrow, Boxing Day, please. It doesn't stop. The first day of the sales. If you thought Christmas was horrendous, wait till you experience the sales. People are queueing up already for the best bargains. A 26-inch widescreen television set for £50.'

'I'll join the queue,' I joked.

'Come and see me occasionally,' said Francis, a wistfulness entering his voice.

'I'd like that.'

A Mexican supper treat was out. I hadn't room for a tortilla crisp but the good claret had made me long for admiring male company, in particular of smouldering DI rank. I wandered along towards First Class Junk, wondering if I ought to open up and catch some trade. Last-minute presents, forgotten aunties . . .

I was just about to put my key in the lock, when Miguel Cortes came out of his restaurant.

'I was keeping the eye open for you,' he said. He looked distraught. His dark curly hair was standing on end as if he had run a hand through it many times.

'Happy Christmas,' I said.

'Ah, yes . . . Happy Christmas. Look, I am in the spot. Will you help me? I will pay double time as it is Christmas Day and you keep all the tips.'

'Me? How? I can't cook. And I'm not much into washing up, not even to help out a friend.'

'I would never ask a fragrant woman like you to wash up. I would do it myself until dawn. And I do all the cooking. It is the serving. One of my girls has not turned up and every table is booked. I even have second bookings at nine o'clock. It's my busiest night of the year, except New Year's Eve. Please, Jordan, help me out.'

His velvety brown eyes were so appealing. Time to swoon. I'd never been called fragrant before. I was a fool but it might be fun. Other people worked on Christmas Day so why not me? I'd had a fabulous lunch and a bit of graft would not hurt. *The Times* once wrote that salvation is to be won by long, hard graft.

'OK. Give me ten minutes to tidy up and I'll be round.'

Miguel threw his hands in the air and blessed me in several languages. I was entranced. Send in the clowns. I was alive and living in Latching. The evening might have surprises.

Fourteen

It was my best Christmas for years and there was a surprise. Sure, I was worked off my pies (Spanish for feet) serving the spicy Mexican food to customers, pouring wine (with festive flourish), asking if everything was all right. I had the jargon off pat. It could have been my vocation. The kitchen was a hive of industrial steam, spicy smells, clattering saucepans, hissing grills. Miguel was overseeing all the cooking, adding a little extra of this and that, giving his dishes the Cortes signature.

I soon picked up how to take orders and pass them to the kitchen, then recognise when to collect the dishes and serve them to the right table number. I only made a couple of mistakes, not knowing my enchiladas from my espadrilles, but no one seemed to mind. It was Christmas.

'One cajun jambalaya, two fajitas, tiger prawn and mushroom and baby corn fillings, one burrito, spicy chicken,' I murmured to myself.

Then the door opened and Sonia Spiller came in with a man. Hotel, Echo, Lima, Papa. Help! Where could I hide? But like most customers, she hardly looked at the anonymous person taking their order. The man ordered. He was about mid-thirties, light brown hair, smartly dressed in blazer and polo-necked jersey, sheepskin coat, pleasant manner. I'd never seen him before. Was this her husband, Colin? They did not seem to be talking much. Sonia twitched nervously like a horse, her long dark hair hiding her face. She was wearing a tight green dress and pearls. Perhaps it was too tight. It did not look the happiest of meals.

'Happy Christmas!' I said brightly, serving their order. 'Enjoy your meal.'

'Happy Christmas,' said the man, looking across at Sonia. She said nothing but unfolded her napkin and smoothed it across her lap as if she was ironing. I poured out their red Merlot. He nodded their thanks. I left them to salvage what festivity they could find.

'Like some crackers?'

'No crackers,' Sonia snarled.

I backed off.

Towards eleven, I began to tire. Waitress legs combined with shop assistant's back did not add up to one hundred percent energy, despite all my sea walking. New Year's Resolution: go to gym. I'd rather go to James.

The patrons were thinning out. I did not see Sonia and her companion leave. The bills were handled by Miguel at his desk. There was a bowl of mints on the desk in case anyone was worried by garlic breath. I wondered if the robbers took mints as well.

I began clearing tables, wiping tops, wondering what the routine was for closing up. But Miguel came over and took the J-cloth out of my hand.

'You don't have to do that,' he said. 'I asked you to serve, not clean. No more work. Sit down and I will bring you some supper. I will serve you myself.'

I shook my head. 'No, thank you, Miguel. I'm too tired to eat, really.'

He looked disappointed. 'The staff always eat together afterwards. We have good time. Plenty of wine. A cup of coffee then?'

'Yes, thank you. Some coffee would be lovely. I'd like that.'

I sat down very carefully, wondering if I would ever be able to get up again. At a pinch I could sleep at the shop, but I really wanted my own bed, my own bath, and eight hours' sleep. If I put my head down on the table I would probably doze off. It was as bad as that. My eyes needed propping open. Pass me the matchsticks.

The last few diners began to leave, fairly merry, calling out Happy Christmases to the staff, wearing rakish paper hats, waving and laughing, blowing whistles from the crackers. They went out into the night and their voices drifted back.

'You have been marvellous,' said Miguel, coming over with two cups of his special aromatic coffee. 'I could not have managed without you.' His eyes were full of warm admiration even though I must have looked a mess and any eye make-up that I once started out with had long since worn off. It was a miracle that the scarf had stayed tied round my hair. He handed me a small brown envelope. 'Here is your pay,' he said. 'And a share of the tips.'

'Thank you. I never realised how hard you work in a restaurant,' I said, putting the envelope in my pocket unopened. It seemed rude to open it. 'It's non-stop.'

'It is not always as busy as this,' he said. 'Tonight was a special night. If you will not eat with us now, perhaps some other would be better? You come in any time, any evening, and it will be my pleasure to serve.'

'I'll come when you all eat together,' I said. Safer. 'That would be nice. I often work late.' Miguel's coffee was excellent. The caffeine began to wake me up. Then I remembered the Boxing Day sales ahead and that sobered me down. 'I do have to go.'

'I will order you a taxi on my account. A lady should not walk alone at night. It not safe. The pubs are coming out and the streets are full of many men who have had too much beer . . . so noisy and disgusting.'

'Thank you,' I said, stifling a yawn. 'I just want to roll into bed.'

Huh . . . wrong thing to say. His eyes sent me an invitation which I pretended not to see. He smiled with resignation and ambled over to the phone on his desk and ordered a taxi. He was indeed a very handsome man in that dark, Latin way.

Even when he was bone-deep tired and he was surely as tired as I was.

'Such a pity,' he said. 'I too would like a roll.'

Boxing Day was a nightmare. I had no chance to do any enquiries of my own. We could have done with twice the staff. Did Francis know what it was really like? Had he ever worked on the shop floor during this stampede? I half expected people to howl like wolves. Some of them certainly behaved like animals. I had to separate two women fighting over a size fourteen gold lamé skirt.

'If you tear it in half, then no one is going to wear it to a party,' I said grimly. 'Give over, ladies. Why not share the skirt if you both like it so much?'

There were some great bargains. I knew they were genuine reductions because I'd been selling them earlier in the week at the original prices. There were also piles of special goods brought in for the sales. I supposed this was normal.

'They're special offers,' I was told.

But other things were happening. Department heads were becoming irritated by replacement goods not arriving. I heard Miss Kent on the telephone.

'I've asked twice for those bathroom sets to come up. When am I getting them? That's not good enough. I want them now, not tomorrow. Mr Oliver would never have allowed this.'

It was the same in Accessories. A consignment of Italian leather wallets and purses was wanted urgently. But they never arrived at the department. The buyer was hopping mad.

'I'm losing sales,' she hissed down the phone. 'And it's all your fault. I shall report you to the general manager.' Then she remembered that the general manager was dead and slammed the phone down to hide her tears.

It dawned on me moving somewhere between bathroom sets and golf umbrellas that Mr Oliver, Oliver Guilbert, the former general manager, son and heir, was the key to many puzzles. He worked for his father and would have inherited it one day. He might have stumbled upon the disappearing stock racket. Supposing he had been removed from a lucrative scene?

Also he'd been seeing Sonia Spiller, the woman who was suing the store for a lot of money. He'd been handling the claim. He played squash. He was a fit young man and upright citizen yet he'd been spun to death on Hell's Revenge. Not his scene, not his style.

No accident. He'd been murdered. It came to me without any doubt. By person or persons who had an interest in both scams. And DI James was keeping it from me. What had he said? Something about a sticky substance? And he mentioned bruising. Manual neck breaking leaves bruises. The arm is hooked across the throat and the head jerked back. The SAS know how to do it. Or it could have been a karate chop, the silent kill.

I needed to know a lot more about Oliver. The clues were somewhere in his lifestyle, his home, his circle of friends. So where should I start? Here and now. As I cruised the staff, I began bringing up his name, dropping loaded questions like miniscule time bombs.

He had known everyone. He had no special friends. He did not chat up female staff. He was not going out with anyone on the staff. All they knew was that he worked hard and often stayed late. He played squash. He drove a red Aston Martin convertible.

An Aston Martin convertible? Where was it now? Hardly the kind of car you could easily mislay. I managed to catch a word with Francis Guilbert as he made one of his lightning tours.

'It was Oliver's pride and joy,' he said, his face lighting up for a second. 'It's a two-door coupé. Six cylinder, twin-overhead camshaft engines.'

Foreign language to me but I tried to look knowledgable. 'And where is it now?' I asked.

'I don't know.' He looked confused. 'It's not in the garage. To tell the truth, I'd forgotten all about Oliver's car. It just wasn't important any more . . . you know . . .'

'Don't worry,' I said. 'I'll find out where it is.'

136

He walked away, looking broken. I'd reminded him about Oliver's death when perhaps, for a few moments at least, the bustle of the store in sales mode had suppressed his grief.

I phoned the leisure centre. The car was not abandoned in their car park. They would have noticed, they said. Nor was it in the store's own underground car park. I checked.

Yet I felt I'd seen it somewhere or a car very much like it. The Aston Martin has a distinctive bonnet line with a flattened air vent, wide grill and laid-back headlamps. An unforgettable shape and length. You can't forget something so unforgettable as an Aston Martin. But I had managed.

I rang up a couple of extra noughts on a pair of pillowcases, charging the bemused woman over £500 for minimum-iron polka dots.

'So sorry,' I said, voiding the whole operation. 'Fingers slipped. Frostbite.'

Who could tell me more about Oliver Guilbert? Sonia Spiller. But I could hardly call on her again after admiring her indoor stencil work so effusively. I sneaked into the loo and got out my mobile.

My voice became coated with sympathy and sincerity. Synthetic treacle. It was pretty awful.

'Mrs Sonia Spiller? This is Tracy Solomon. I am so sorry to intrude at a time of grief but I am writing a piece for the staff magazine about Mr Oliver Guilbert and I wondered if you could add anything to it.'

'Me?' She seemed genuinely taken aback. 'But I hardly knew the man.' But she knew he had died.

'He spoke very highly of you,' I lied. 'As a fellow squash player.'

'Squash? Yes, we occasionally played together but I was hardly in his class. He played very well.'

'Can you tell me anything about the case in which you were involved? You know, the plastic bag you slipped on.'

I heard a sharp intake of breath. 'I can't see what that has to do with the accident,' she said.

'Yours or his?' I asked innocently.

'I'm sorry?'

'Are you talking about Oliver Guilbert's accident or your own accident in the store?'

'What has this got to do with writing a piece for the staff magazine?'

'I wondered if you found Mr Guilbert sympathetic or helpful in your claim.'

Sonia was losing her cool but seemed unable to do anything about it. Any minute now she was going to say something she would regret.

'Look, Miss Solomon or whoever you say you are, I resent this intrusion. I know nothing about Mr Guilbert's accident or how it happened. He was not a friend of mine. And it's none of my business how he died.'

'If you'll recall, I have not asked you anything about Mr Guilbert's accident.' I was such a smoothie at times. 'I thought we were talking about your accident, slipping on the plastic bag that you say was on the floor.'

'If I say there was a plastic bag on the floor, then believe me, young lady, there definitely was a plastic bag. And you can't prove anything different.'

'What kind of plastic bag was it?'

'I've had enough of this.'

'Thank you for being such a help, Mrs Spiller. You have given me a very useful insight into Mr Guilbert's character,' I said before she could slam the phone down.

'I don't know what you mean,' she flared.

Someone came into the lavatories and so I switched off the phone and flushed the loo. I came out and washed my hands. I looked at myself in the mirror and didn't like what I saw. What a job. Phoning people up and pretending to be someone else. Lies and more lies. Still, I could hardly have asked her outright what was Oliver doing in her house the afternoon the RSPCA inspector checked on Jasper in the car? And only Sonia could tell me.

Alan Preston was looking more harrassed than ever. He was losing control of the stock. It was disappearing as fast as it came in. He stood there, wringing his hands and pushing his specs up, both at the same time, if possible.

'I don't understand what is happening. The goods are vanishing before my very eyes. I sign for most of the delivery notes. Look, that's my handwriting.' He waved a pile of notes at me. They were crumpled as if he had checked them over and over again.

'And who sees the goods in? Who actually carries them in?'

'They are usually loaded onto a pallet or trolley and wheeled in. Smaller items are carried by one of my warehouse staff. We have three good strong lads.'

'Where are they now?'

'Well, there's only two in today. Over there, unloading those crates. Daffy is off sick, so he says, probably out late at the pubs last night. Knowing him, he'll be off a week.'

'What has come in those crates?' I asked.

Preston unclipped the last of the delivery notes. 'Duvets. Single, double and king-sized, and pillows, goose, feather and synthetic. Standard quality. Not luxury.'

'Will you check the crates now,' I asked. 'I know you're busy but I'd like it done right away.'

'Certainly. Nothing wrong with this delivery, I'm sure. A most reliable firm.'

The tops were prised off the crates as they were stacked on the concrete floor. Crates one, two and four were full of duvets and pillows packed in plastic bags. Crate number three was also full of plastic packs. But nothing else. The bags were empty. It was a fake delivery. I closed it quickly so that only Mr Preston and I had seen the contents, or lack of them.

I told Alan Preston about the consignment of CDs which I had taken. 'He was actually about to drive away without leaving the delivery.'

'A mistake, I'm sure . . .' Alan Preston was too trusting, too good-natured. 'This could be a mistake too, you know, in the Christmas rush.'

'Maybe,' I said. 'But I suggest you check the contents of everything as it comes in. And check some of these other deliveries which have not yet been unpacked. You may get some surprises.'

'I hope not,' he said wearily. 'I don't want any nasty surprises.'

I went outside into the yard. The air was sharp and bracing, the sky granite with laden clouds. It was the best place to make a private call to Frances Guilbert in his office.

'Mr Guilbert? It's Jordan Lacey. I'm outside the warehouse. First I must thank you for that very pleasant lunch yesterday. I didn't mention it earlier on in front of everyone.'

'It was my pleasure, young lady.'

'I think I have discovered how your stock is disappearing, but not who is organising it. It feels like the work of a well-organised gang, operating in several towns, maybe widespread thieving throughout Sussex. I don't think it's a member of your staff although one of your warehouse lads could be being paid to keep his eyes closed to the goings-on.'

'How am I losing the stock?'

'Firstly, some of it is never actually delivered. It's signed for but no one checks that it has in fact been carried into the warehouse. Secondly, in a big consignment, boxes or crates are being switched somewhere along the line and empty ones brought in among the genuine deliveries. We've found one just now, an empty crate that should contain duvets and pillows.'

'I'll be right down.'

'No, don't do that, Mr Guilbert. Play it cool and we may be able to catch them red-handed. But I do think I have to inform the police. As I said, you may not be an isolated case.'

There was a momentary silence. 'I understand. Yes, you may inform the police, Jordan. But it must be discreet. I don't want any heavy-handed police guarding the store and frightening away customers.'

'From my previous experience,' I said, as if I was always arranging police presence at crime scenes. 'They will probably

140

plant an officer here in the warehouse, plain clothes, brown overalls. No one will notice him. Only you, I and Mr Preston need know who he is and why he is here.'

'I leave it in your hands,' said Mr Guilbert with a deep sigh. 'I am relying on you.'

A phone call to my favourite Detective Inspector, some quick talking and an hour later, DS Ben Evans appeared at the warehouse entrance. He was in scruffy, paint-sploshed jeans and a torn sweatshirt.

'I understand you are looking for temporary warehouse bods,' he said, trying to look unemployed and short of money.

'Come in, lad,' said Mr Preston. 'Yes, we're short-handed. I'll show you what to do.'

Fifteen

After the store closed its doors on Boxing Day, everyone was too tired to talk or even go for a drink together. The cashiers had to stay and count the money. The assistants wanted to get home, soak their feet and unwind.

'Goodnight. Goodnight,' they called to each other.

'Goodnight, Jordan,' said Miss Kent, sweeping out in a fur-trimmed coat. 'You've been a great help. We couldn't have done without you.'

Praise indeed. 'Thank you. Goodnight, Miss Kent.'

I went home to my bedsits. They had a neglected, boarding-house look about them. I'd only slept there, none of the usual living around. No books, tapes, newspapers on the floor or washing-up waiting to be done. My plants were dehydrated, drooping visibly. I toured the pots with water and encouraging words.

'Come off it, you're putting it on. You can't have died yet. It's only been a few days.'

It seemed like a lifetime since I'd had any life of my own. I started at Guilberts on Saturday morning and now it was Wednesday evening. The store had taken over. Sunday had been a working day, and I'd been to the midnight boot. When did I last open my own shop? I could hardly remember where it was.

But I wasn't finished yet. I wanted a serious talk with DI James. I'd neglected my friends over Christmas. And I had to see Mr Guilbert and ask him more about Oliver. But when? Oliver's funeral would be soon. I would have to go to that.

Now. It had to be now. I phoned Mr Guilbert and asked if a brief visit would be convenient. He seemed pleased to hear from me.

'Sure, Jordan. Come round and have a drink. The house seems very empty.'

'In half an hour, then? I want to shower and change. It's been a hard day.'

'Make it an hour's time. I may catch a little snooze.'

It took a whole hour to get ready. I slowed down to a frail snail's pace in the shower, washing my hair slow-motion, rubbing in and rubbing off masks and rejuvenating samples given to me by the cosmetics lady who hadn't given up on my appearance.

'You have such flawless skin,' she'd enthused. 'You must not let it wrinkle. And that bone structure. It simply isn't fair.'

I looked at my unfair bone structure and saw nothing special or different to any other face. Except that it was wan and manless and hadn't seen the jazz trumpeter for weeks. Perhaps my fate was to become an old man's darling.

I hung up my black dress which also looked dispirited and creased. My best dress now. My only dress. I'd gotta a real dress in my wardrobe. And a pricey one. I hadn't chosen cheap.

I appeared at Francis Guilbert's front door in the same indigo jeans, black jersey and leather jacket. He would start thinking it was a uniform. But my damp hair was in two squaw plaits either side of my face. Very youthful. No make-up. The scrubbed look.

His face was sunken and hollowed-out, bruised with pain, his soul bankrupt. The lines had deepened. And I was about to make him feel worse. I made as if to go.

'No, no, Jordan, come in. Please, I need some company. I've had a little sleep and whenever I wake up, Oliver's death hits me hard, every time. I suppose it always will. I'll never wake up without thinking that he has gone.'

I didn't know whether to say it. 'My parents died in a car crash, together, when they were on holiday in France. A wedding anniversary holiday. I felt as you feel, for a long time. Please don't take this the wrong way, but the pain does fade. It never goes away, but it does lessen in intensity. Then sometimes it comes back and hits hard, just as strong and painful as if it only happened yesterday.'

'My dear. How awful for you. Both parents. I didn't know, of course.'

'This black leather jacket, it's real leather,' I went on, to distract him. 'They gave it to me for my twenty-first birthday. I still keep their little card in the top pocket. It gives me comfort to wear it.'

I took out the little birthday card, but did not show it to him.

'Jordan, thank you for telling me. We all have sorrows to bear. It's what life is all about, I suppose. The way it moves on in its unfathomable way, making waves. Come in. I shall open a nice bottle of wine. What did you think of our Boxing Day sales?'

'Madness,' I said, shedding my jacket on a hall chair. 'I couldn't believe that people still had money to spend after the Christmas excesses. Nor the energy to go shopping.'

'Shopping is the new leisure pursuit,' he said. 'There's the soaps, the pub and shopping. I don't mind being third on the list.'

His colour was improving. Francis Guilbert had guts. He might be disintegrating inside but he wasn't going to let it show. He should have had a family of sons, not just one.

We took the wine and glasses into his study. It was a smaller, cosy room with dark tapesty armchairs pulled up to an open fire. Not exactly book-lined. He did not have much time to read. But there was a desk piled with paperwork that he could not leave at the office.

'My housekeeper, Mrs Waite, is still away, so I can't offer you anything to eat. Her home life is a problem. I've opened a packet of crisps. Bacon flavoured.'

I didn't laugh. I drank some wine and we talked about DS Evans in the warehouse. I reassured Francis that he was discreet and very bright. He was the right police presence. We got round to talking about Oliver.

'I feel like Al Fayed,' said Mr Guilbert. 'I don't believe that my son's death was an accident. He would not have gone for a ride on this so-called Hell's Revenge. I ask you, Jordan, does it seem likely?'

'No, Francis, it doesn't add up. And I don't believe that his death was accidental either. Something is quite definitely wrong. It doesn't ring true. I know this is an imposition, but may I see your son's room?'

It was the wine talking. I could never have found the courage on my own.

'You want to see my son's room? Just as he left it?'

Oh dear, what would I find? Teddy bears and Spice Girl posters?

'Please, if you don't mind.'

Francis took me upstairs. But he paused on the landing for a moment. It was still difficult for him to even open the door . . .

Oliver's room was on the front corner of the house with two large bay windows, one facing south and the other facing the setting sun. The view did not quite include the sea, but it was there, twinkling away in the distance and the horizon line was clearly defined.

It was a plain room, all navy and mahogany and lots of brass naval touches. He had not changed the furniture for years. But the curtains were a modern navy and cream design and the matching bed cover (Guilbert's best) was top quality. The carpet was navy, inches thick with the odd red rug thrown for contrast. The pictures were all of the sea which I would have expected. Everything neat and tidy as if the absent housekeeper had been at work and Oliver was expected back.

Surely not as Oliver would have left it? Not a sock in sight, not a letter or magazine. Only some crime novels on the bedside table.

'Have you noticed his trophies?' said Francis, his voice full of pride. He had recovered slightly. 'Oliver was junior county champion.'

The silver cups in the case were county squash trophies. He was a good player, hardly Sonia Spiller standard. Weird.

I duly admired them. The room did not tell me much about him after all. I needed to look through the sturdy chest of drawers and three-door wardrobe. Bottoms of drawers often held secrets.

'Did Oliver have a girlfriend?' I asked, thinking about Leroy Anderson, who would have been just right.

'Not as far as I knew,' said Francis Guilbert. 'He didn't mention anyone special and brought no one home. But then he didn't confide his private life to me. He lead a separate existence even if we shared the same roof.'

'Very normal,' I said, as if I knew all about it. 'Is his funeral soon?' I added, putting my size sixes well into it.

'On Friday. You are welcome to come. I shall be closing the store as a mark of respect.'

I nodded. 'Of course. Everyone will want to be there. Oliver was so well liked.'

'Jordan, if you ever find out anything more about my son's death . . .' he hesitated, '. . . you will tell me, won't you?'

Was he asking me to investigate? It wasn't clear. But I nodded. 'Yes, I will.'

Later I made scrambled eggs on toast for both of us in the kitchen. The height of my culinary skills. He seemed grateful and we ate them at the kitchen table with salt and pepper, tomato sauce and the wine.

'I enjoy your company,' he said. 'I'm almost tempted to pay you to visit me. But that would be unacceptable, wouldn't it, even for a working girl?'

'Not very ethical.'

'I shall invent cases for you to solve and demand weekly reports in person.' His eyes twinkled.

'Outrageous.'

It was after eleven when I left. He didn't order me a taxi, perhaps not knowing the Latching scene late at night. I walked home fast, no short cuts or twittens, keeping to well-lit streets, one of his kitchen knives clasped in my hand just in case. I'd lifted it. A kitchenlifter.

I knew I wouldn't use it, but the light from street lamps on the steel blade was reassuring.

When I awoke, I didn't care if I was supposed to go into the store or not. I was not going. DS Lyons was there. It was his case now. I'd done my bit.

First Class Junk looked as if it had been closed for months. It had been repossessed by spiders and moths. Dead flies redesigned the window dressing. I rushed round with J-cloth and broom, door wide open for fresh air, coffee percolating in the background, a tape of Benny Goodman blowing his clear clarinet into the street. 'Autumn Leaves', 'April in Paris'. Where was my jazzman? Why had he left it so long to come and see me? If anything had happened to him, it would have been in the papers . . . but when did I get the time to read them?

A single rose in cellophane lay on the shop floor. It had been posted through the open door. There was no label. I picked it up, sniffing at the petals, expecting scent, but there was no perfume. DI James had remembered me after all. That's all that mattered.

There was a single-bloom vase out back and I put the rose in the window, pride of place, a way of saying thank you.

I had a steady stream of customers and browsers. I sold a bumper bundle of paperbacks, knock-down price, several small china ornaments (didn't people have enough?) and a couple more of those cap badges. Not a bad morning's work.

'And how's Mavis?' I asked Doris, diving into her grocery shop for a carton of soya milk. She was stocking it now, just for me.

'Not so bad. I spent Christmas Day with her. She's getting over it and her face is healing,' said Doris.

'I meant to call, I did. I really did.'

'Don't worry. She knew you were working at Guilberts. And

I saw you, all dolled up like a dog's dinner, rolling gold paper round things like you knew how to do gift-wrapping.'

'Is there nothing, nothing that you don't know?' I grinned. 'You should be running my business. Wanna take it on? I'd make more money serving in your shop.'

'No, thank you. Too dangerous.' Doris was trying to stick an extension onto a broken nail. She liked nails inches long. Lethal. 'I wouldn't like to be mixing with the sorts that bashed Mavis up. Have you found them yet?'

'Not exactly but we've good descriptions of them. They tried to hold up one of the funfair cash kiosks, but I got the money back even if they got away. They escaped on a fishing boat waiting for them under the pier.'

As I said the words, the fifty pence coin dropped. I wondered if Doris had the same thought. It had puzzled me why Maeve's Cafe should have been robbed of its takings. Not a lot by any means. But the fishy connection suddenly connected.

'Has Mavis got a fisherman boyfriend who is married or very much in a relationship?' I asked.

Doris would not look at me. 'You'll have to ask her,' she sniffed. 'None of my business.'

'It could be the reason why she was beaten up.'

'Ah . . . you mean another Hell's Revenge? Some wife or girlfriend wanting her swarthy fisherman back? All that sun-bronzed skin. Or making sure he would not stray again?'

'Exactly. One of the two funfair robbers was called Chuck. They both match Mavis' description and those of the Mexican restaurant robbers. It's the same pair without any doubt.'

'Miguel give you a nice tip?' Doris winked. 'I saw you serving tables. Get around, don't you?'

I grabbed the carton of soya and put the money down on the counter. 'Doris, that mind of yours. It's going to get you into trouble.'

But I didn't mind the teasing. The trouble was it was one-sided. If only I could retaliate with the odd barb. 'Thank you for the herbal tea. I'm sorry I didn't get you anything.'

'I'll hold you to that.'

Lunch time I shut shop and went along to the police station. Sergeant Rawlings looked really hungover. Had they had a late station party?

'Hey,' I said. 'I didn't get invited to the party.'

'What party? We didn't have a party,' he said morosely. 'But everyone else in Latching did. We were called out to five domestics, two pub fights, three stolen cars, one shop ram raid. And what were you doing last night, PI Jordan Lacey?'

'Cooking scrambled eggs for a client.'

'How sensible. I suppose you want to see DI James?'

'Is that possible? Or is he sleeping it off?'

'I never get time to sleep,' said a voice I could die for. DI James stood there, his usual serious expression, yet with a glimmer of welcome, as if I was light relief. He was washed out with exhaustion. A double shift on Christmas Day. Boxing Day sounded a barrel of fun. He waved me upstairs to his office. It was littered with take-aways and polystyrene coffee cups.

'Don't you ever have anything proper to eat?' I said, surveying the debris.

'Maeve's Cafe is closed.'

'She's getting better. I'm sure she'll open again soon.'

'Good. I'll wait.'

He poured me some coffee from the machine. I took it. How I had missed him, these last few days. I had not seen him over Christmas, that special time for people together. Work for him, work for me. I smiled at him, relieved that he was still alive, that no stray bullet had stolen him from my life.

'Thank you for the rose,' I said.

'The what?' He was not going to admit it.

'Here's your Christmas present,' I said, pushing a slim holly festooned package across his desk.

'I didn't expect anything,' he said, looking at the package. That solemn look. It got me. Then sometimes he smiled and the sun broke through. I like the sternness in his ocean blue eyes. I

149

need that kind of discipline. When was he going to come in to my life, take over, take charge?

'So? Does it matter? This is my present to you,' I said.

'I've already got three slimline diaries.'

We looked at each other and then began laughing. That's what he thought was in the package. And I knew differently. Music surged into my heart. This man was a soulmate, but he did not know it.

'Open it, you twit. Show some enthusiasm. I spent valuable hours cruising the shops searching for that present.'

James opened the package carefully as if he was going to save the wrapping paper. He liked what he saw. A book of one-liners. Wit and wisdom. He opened it at random.

'There aren't enough days in the weekend,' he read. 'Anonymous. Ask him the time, and he'll tell you how the watch was made. Jane Wyman of ex-husband, Ronald Reagan. Thank you, Jordan.'

'For the man who has everything, but no time to read,' I said flippantly.

'For the man who has nothing,' he said.

It was all in his face yet he would not allow me anywhere near. Some woman had hurt him so much. That wife that he never mentioned. He did not trust me. I was that sassy Jordan Lacey, PI irresponsible, wild, reckless, always in need of rescuing. Not someone to take seriously.

'OK. Christmas is over. Back to work. Oliver Guilbert. I'm still working for his father. How did Oliver die? I don't believe Oliver died on Hell's Revenge. Or if he did, how did he get there? Something is totally wrong. And where is his red Aston Martin convertible? It's gone missing.'

'Jordan, slow down. I know you're Latching's Wonder Woman. How many cases are you working on? Or how many do you think you are still working on? I'd really like to know. Then we won't clash or we could collaborate.'

I had to think hard. 'Oliver Guilbert employed me to follow Sonia Spiller. She's suing Guilberts for a lot of money for slipping on a plastic bag and dislocating her shoulder. No actual evidence of this plastic bag as far as I can make out. Francis Guilbert is employing me to find out how stock is disappearing from his warehouse.'

'Anything else?'

'No. I took on the robbery myself. Mavis is my friend. I was outraged.'

'But now you've turned Guilberts over to us, having asked for a police presence, i.e. DS Ben Evans is in place. It's our case now. And Oliver Guilbert is dead so I presume he is no longer employing you?'

'It seems I am no longer employed by anyone.'

I had let the coffee grow cold. No one had paid me either. Oliver hadn't paid me, obviously, being dead. And Francis had put me into some office system for the shop assistant work which had not yet surfaced. The only money I had earned recently was in the small brown wages envelope, unopened, given to me by Miguel Cortes. It had felt quite bulky. Several folded notes.

'You haven't answered my question. Do you know how Oliver Guilbert died? Was he killed by being spun round in the funfair? Or was his neck broken manually? It could have been a really nasty karate chop delivered to the front of the neck by the outside of the hand. It compresses the vagal nerve and causes the heart to stop quite quickly. Surely you know by now, James.'

'And you know, just as surely, that I am unable to give you this information, Jordan. Nor do you need it. The cause of Oliver Guilbert's death can't be established. We are waiting for the coroner's report. You'll have to wait like everyone else. Then there may be an inquest.'

'That's not good enough, James. I give you lots of information. You can't deny that. I'm your secret weapon. You'll probably solve half a dozen cases in the county with my lead from the warehouse. You'll be promoted.'

'Those Sonia Spiller tapes,' he said, deftly changing the subject.

'Going to pay for them?'

He ignored the suggestion. 'Her dog, the labrador puppy that she takes for walks . . . Do you know anything about dogs? Can you recognise them?

'Four-legged, jumping about, face licking. Yes, I can recognise a dog.'

'Come and see this one. It was found last night, wandering on the beach in a distressed state. We're waiting for the RSPCA to come and collect it.'

I followed his tall figure out to the back of the station. They'd tied the dog to a radiator but with food and water bowls within reach. It looked forlorn, head resting on front paws, doggy eyes blank with misery.

'Hello, Jasper,' I said.

The brown eyes lit up at the sound of his name. Jasper went into his mad dog routine, jumping and barking, trying to reach me. He sent the water bowl flying. I went down on one knee and he immediately decided to lick my face clean.

'Hold on buster,' I said, trying to restrain him. 'I've washed already this morning. *Down, sit.* Good boy.'

He looked astonished at the stern command, quietened and sat, tongue lolling, eyes bright with expectation.

'Is this Sonia Spiller's dog?'

'I'm pretty sure it is. She couldn't handle him. She's probably thrown him out. Or tried to drown him. Poor old thing.'

'I'll give her a call, then ask the RSPCA to rehouse him. Lots of pets are abandoned over Christmas.'

'There's the husband, Mr Spiller, although I've never seen him. Perhaps it's his dog. You need a dog,' I rambled on, stroking Jasper's head. The dog turned so that my hand found a special place behind his ear. 'Something to take for walks. Company in the evenings, someone to talk to.'

'You know I'm never at home.'

'Where's home?' I asked, seizing the opportunity.

'Sometimes I don't remember where it is and have to look for it. Just rooms, Jordan, not a home like your place. I envy you your two bedsits. You've made them a real home, all your own, full of your personality, pictures and plates and things.'

I was stunned. Four whole sentences. James had actually spoken to me, for once, like a real person, noticed what was in my home. He was standing way above me so I could not see the look on his face. I could only see his trousered knees. Dear knees. I wanted to write the words down so that I would never forget them. I wanted to hug his knees, lean my head onto their bones.

'I can't have a dog,' I said, like an idiot, to cover my frailty. 'Not in two bedsits.'

'No, of course not. Far too small. Jasper would break all your treasures in five minutes. He's not your problem. I'll phone the RSPCA.'

'But I know someone who would like a dog,' I said, standing up. My knees were damp and stiff from kneeling in a puddle. 'Someone who needs a dog. Can I take him?'

Sixteen

M avis was surprised at first but then delighted. She and Jasper took to each other like long lost friends. She did not mind having her face washed.

'Of course I've got room for him. He's a smashing dog. He'll have to be taken for lots of walks and that will get me out again. I'll take him to the cafe every day and keep him there with me, out back, away from the food. He'll learn. I'll train him, feed him up, make him obey me. And if I say attack, then he'll *attack*.'

I was not so sure about the attack command. Jasper would probably lick a robber to death. But if it made Mavis feel more secure, then it would work for her.

'At the moment, I'm not sure if you will be allowed to keep him. He was found wandering at night and the owner says she does not want him any more. But the RSPCA may have to vet you to see if you are a suitable home.'

'You bet I'm suitable,' said Mavis, growing inches, guts coming back, mental mascara being applied. 'No one dare say I'm unsuitable. And I've got friends who'll vouch for me.'

Friends . . . hunky fishermen. Brawn and bronze. They'd say she was suitable, take Jasper for power walks along the beach, teach him to obey, have the time and patience. They have to be patient to fish. It's all those long hours alone at sea.

I knew I had done the right thing.

'I'm sorry I didn't come and see you on Christmas Day. I don't know where the time went. Boxing Day I was working at

154

the store. Sales time, you know. The stampede of the century. I meant to come, but I didn't.'

'Don't worry, Jordan. I know about all the pressures you've had. Doris tells me what's happening. She knows everything. You look thin. I must get back and feed you.'

'James is missing your good food. He hasn't eaten anything except take-aways since you closed. Open up for him, please.'

Mavis threw me a lancing look I had never seen before. She knew how I buried myself in longing. Perhaps my torment is close to her torment, only she gets better results.

'I hate to ask you this, Mavis. Please don't get upset or be angry. It is important in my enquiries. But your friends, your fishermen friends . . . what do you know about them?'

She made an indignant move as if to stop me but I fenced my hand and went on. 'I know they are special and nice and extra hunky, and I don't blame you, heavens no, for encouraging them, not for a moment. I am not making any moral judgement. But might it be possible that one of these fishermen has an extremely jealous wife or girlfriend or partner-type female?'

The seconds hung in a stiff silence, broken only by Jasper wanting to jump around and explore his new home. Mavis did not know what to say or where to look.

'Well . . . there might be. What makes you think that?' she said at last.

'Chuck, one of the men who robbed you, and his mate, were picked up under the pier by a local fishing boat, after they had attempted to rob a funfair kiosk. Now, that starts to look like some sort of pressure to me. The fishermen are ninety-nine percent honest, measuring their catches in case a fish is half an inch too long. But supposing a jealous woman employed these two thugs to bash you up, then threatened her fisherman husband so that he had to help the robbers escape or you would get bashed up again . . .'

Mavis was trying not to look at me.

'You're right,' said Mavis, visibly shaken. 'There is a woman who would do that. I know her all right. She's as jealous as a green cat. Got red hair, face to match. She'd pay. Yes, she'd pay anything to keep . . . to keep him . . . this man . . . well, you don't need any names, do you?'

I let her off the hook. 'No names, Mavis. As long as I am on the right track.'

There were only so many fishermen along Latching beach. It was a dying trade. It would not take long to weed out the pensionable, the paunchy and those over the hill in bed. The hunks in yellow waders were few and far between, winching their boats up the shingle at dawn. Very few.

'Yes, you're on the right track, Jordan. So that's why I got a face like this.' She touched her bruises with care. 'They weren't after the cafe money at all, I can see it now. The money was petty cash. They'd been paid already.'

Jasper was bored. He wanted action, strained at the lead to make himself noticed. Mavis moved the glass mermaid I'd given her on to a higher shelf.

'Come on, old fellow. Like a nice walk? How about twice round the pond for starters? That'll give the ducks a fright.'

Jasper was all for a walk. He followed Mavis with complete confidence and trust. If she'd suggested a walk to the moon, he'd have gone along for the fun of it. They were on the same wavelength.

We cruised the pond a couple of circuits. Jasper was near hysterical with excitement, ecstatic tail thrashing weeds. He'd never created so much fuss. Ducks were a lot noisier than seagulls.

'I can see this one needs a firm hand,' Mavis grinned. She was already looking brighter. The brisk walk was bringing colour into her cheeks. 'But I'll manage him. I had a dog when I was a girl. It takes time and patience and I've got plenty of both.'

I gave her a hug and a girl kiss and she promised to open the cafe soon. Doris had some theatrical make-up that would cover the bruising, she said. I drove away, well pleased.

There was still a lot to do. I drove back to my shop and immediately knew something was wrong. My nose told me. My stomach shrank. The stench was awful.

I parked the ladybird in the rear yard and went in the back way, holding my hand against my face. It was not easy to make myself go through the office into the shop.

A pile of rotting fish lay on the floor. They had been posted through the letter-box. By the bucket. My stomach, the most delicate part of my anatomy, could not stand the sight nor the smell. I rushed back outside into the cold air, holding onto a wall, until my breathing eased and my brain took over. Instant shopping list: mask, disinfectant, lavender oil, new film.

I made myself take photos. Lesson recently learned: always take photos of the evidence. Wearing the mask, I cleaned up and disposed of the same, well wrapped, in distant bins. The lavender oil was on my pulse points and near my nose. It was the only way I could cope. Then when the floor was damp but cleared of debris, I scrubbed every inch with strong disinfectant. The fish fluids had soaked into the floorboards, taking off the polished stain. I wondered if I would ever rid the shop of the smell.

'Hell's Revenge,' said Doris, pausing at my doorstep, nose wrinkled in disgust. 'Fish guts.'

'A ton of them,' I said.

'You've upset someone,' said Doris, backing off.

'Did you see anyone near my front door this morning? Someone with a barrow or a Land Rover or van?'

'I saw a red convertible,' she said.

I groaned. 'No . . . I don't believe it. Not a red convertible. Was it an Aston Martin?'

'Come off it, Jordan, I don't know makes of cars. They've got five wheels, one at each corner and one at the front and that's about all I know.'

'That car's a stolen car. Someone's got hold of it, but who and how? His father hasn't seen it for long enough. Now it arrives at my doorstep and delivers a load of stinking fish.'

'You'd better leave the door open, get rid of the smell.'

'But I'm so cold. It's winter.'

'Put on another jersey. Who's father?'

'Oliver Guilbert's. Oliver had a red convertible.'

157

Doris paused and thought, crinkling up her Joan Crawford brows. 'That means that Oliver's death is in some way linked to the two morons who painted by numbers on Mavis's face and then robbed the funfair kiosk. Are you missing something, Jordan?'

'I'm missing a brain,' I said. 'Thank you, Doris. I'll call on you again when I need help.'

Doris was right. There must be a link. The three robberies were linked to Oliver's death. Or whoever paid Chuck & Co to re-arrange Mavis' face had somehow come into possession of Oliver's car. If I could find out when he last had the car . . . his last day alive. The trail could go cold so quickly but the clue must be there somewhere. And fish again. This time through my letter box. It would take me some while to face fish on a plate.

The fair had arrived that day. Oliver had visited Sonia at her listed cottage. Where had he parked the car then? Suddenly I knew, at the health club opposite. A man who played squash so well would pump iron. Later I'd seen Sonia hurrying some-where, followed by a man who could have been her stalker. She'd sat in the cafe, Macaris, then thrown a bag off the end of the pier. Oliver had been found on Hell's Revenge with a broken neck. Brother, was this getting complicated.

The disinfectant and the lavender oil were winning against the fish. No customers today for sure. No one would pass over my threshold. But perhaps DS Ben Evans had a blocked nose because he made the leap.

'Got a leaking pipe?' he asked, stepping over the wet floor. 'Looks like you've been flooded.'

'I got flooded with a pile of rotting fish. Sorry about the smell. I've done my best. That's why the door is open. Come through to the back. I've some good coffee brewing.'

'This is better than that station stuff,' he said, moments later, perched on my desk, looking very much at home. 'Brown mud, I call it.'

'Coffee is one joy in life that must be enjoyed slowly and

seriously,' I said. 'It should always be good quality and made with care.'

He grinned at me. He had a nice face, openly attractive, regular manly features. The WPCs must be swooning in their black tights. A bit young for me. I really prefer that older, mature DI James look, his knit of anguish. And my jazz trumpeter who I had not seen for ages. Perhaps he was in the States, blowing his horn for a pocketful of dollars.

'I can think of a few other things that should be enjoyed slowly and seriously.' He was teasing but it suited me to make out that I did not understand. It was so long since I had slept with anyone. And that had been a single horrendous mistake. Mistakes are easy to make when your hormones are aroused and it's too late to stop.

'So, is this a social call? Did you smell the coffee? Or do you want to ask me something?'

'All three,' he said. He'd been on a diplomacy course. 'You were working at Guilberts. You spotted that the goods were not being delivered, only signed for. You also got consignments checked and found the empty crates. What else do you know?'

'Did DI James send you?' I've such a suspicious mind.

'Do you know anything about the outlet? Where the stolen goods are sold? OK, it may be country-wide. A few container lorries full of stuff and twenty-four hours later it's on sale in the north. But what about locally?'

'There's a midnight boot,' I said. What was the purpose in keeping quiet? But I did not want to involve Jack. He was an innocent customer. 'Out near Ford, in an old barn. Don't ask me how people find out it's on. Loads of dicey stuff. I recognised merchandise from Guilberts . . . well, I'm almost sure it was from the store.'

'You should have bought some of the goods. It could have been checked.'

'What was I suppose to use for cash?' I scoffed. 'Monopoly money? I don't carry a wad. It's up to you. And I can't find this place again. It was in the dark.'

Suddenly I remembered the parking yard. I remembered the cars and vans parked in the dark, among the dense bushes and hedges. There had been a red car, long and low, its colour turned almost black in the shadows. I remembered the long bonnet and air vent. Oliver's car. But he was already dead. Someone else had driven it there. I felt a headache coming on.

'Thanks,' said Ben Evans, rising. 'I owe you. Want to come for a drink some evening? I hear you like jazz. There's jazz at the airport terminal every Sunday evening. Like to come along next Sunday?'

I nodded dumbly. I'd go anywhere for some real jazz. My soul needed a transfusion. It was near to body breathing. The music would infuse me with glorious flames. Jazz began in the fields, men and women working, needing pulsating sound and beat to lift their worn spirits.

'Sure. Phone me.'

I tried not to sound too enthusiastic. If DI James learned that Ben Evans had taken me out, then he might think I was spoken for. And that was definitely not the case.

'Perhaps some of your mates might like to come along,' I added. 'The more the merrier.'

'Your flood is icing over,' he said, leaving. 'Perhaps you'd better close the door.'

A thin film of ice had formed on the floor. Iced fish juice. I'd never get rid of the smell till the summer. I might as well close the shop and go for a walk. The sky was heavy. I didn't like the look of the clouds, too dark and moving so fast. It was a northerly wind. Time to batten down the hatches.

I took a narrow short cut down to the beach. These lanes were only wide enough for a fisherman and his barrow, used daily by fishermen, nightly by the smugglers from the past. Only tourists used them now. And dogs. And seagulls. Canyons between houses, eerily empty, dark, cobbled walls. Field Row was haunted, they say. I'd never seen anything . . . yet.

The sea was churning, huge waves towering over the shingle. The pier had been closed already. The sound of the restless sea was ominous, torment of a seabed being uneasily disturbed. A storm was on the way. Somewhere isobars were wrecking havoc with the tides. People were scurrying home, heads down, not wanting to be caught out in it.

I pulled up my collar, jammed down my ski-hat and thrust hands into pockets. Perhaps twenty minutes' ferocious fight with the elements would clear my mind. I had to lean into the wind to make any progress. Breathing was hard work.

It puzzled me how seagulls could fly in a storm. They are merely puffs of feathers, yet somehow they find thermals in which to wing it. They had more control than a human. You never see a seagull being tossed about like debris.

Some people were coming down to the sea with video cameras, keen to film the raging seas. A few brought toddlers in pushchairs. I wanted to warn them but knew there would be parental abuse. Those babies were at risk.

The beach guard driving his four-wheeled buggy was clearing people off the shingle. They were expecting a high tide. The sea was bucking and rearing like a nervous horse. But the sound was more like that of an enraged sea monster emerging from an underwater lair after centuries of imprisonment.

Rain clouds from the north opened up, drenching Latching with nasty stinging bolts of icy rain. The weather was getting worse. I could hardly see where I was going, keeping my eyes on the ground ahead, avoiding puddles, putting one foot down after the other with deliberation. My boots were sodden, the rain soaking through the stitching. The wind was determined to blow me over. I strained ahead, tried to cross the road but the wind made it impossible. The lower level from the front was like a wind tunnel.

'What the hell are you doing out here, Jordan?'

The wind whipped his words away but I got the gist from his face. DI James was done up in a patrolman's black bad-weather gear. Wind and rain resistant fabric, the kind they wore in the Falklands. He did not seem to have a patrol car.

'I could ask you the same,' I said.

'The patrol car's broken down,' he shouted. 'I'm walking back. Why aren't you at home? It's not safe to be out.'

To emphasise his warning, a dustbin came rolling across the road, its contents blowing all over the place. I hoped it didn't contain a package of rotting fish.

Rain was streaming down my face. I was hardly Kate Moss but James had the arms and legs of a rescue team and I needed help. Not like when I was choking to death in an old cinema or locked in a hermit's hole, but something simple, elemental, like being totally unable to cross a road without help.

He took my arm. It was not a lover's caress but more old lady across a road type assistance. I took what pleasure I could from his closeness, even wet closeness.

'Mavis is going to open her cafe soon.'

'Good, I'm hungry.'

Before I could offer him ginger and lentil soup, a car came screaming round the corner, far too fast, heading straight for us. I was transfixed. James yanked me back onto the pavement, only seconds to spare, almost wrenching my arm out of its shoulder socket. It was a reflex reaction. The spray from the car wheels spinning through a deep gutter puddle drenched us both. I felt displaced air batter my face, sting. The car righted its spin with a screech and careered down the road.

'Damned fool,' James shouted again, his face angry. 'He could have killed us. Are you all right?'

I hung onto his arm, swallowing hard, shaking. 'They meant to,' I choked. 'They meant to kill us or kill me. They were after me.'

'Jordan? Get your head on straight, for goodness' sake. Stop imagining things.'

'See that car that nearly hit us?' I said, grimly, biting my lip till it bled. 'That's Oliver Guilbert's car. How many red convertibles are there in Latching? How many red Aston Martins? It's a stolen car. It's been missing since the day Oliver died. That's his killer driving it.'

DI James took out his mobile and shook it. 'Damned

battery's gone.' I didn't know if he was listening or taking any notice.

'He was trying to k-kill me, I tell you,' I whispered, teeth chattering. I could barely speak. My legs didn't belong to me. They had gone walk-about and not in my direction.

'But he didn't, did he? He missed. If the driver was aiming for you then he was only trying to scare you. A killer driver would have mounted the pavement and slammed you against the wall. Splatter. End of Jordan Lacey.'

I nodded stupidly, wanting to believe he was right. 'But that's only what you think, and you don't know. Perhaps he saw you and changed his mind at the last minute. I've got a mobile that works. It's in my left pocket. You can use it.'

His hand went into my pocket, felt around and took out the mobile. 'First sensible thing you've said in years. Let's hope it works.'

His hand had touched my hip. It was almost worth dying for.

Seventeen

Sergeant Rawlings rolled out the VIP treatment, tea in a china cup, not a polystyrene burn-your-hands beaker. He opened a packet of low-sugar digestives, not a speck of fluff in sight. I was still shaking.

'Can we dry her off?' DI James asked as if I were a creature not a person, something just fished out of the sea.

'The warmest place is by the radiator,' said Sergeant Rawlings. 'We don't have any female clothing around.'

WPC Patel produced a scratchy towel and I dabbed at my hair and face, not really caring. My boots were sodden. Everything dripped. I took my boots off and put them near the heat. It would probably ruin the leather. I draped my anorak over a chair and the sleeves hung like washing, dribbling onto the floor. I could hardly strip off my jeans. They clung to my legs in folds of wet blue blotting paper.

DI James sprinted upstairs to his office. No prizes. He had dry clothes in his cupboard. I used to keep spares in my locker. I wondered who was using it now.

I drank the tea and continued dripping on the floor. A small pool formed. Steam was starting to rise from my boots.

'Why can't I go home?' I asked. 'I'm all right now. I'm not injured.' Except for a bruised arm, a trophy of uncertain value.

'We may want a statement, Jordan,' said Sergeant Rawlings, giving me a refill. 'You might need protection.'

'Sure,' I scoffed. 'The West Sussex Police Authority has plenty of spare manpower, yes? I don't think so, matey. Anyway, I can take care of myself. I'll be careful.'

164

I thought of Mavis's face. No joke. I might be next on the hit list.

The station was filling up. The usual night's sweepings. A couple of homeless and smelly drunks; a domestic still going at each other, hammering and tonging; a driver whose breathalyser test had soared. He was in for a blood test. Relations, witnesses, solicitors, doctors . . . it was worse than ER, worse than the Guilberts Boxing Day sales.

DI James came downstairs, pulling a black jersey over his head. He had towelled his crew cut dry. It stuck out like a small boy's.

'I've got to go out,' he said to Sergeant Rawlings. Then to me, 'Stay here and I'll be back.'

I can't help it. I was born to snoop. Indicating to Sergeant Rawlings that I was going to the loo, I wandered out and took a sharp left turn and raced upstairs. Everything had changed since I last worked there. It used to be cramped little offices, hardly room to swing a warrant. Now it was all open plan and plants that needed watering. But there was still the same shabby furniture and desks piled high with paperwork.

It took me a few minutes to identify James's desk. Wet clothes slung over a chair, tidy desk, no photos, nothing personal. I ached for his hurt. But it did not stop me looking through the papers and files on his desk. I wanted information about Oliver Guilbert's death.

Then I found the file that I wanted and extracted a two-page document. Another file caught my attention. I looked round for a photocopier and ran off copies of several pages in as many seconds. Brilliant. I could barely keep my excitement from showing. He'd kept this from me. Why? Was he trying to protect me, or drill me into the ground? I returned the two files to more or less the same position on his desk, then went downstairs and back to the chair, trying to look as if drying my hands had taken a long time.

'Sorry,' said Sergeant Rawlings, apologising for his lack of attention. He had not even noticed how long I'd been gone. 'Been a bit busy.'

'Par for the course. Usual night's trawl.'

The photocopies were folded inside my sweater, giving my bust an angular shape. I hoped he would not get suspicious. But he was far too busy to investigate my lopsided bosom. Besides he was a gentleman (almost) and married (very).

'What's happening?' I went on, draping myself over the radiator. The photocopies crackled.

'Don't ask me,' he groaned. 'Latching has erupted into a tidal wave of minor criminal activity. And in this weather, too. You name it and it's happening. I don't think DI James will be back for hours. He's gone out to a nasty pile-up on the Arundel Road.'

'I'll walk home,' I said. 'I feel better now and I've dried off a bit. Some warm clothes would be nice.'

He didn't argue. 'We don't have a car available to take you home. Sorry. But you can borrow a waterproof and take my torch. There's been a power cut. No street lighting.'

He'd forgotten about the statement. It had taken a back seat.

The waterproof was six sizes too big, came rustling down to my knees, but was ample protection. I forced my feet back into wet boots. They felt like soggy socks.

'Thanks, Tiger.' I grinned, reminding him of his face painting on the pier. 'I'll return it tomorrow.' Then I remembered that tomorrow was the day of the funeral. 'Or sometime tomorrow, after the funeral.'

'OK, Jordan. Anytime. We'll issue a warrant when it's overdue.'

It was spooky outside without street lighting. The station had been using an emergency generator. They couldn't have villains escaping in the dark. Nearby houses and flats were darkened too, some windows illuminated by wavering candlelight. The Christmas decorations were off, as were the garlands of bright fairy lights strung along the seafront. Inky Latching was a different world, as if struck by some major disaster. Very few people had ventured out. The twittens were deserted. The sooner I got safely home, the better.

I transferred the photocopies to pockets in the waterproof in case they fell onto the wet pavement. The storm had abated but it was still raining heavily. I held the torch at the ready like a weapon. I didn't trust anyone these days. Every approaching car gave me a fright, headlights sweeping my feet into panic mode. They all looked shades of red. My two bedsits were shrouded in darkness but I raced for them.

I knew exactly where I kept the candles and matches. I crept upstairs, feeling around like someone newly blind. The flame ignited a wick and I steadied the candle in its holder and walked about as Florence Nightingale had in the Crimea. The shadows revealed no intruders. No one had broken into my fortress. The hit-and-run had unnerved me. Even Derek would have been a comfort as long as he did not hassle me as I peeled off my damp jeans and changed into a fleecy tracksuit. I heated some soup and poured it into a big white bowl.

A ring of candles threw light onto the coffee table and I flattened out the photocopies, squinting at the crumpled lines of black printing. The pathologist's report on Oliver Guilbert was two closely written pages, the language half legal, half medical.

The sticky substance on his face was the residue from heavy-duty parcel tape. There was bruising on his throat with damage to the thyroid cartilage and the hyoid bone was broken. This was shown both on X-rays and found in the autopsy. Wounds on the hands and arms were defensive. Oliver had fought off his attacker.

The pathologist deducted that Oliver Guilbert had died of manual strangulation, in particular from an arm-hold across his neck, jerking the head back. The breaking of this small hyoid bone was a strong sign of manual strangulation even if there were few other visible signs. At some point a surgical neck collar had been placed on him. There were traces of the foam material.

From blood displacement and lividity, it was deduced that Oliver had already been dead before being placed in a sitting position in a car on Hell's Revenge. His head had been taped to the brace and headrest for the spin, then the tape removed as the ride slowed down and the attacker made his escape.

The report then listed the different fibres found on Oliver's clothes. My eye caught on two words: scales, fish. Two minute scales had been found, identified as huss, Latching's staple catch.

Fish again. But what was the connection with Oliver? He hardly knew Mavis, apart from the occasional chip shop treat. Sonia surely did not know Mavis. I couldn't imagine her in Maeve's Cafe. Nor her husband . . . if the man treating her to a festive Mexican meal was her husband.

Mavis wasn't giving me the name of her current lover, the fisherman with a jealous wife. What possible connection could there be between these people? Fishermen didn't shop at Guilberts or their wives. They trundled round Tesco's and Quality Seconds looking for bargains and special offers.

This was making my head ache. A candle spluttered.

I turned my attention to the second stolen photocopy. Stolen. The word shocked me. One could hardly call them borrowed or accidentally acquired. It had been a deliberate theft.

This was not my case either, but the part destruction of Latching Bowling Club's pavilion was of interest as was the gruesome find in the bucket/scoop/shovel. A second arm had been washed up on the west bank of the River Arun by the tide. Did they belong to each other? Had they been identified? I was just plain nosey.

By the time I'd finished reading the report, I was also plain nauseated. It served me right. The detail made me feel ill. I should have left the report where I found it.

The arms did belong together. They had been identified by fingerprinting, DNA, skin-scrapings, a ring, a watch and naval anchor tattoo on the left wrist. But no one had reported this man as missing. I read on, hardly breathing. The man who partly ended up in the shovel of a yellow JCB was Ronald Arnold Hamilton, aged fifty-four, antique dealer and husband of Mrs Brenda Hamilton, secretary of Latching Bowling Club and giver of lavish, but foodless parties.

Music, bath, lots to drink. All at the same time. I was severely dehydrated despite getting soaked. I put on some smooth jazz, Stan Kenton playing Dorsey, ran a bath laced with aromatherapy oils, lavender and neroli, to soothe my tattered nerves, drank several glasses of water. I couldn't tolerate alcohol.

How could Mrs Hamilton give a party when her husband was dead and strewn around the county? Perhaps she didn't know. Husbands often walked out and the wife kept quiet about it. Who had been the silver-haired man handing out drinks, greeting people like a good host? Of course, a hired butler. What was going on? Another household that was not what it seemed on the outside.

But none of this was my concern. Not my case. I had to get my priorities in order. I had only to find out if Sonia Spiller was faking her claim and explain the disappearance of goods from Guilberts. I'd set the police on the right track of the second investigation. I was no longer employed to follow Sonia Spiller but it would keep my mind occupied if I brought that case to some conclusion. Picket surveillance was the answer. Anticipate where Sonia is going and be there first.

The three roberies were strictly police business even if I had a personal interest in Mavis. I could just leave it all to DI James and DS Evans and his brilliant band of men, concentrate on my shop and lost tortoises. I'd given Mavis a dog. That's what friends are for.

But the hit-and-run car had been after me. That was a sobering thought. They obviously thought I was on the right track of something. If only I knew what it was.

The next morning I dressed soberly. The funeral was at eleven o'clock at St Michael's, private cremation to follow. I wondered why the body had been released when the death had not been accidental as at first thought. Perhaps they had taken all the evidence and samples they needed and could let the body of poor Oliver go to his rest.

The church was packed and I was able to slip in the back unnoticed. This was fortunate as funerals upset me and I did not want to be seen sniffing into a damp tissue.

A few rows in front of me sat a woman with a mane of dark hair on her shoulders. As she moved slightly, I saw it was Sonia Spiller. I could not believe it. She was at Oliver's funeral, bold as brass, and to add to it, she was wearing a neck collar. This was outrageous. She really did have a nerve. Perhaps she thought this public appearance would manufacture some sympathy from Francis Guilbert.

I couldn't bear to look at the coffin as it was being carried in. A wreath of white lilies had been placed on the lid. It bore no resemblance to the Oliver Guilbert, so boyish and handsome, that I remembered coming into my shop not long ago. I could even hear his voice apologising to me: I've got suspicious of everyone. This business has really upset me. You don't know who to trust . . .

Had he meant that he had suspicions about someone he knew at the store . . . now that I could no longer ask him, his words took on another meaning.

Francis Guilbert was one of the pall bearers. Carrying his son now in death, as he had once carried him in life, as a small boy. I found this unbearably moving. I had to blink away the tears. At this rate of disintegration, I'd have to leave the church before the service was half over.

The music was inspired and saved me. As well as two traditional hymns, Francis had chosen some of his son's favourite pieces. A tape played Queen, Elton John, Madonna. It cheered everyone up. I recognised many of the staff from the store. Several smiled at me.

It took ages to file out afterwards. Francis Guilbert stood outside, shaking hands with everyone. Oliver had already left in a black Daimler for his last journey. Francis even shook hands with Sonia, briefly but politely. They barely spoke. But when he came to me, he clasped my hand warmly.

'You didn't come into work yesterday,' he scolded me lightly. 'We were expecting you.'

'I thought my job was over,' I said, hoping I was not being overheard. 'Seasonal temp, you know.'

'But you were so good. I'd offer you a permanent position anytime. An asset to any establishment.'

'But I've got my own shop and a business,' I said, gently reminding him of First Class Investigations.

'But we are hardly competition!' He tried a slight joke. He was trying to put me at ease. The man was made of stern stuff. I really ought to introduce him to Hilary Fenwick. She was a sweet woman and lonely. 'Don't forget to pick up your pay packet for *all* your work for me,' he added.

'No, I won't,' I said, slightly confused. I presumed he meant for the FCI work at the store, although I had not yet sent him an invoice. 'I also have some unfinished business . . . for Oliver.'

'Ah yes . . . I should be grateful if that could be completed at some time. No hurry.'

'I'm so sorry again,' I said, moving down the steps.

'I know you are, my dear.'

I wondered if he knew about the arm-hold and broken hyoid bone. I hoped not. Better to think it had been an unfortunate accident and that his son had died in a moment of Christmas high spirits.

Someone was following me. My fingers closed on Sergeant Rawlings' torch, which I still had. I was becoming paranoid. The footsteps quickened. I heard fast breathing.

'Hold on, Jordan. It's only me. Slow down . . . it's not a marathon. I want to talk to you.'

DI James caught up with me. He was wearing his up all night look, his eyes weary. That pile-up on the Arundel Road had taken longer than anyone expected.

'You look tired.'

'Sorry, I never made it back to the station,' he said. 'You got home all right, then?'

'With the aid of Sergeant Rawlings' trusty torch.' I drank in his apology. Another first. I didn't remember James ever apologising to me before. If only I could take him home now, feed him breakfast, all his favourite things, then let him flake out on my comfortable bed. He might not even notice the rose patterned duvet. He could sleep as long as he liked. I'd divert all calls. 'DI James is unavailable,' I'd say sweetly to his mobile callers. 'He will be unavailable all day.'

'All day what?' DI James asked.

'Er . . . talking to myself. Nasty habit. Sign of dementia. Were you at the funeral?'

'Yes, on the far side. I wanted to see who was there. Check on a few faces.'

'Have you checked on his friends? Found out who suggested a visit to the funfair?'

'Of course. He hadn't seen any friends that day. It was a normal working day at the store. They were busy at Guilberts, getting ready for the last-minute Christmas rush.'

Not all that normal. He found time to go and see Sonia.

'Sonia Spiller was at the church,' I said. 'A bit odd.'

'I saw her. That woman never smiles.'

'It's supposed to be a look of pain. All part of the charade.'

He did not comment. I suppose he couldn't. It would not be right.

'A red convertible, an Aston Martin,' he said. 'We found one last night in a ditch off the Arundel Road. It had been dumped. There was no one inside. We checked the PNC for vehicle registration. It belonged to Oliver Guilbert, personalised number plate. You were right. Forensic are going over it now with a tooth comb. Perhaps we'll find out where it's been since Oliver died.'

Fish scales. They might find a few fish scales. I was certain it was the car that made an unwelcomed delivery to my shop. DS Ben Evans might have told James. But then again, he might have forgotten.

172

'Is it the car that drove at us last night?'

'Difficult to be sure, Jordan. But it's fishy that it was abandoned soon after.'

'It was raining too hard to see the number plate,' I said. 'Nor did I see the driver. But Oliver's father, Francis Guilbert, said the car had been missing since his son's death. And he didn't know where it was.'

'Someone has been driving it around since then. It got a parking ticket on Christmas Eve in the High Street. It was illegally parked outside the health food shop.'

'Stocking up on vitamins?' I suggested then bit the words back. It wasn't funny. 'Sorry. I remember something about the hit-and-run car . . . it's not much . . . it all happened so fast . . . but . . .'

James waited expectantly, almost patiently. That showed how tired he was. 'So . . . ?'

'It had an old-style GB plate on the back bumper.'

'Better than nothing, I suppose,' he said. He nodded, turned and walked away without another word, leaving me as always, bereft.

Eighteen

I t was on display in the front window of a Heart Foundation charity shop. Heavens, and so soon after Christmas. People usually get rid of unwanted Christmas presents after a discreet interval but the boy's mother had thrown it out immediately. If in doubt, throw it out was her motto.

I bought it back, of course. I hadn't wanted to sell it in the first place. The Edwardian beaded evening bag that I would never use. It was my Girl Guide streak. Be ready, just in case. I paid more for it than I had charged the boy, but that's life.

And I had a black dress and the shoes. Shopping list: nil. It cheered me up no end.

So Francis Guilbert wanted me to continue following Sonia Spiller. But no windy walks along the front. What would she do with her time now that she had got rid of Jasper? More squash? More interior decorating? Her poor shoulder made it impossible for her to go back to work at school, all that lifting of heavy exercise books and marking pens.

I was determined to catch her out. I checked the video camera, having almost forgotten how to work it in my brief career as a shop assistant. Picket surveillance. I drove to the leisure centre out of town and parked, checking on the other parked cars. Bingo. Her white Toyota was already there.

I paid my entrance fee and wandered about, completely in tune with the surroundings in casual grey tracksuit and trainers. Who would notice that I never went on a court? The camera was in my Adidas sports bag, another charity shop purchase. It also contained a bottle of water and a packet of oatmeal biscuits, in case it was a long siege. Also the unreturned Rawlings issue torch. I did not feel safe without it.

From the visitors' gallery I watched her play. Yes, she was left-handed. But for all that, her mobility seemed excellent. Not a twitch or a wince. She looked fit to me. In the cafeteria she carried a tray of snacks without trouble, moved chairs, reached for things, nodded and talked to people sitting behind her. She'd be even more mobile if Guilberts had to pay her £150,000 compensation.

I took some boring shots of squash.

I couldn't even imagine having that much money. What would I do with it? Move? No, I liked my two bedsits. They suited me. Anyway, who'd do the housework in somewhere bigger? Buy lots of new clothes. What for? I had enough to wear. I might buy a new pair of boots since last night's soaking had taken the gloss off mine. They looked past their best now. Get a bigger and better car? Never! The ladybird and I were bonded for life.

Could I seduce DI James with loads of money in the bank? I doubted it. He would just shrug off offers of weekends in Paris, cruises in the Med, sun-soaked beaches in Barbados. He might accept a Mexican at Miguel's but that would be all. He'd leave me at my door, go back to whatever he called home at the moment, forget me.

Then I saw the stalker. Someone else was watching from a table at the far side of the cafeteria. Sonia had not been lying. A man was definitely following her. Again that uniformed look, yet I could not see his face or define the uniform, dark material, shoulders padded. He was keeping out of her sight. I began following him, following her. It was uncanny. She went to her car and he went to his, a Vauxhall. I went to mine. This was ridiculous. I started the engine. My ladybird throbbed to life immediately.

The three cars manoeuvred towards the exit. It was like a computer game. I wondered where it would lead me to. I had to tell DI James, just in case. The hermit's hole haunted me. I left a message on his answer phone. A rambling sort of message, but I hoped he understood the gist.

We drove in a raggedy convoy. I tried to note which roads we were taking but it was impossible. These people knew inland Sussex better than I did. Strictly against the law, I drank and ate as I drove. I was feeling in need of energy. Mavis, please open up!

Then, suddenly, I lost the stalker, the Vauxhall. I was following the white Toyota but the man had gone, taking an earlier turning towards Gatwick. I never saw it happen. Damn. Still, I was following Sonia and that's what I was (hopefully) being paid for.

She slowed down and took a left turning down a lane, then another, bumping over an unmade road.

'Sorry,' I said to the ladybird. She was not built for bumpy lanes. The leafy track, meandering under arches of branches, led to an idyllic spot. Sweeps of green grass, weeping willows wept over the water, ducks and swans paddling about, shaded by ancient trees. And there, lording it over all, was a water-mill.

The wheel over the water was a ten-foot-high steel structure, the lower slats immersed in the river. The eighteenth-century part of the building was built of dark wood. I was not sure which bit of what river we had reached. Sonia parked but I couldn't do the same. I reversed back and left the ladybird in a secluded copse. What on earth was Sonia doing here? Only a few people were wandering about. It was a tourist spot in the summer. One of the last working watermills in Sussex. There were bags of stone-ground flour on sale in a small shack. I tried to look like a tourist, taking pictures.

Sonia was walking determinedly towards an area where a few valiant souls were trying to have a winter picnic. Soup in thermoses, sausages in foil. She stopped at a wooden table where another woman was sitting.

The other woman was huddled up in a sheepskin coat, close-knitted cap pulled down over her hair, thick scarf wrapped round her neck. She seemed vaguely familiar in an odd way. I thought I had seen her before. She greeted Sonia tersely as if she had been waiting a long time.

Sonia and the woman began talking. She poured Sonia a drink out of a thermos. It looked like coffee. She had some packets of sandwiches and they unwrapped them. They seemed to be on reasonable terms, yet Sonia was tense, not that at ease.

I took some video shots, at a distance, in case Sonia started to climb a tree. I did not know what I was doing here or where I was. The people who paid me money were so trusting.

The two women seemed to be having some kind of argument. Their voices were raised. Sonia turned white with anger.

'I never said anything of the kind. Why should I give you half? You've done nothing special.'

'Come on, Sonia, we wouldn't be where we are now if it hadn't been for me,' said the other woman, her face like thunder. 'And don't you forget that.'

This was too good to miss. I crept nearer, taking a round-about route so that I was never in direct view. Everyone else seemed to be going home. I was far too close to the slippery edge of the river bank, but the risk was worth it. I held onto some overhanging branches. The veined leaves brushed my face with wet fingers.

'But I never said half, Sara. You're being plain greedy. You always have been greedy. You wanted the nicest clothes, the best bed, the front seat in the car. I've always come second, but not this time. I'm the one dictating the terms.'

There was a moment's silence but I could feel the tension in the air between the two women. Neither of them were eating now, sandwiches left on the table.

'My dear Sonia,' said Sara, the other woman, smoothly. 'You should mind what you are saying and how you put it. Just you remember, I could blow the lid off the top of this whole unsavoury scheme and then you'd get nothing, zero, zilch without my skiing injury . . .'

The next words chilled me. I even shivered and the branches sent raindrops flying. Sonia's voice dropped low.

'And you should be very careful what you say, Sara dear. You might have an unexpected accident, something quite out of the blue, something unexplainable.'

An unexpected accident like Oliver's? Surely not? A woman could not have inflicted that arm-hold on Oliver, unless she was combat trained. Had Sonia been in the armed forces? Check a.s.a.p. She looked more like a witch than an army officer.

Part of my mind was aware of footsteps. Suddenly I went flying. I just had time to register the swift hard thump of hands flat on my back that knocked me off balance. I slithered down the bank, trying to grasp at anything, weeds, stones, mud. I plunged into the river and the coldness of the water took my cry for help out of my throat.

'You've stalked me once too often,' came a female voice from above. I couldn't see anything but I knew that voice well enough. 'Perhaps a ducking will teach you a lesson.'

In seconds the fast-running current swept me away from the bank. Last night's downpour had filled the river to capacity. I struck out but my clothes hampered me and the water was full of swirling debris. I hung onto a broken branch, gasping for air, paddling with my legs. I knew how long people lasted in icy cold water. About ten minutes.

I tried to call out but no one was around. Even my arguing aggressor had disappeared. The dark waterwheel loomed ahead, thrashing the water, the slats of the wheel turning and slicing. If I could catch hold of one of them, it would lift me out of the water, taking me high enough so that I might be able to jump from it onto the safety of the bank. So I thought. It was worth a try. I'd be dead long before the river washed me ashore on some low bank near the coast.

The timing was not easy and I'm no athlete. I might get only one chance. The noise of the wheel became louder and louder. I could feel its pull. The slats were above me now as they came out of the river, cascades of spray sliding off them in a series of waterfalls. I caught hold of the slippery wood, half expecting my hands to be flung off. But the opposite happened.

It happened with the speed of sound. Only I didn't have time to make a sound.

The momemtum of the wheel tossed me up into the air, legs flying, and I fell against the next rising slat, shattering the rotten wood. I remembered falling into churning water. My feet were being taken away from under me by some force that I could not control.

I was being tumbled round and round in the drum of a washing machine. I was being battered by slats. It was minutes before I could get up, stumbling, struggling.

Above me was the slate sky, dissected by movement. I tried to find something to hold onto while I gathered my wits. There was some kind of central rod, a sort of spindle, which was turning more slowly, slow enough for me to hold onto if I kept a hand over hand movement going. Somehow I forced myself to stand up, dragged myself to my feet but there was nothing to stand on.

Then I saw where I was. To my horror I realised that I had landed (if landed is the word) inside the waterwheel. If I did not want to become sliced meat, I had to keep running. I had to keep up with the wheel. By linking my arms over the rod and keeping a rhythmic leaping stride from slat to slat. I could just about stay upright and alive. I had to jump from one slat to the next one coming up. It was exhausting, beat ten visits to the gym. The alternative was to drown or be cut in half. No choice really.

The sky was darkening with more rain clouds. Spatterings hit my face. I was already soaked so another couple of pints made no difference. But I put my tongue out to catch raindrops. There was water everywhere but I needed some inside my body. Fear had dehydrated me. Exhaustion was fast catching up. This was one marathon that I was not going to finish.

Then I remembered my phone. God bless the mobile moguls. Would it be wet-proof? Without letting go of my hold, I twisted my hip up so that I could manoeuvre the phone out of my zipped-up pocket and into my hand. I could barely see what I was doing. My lashes were soaked and glued. The DI James number was on memory. I pressed the right code. He wasn't there. Damn the man. I got his answering service again.

'James . . .' I shouted against the noise. 'I'm . . . trapped. I can't . . . get out.' My voice jerked, words incoherent, disjointed. He would not be able to make anything of it. I tried again. 'The old watermill. Sonia . . . pushed me in. James! James!'

My voice rose to a shriek as I almost lost my balance and the phone went flying out of my hand. The river sucked it up. I was gasping, hanging onto the rod grimly, legs numbed with cold now, trainers shredded. Had he heard enough? When would be listen? Did he check his calls regularly? He might be the other side of the county, on some case, concentrating on something else, not checking calls. There was nothing more I could do except hold on, pray, try to think straight.

I could see it all now, although it was almost too dark to see anything else. Half of my brain was working. Sonia and Sara were sisters, maybe even identical twins. They looked very alike. Sara was the one with the genuine shoulder dislocation; she'd attended the medicals, got the doctor's certificates. I might even have followed her at times. She was the woman wearing the neck collar at the funeral. But Sonia was the one claiming the compensation, walking Jasper, playing squash, decorating her listed house.

What had happened that day when Oliver called at number eight Luton Road? Had Sara been there? Or Sonia, or both of them? Had Oliver put two and two together and come up with one hundred and fifty thousand? There must have been a very nasty scene. Perhaps it was then that Sonia decided that Oliver had to go, via Hell's Revenge. Perhaps she suggested a walk to the front to the Christmas Fair to talk things over, down a lonely twitten. Perhaps she bought some parcel tape on the way.

My hands were becoming raw but there was nothing else to hold onto except this turning rod, my feet running beneath me. I tried lifting a foot at a time and holding it up, to give the muscles a rest, so that I was not pacing each slat, but every other slat. It was some relief. My breathing got regulated so that I did not waste energy. Sergeant Rawlings once told me that energy is breath.

Sergeant Rawlings . . . his unreturned torch was in my pocket. I needed light. So I still had some means of attracting attention. I removed it with slow-motion carefulness and turned it on with my nose. I did not want to look around at my predicament but kept the thin white beam pointed straight upwards to the sky. Surely the watermill had some sort of keeper/miller type person? Someone had to lock up, shut the shop, count the money. At least once a day . . . or night . . . I'd lost track of time. It might be afternoon now or evening.

If someone came, they'd see the light, even if it was too dark to see me. A small figure, shrunken with cold, half-submerged in water. I was not simply half-drowned. I was sodden, drenched, saturated, waterlogged. My fingers were numb. I would not be able to hold on much longer.

I didn't hear the voices or people running. I was vaguely aware that the waterwheel was slowing down or had my feet fallen off? Then the wheel stopped turning. I still hung on to the rod, even when arms were lifting me and trying to prise my fingers away. Several figures were sloshing about, balancing on slats, swearing, holding me up. I wouldn't let go of the rod or the torch.

'It's all right, Jordan. You can let go now. We've got you.'

But I was still dreaming, lost in a mist. My brain had let go of reality and taken me to another world. Perhaps I had died and was drifting away and it was safe to give in. I let go.

They wrapped me in anything, coats, blankets, towels. The relentless movement had stopped, though my head was still going round. I was being carried somewhere.

'I always wanted a hamster,' said DI James. 'But not one this heavy.'

Nineteen

They thawed me out and dried me out in hospital. Thank goodness it was not my best tracksuit. It was ripped to pieces. Could I charge it to expenses? My feet were in poor shape, too. Couldn't charge for feet. Flowers arrived from Francis Guilbert, freesias and spray carnations, shades of pale yellow and mauve. I was touched. How did he know where I was? DS Evans, I suppose.

I didn't remember being carried from the watermill by DI James, which was a shame. Such a unique experience ought to be indelible on my memory. But I barely knew who it was. The A & E doctor said I was in pretty bad shape but it was only cuts and bruises in the end. My feet and hands were the worst. Both were bandaged and *sans* sex appeal. They kept me in overnight, then lent me some huge plastic slip-ons to wear going home. I was a cloddish monster, clumping about, feet about a foot long, all white and crackling. I needed furry doggy slippers with cuddly faces. They ordered a taxi.

'Don't say anything,' I said to the driver, clutching my flowers. 'I got caught in a meat mincer.'

'Rather you than me,' he said, averting his eyes.

I felt as if I had been away years. Hospital always does this to me. There's a sort of mental cut-off point. Hospital is a no-man's-land where time does not exist. They said I could go home on condition I washed my feet and hands in salt water twice a day and put fresh dressings on.

It took me half a day to write up my notes, seeing as I could barely hold a pen. I was convinced now that Sonia was involved

183

in Oliver's death. If she and her sister were together in this compensation fraud and Oliver had found out, it followed that Sonia had to get rid of him. I re-read my two lists of reasons for paying out and not paying out.

I hobbled over to the window, looking at the rain-filled sky, watching the clouds. The scent from the freesias was gorgeous. I ought to buy more flowers. A familiar red and black spotted shape was parked outside, roof glistening with rain. My ladybird! Some kind soul had returned her to me. I must have left the keys in the ignition. All the pain of the last hours was wiped out by that generous gesture. I had to go out in her.

It took a bit of negotiation. My oversized feet were not meant for foot pedals. I only managed a sedate drive as far as my shop. I parked carefully outside, got out and hopped along the road.

'Got any dressings?' I said to Doris. She immediately shut her shop and sped down to Boots (now open on Sundays) where she bought mountains of surgical dressings, all shapes and sizes. Then she made me sit down in my office and put my feet up while she tut-tutted and lectured me on the dangers of my chosen profession.

'I think she has already murdered one person, so one more wasn't going to make any difference,' I said cheerfully.

'Jordan, this just won't do. It's all right chasing up people about lost tortoises, trivial sorts of things, but not murder. It's not for you. Leave that to the experts. Detective Inspector James and his lot. You keep to chasing errant husbands and serving writs. At least you won't get half-killed in the process.'

'Divorce can be just as dangerous.'

'Nonsense. This woman tried to kill you for £150,000. Now bath your feet, put some fresh dressings on and I'll phone Mavis for a table this evening.'

'Is she open?'

'Re-opening today. She'll do you a supper to die for.'

Not quite the right words but I got the message. I had nothing to wear. I was still trailing the borrowed hospital dressing gown. Hopefully my charity box would produce something wearable for supper. Cinderella's fairy godmother never had a name, but nevertheless I called on her for help. I slept most of the afternoon in the Victorian button-back chair, my feet up on a cardboard box of books.

Maeve's Cafe was festooned with ballons. Jasper was on guard by the door. He gave me a foolish grin and thumped his tail. There was a long table, draped with streamers and crackers and bowls of nuts. Red candles stood in holders, their lights wavering uncertainly each time the door opened and more people came in.

I could not believe it. There was Leroy Anderson and Mrs Fenwick, Mrs Drury and my book expert, Mr Frazer, Cleo Carling and her stepfather, Arthur Carling, both looking prosperous and content. How had Doris and Mavis managed to get in touch with all my friends? Except no jazz trumpeter. He had been missed out. They wouldn't know about him. Nor Jack, the owner of the pier amusements, or maybe he had to work nights.

Both Cleo and Leroy loved their silk scarves and thanked me. Mrs Fenwick thanked me for the antique flowered teapot.

'It was the perfect present,' she said. 'What an inspired choice. Thank you, Jordan. I'm sorry I didn't get you anything. I couldn't think straight this year.'

Parcels look much the same when wrapped. I'd given Mrs Fenwick the wrong one. I didn't think Mrs Drury would be so pleased with the high-tech egg coddlers, but I was mistaken.

'Absolutely spiffing,' she said, giving me a hug. 'I've used them twice already. Saves me loads of time.'

'My son, Ben, has phoned,' Mr Frazer confided, not hiding his pleasure. 'A Christmas call from London. Wasn't that nice?'

'I'm really pleased, Mr Frazer. That's wonderful for you. He'll call again, I'm sure, now the ice is broken.'

'I hope you're right, Miss Lacey. He said he was working in the catering trade.'

True, he was serving sandwiches and coffee in a snack bar. I'd seen him and spoken to him. I was glad he'd phoned at last.

Then in walked DI James and DS Evans and my evening was complete. James had upgraded his usual gear. He was wearing a grey polo jersey and dark jacket and slacks, human and civilised. It was almost more than I could bear. Ben Evans was his usual amiable self, glasses glinting, and was soon chatting with everyone. James smiled gravely at me. I could read that smile. He was amused at my feet. Thanks, buster.

Everyone sat down and Mavis produced the most succulent heaps of fish and chips this side of the Atlantic. Her face was healing well and she joined us for the meal. No one worried about my big feet under the table. Doris cut up my food. I could manage using a fork.

'You're looking better,' said DI James, tucking in as if he hadn't eaten for weeks. He was sitting the other side of me. A devious manoeuvre engineered by Doris, matchmaker in chief, bridesmaid in waiting.

'Thanks to you,' I said. 'Did you rescue me?'

'Guess so, but I couldn't hear a word that you said on your mobile. The noise of the watermill drowned everything. But the water was the clue. Only one place sounds like that. Luckily we were not too far away. Niagara Falls are on the Canada-US border. I knew you weren't there.'

'I could have died,' I said. He wasn't asking me how I got inside the watermill. Didn't he want to know if I fell or if I was pushed? If he didn't want to know, then I wasn't going to tell him.

'But you didn't. You've got work to do. And that, my girl, is what you are going to do as soon as you are better. Sort out all of Latching's problems.'

I couldn't believe his detachment. Did he think I'd gone paddling? He was keeping something from me.

He couldn't see my feet beneath the black cotton caftan that I was wearing. I'd pushed my hair up into some sort of bird's nest. It was the best I could do with bandaged hands. DI James seemed to like it. Mavis produced several bottles of red wine, plonk variety (aromatic, zingy, hint of raspberry) and everyone toasted me. I couldn't really stand up as my feet were too bulky. It was all very embarrassing. The red wine was a bit sharp, not my favourite but I was too relaxed to care. I decided I was still dehydrated so another glass wouldn't hurt. Someone would see me home. Maybe James . . .

'Did you arrange for my ladybird . . . ?' I asked cautiously.

'Drove her myself,' he nodded. 'Not much leg room.'

'That was very kind.'

'Reciprocal gesture. We're getting good results on our enquiries about the stolen goods from big stores, thanks to you. It's a widespread organisation. We should be able to catch the gang any day now. Both your leads were invaluable.'

'Both?'

'The midnight boot. We found the whereabouts of that, too.'

'Great . . . I don't even know where it is. And what about the JCB?' I had to be careful on this one. 'Any news?'

He shook his head. 'The JCB was stolen from a local building site, that's all. We've no leads.'

'And the . . . er . . . arm?'

'We're working on it,' he said vaguely. Liar. He obviously wasn't going to tell me that it had been identified.

'I'm still curious about Oliver,' I began.

'You're far too curious about everything,' he said. 'But I will tell you one interesting thing. His red Aston Martin. The lab lot have been over it and guess what we found?'

'Fish scales.'

He looked at me incredulously. 'Jordan, are you sure you're feeling all right?'

Whoops. I had nearly let on that I knew about the discovery of fish scales on Oliver's clothes. 'Light-headed,' I said. 'Lack of food and post traumatic stress.'

He seemed convinced. 'We found a hair, a long black hair in the car. Female, no doubt.'

I knew one woman with long black hair and in my mind she fitted the bill. 'Sonia Spiller's, I bet. How can we find out if that woman had a lift with Oliver in the car before he died, or has been driving his car around since he died? Maybe even indulging in a spot of hit-and-run?'

'We don't know, Jordan. You're speculating. No more shop talk. Not tonight. This is supposed to be a celebration.' He filled glasses in all directions. 'A toast, everyone. Here's to Mavis! And the best fish and chips in Sussex!'

'Here, here!'

'The best fish and chips!'

'To Mavis!'

Everyone stood and toasted Mavis, that is, everyone except me. I mean, I toasted her but didn't stand up. She was grinning all over her face and looking more like her old self. The company was doing her good. Mavis was serving apple pie and ice cream now but I was too full for any more. People started changing seats and I lost James. Still it was nice to talk to Cleo and Leroy and hear all their news. Then Mrs Fenwick started to tell me about her evening classes in French cookery, and Mrs Drury gave me the latest recruitment figures for the WI. It was all very pleasant.

The front door opened and a gust of cold sea air blew in. Mavis froze. A woman with spikey magenta hair stood in the doorway, her face twisted with anger.

'Back in business, are you?' she sneered. 'Well, I bloody well don't think so!'

She made a lunge towards Mavis. I stuck out my twelve inch, plastic shod feet. The woman tripped and went flying. Ben Evans was up and out of his seat in seconds. He held the woman down on the floor with his big hands.

I didn't see what happened next. The pain was excruciating. I think I fainted. Or perhaps it was the wine.

Everyone said that the party was terrific especially the cabaret afterwards. Ben Evans was sitting on one red-head (magenta) and James propping up another (tawny). Such fun. Four mobile 999 calls were made simultaneously.

'No need to phone,' said James, irritated. 'We are the police. We're here.'

I didn't pass out for long although I would have liked to make it last a bit longer. Considering the proximity of DI James and his strong arms around me. I didn't even have time for a ten-second fantasy of his face coming closer and his hands tenderly brushing my hair back. The bird's nest had fallen down.

He hauled me upright. 'Too much wine?'

'Too much feet,' I groaned. They were throbbing, the intense pain pulsing up to my brain. I wanted a painkiller. I didn't care that they don't mix with alcohol. I wasn't going to be driving a tractor.

'Quick thinking, Jordan,' said Ben, pushing his glasses back on his nose. 'Well done. Shall I cuff her, guv? She's calming down.'

Mavis was still shaking. 'That's the one. She's the cause of all this. That's Tracy Jones, jealous bitch. She won't let him go.'

'He's my husband,' the woman on the floor spluttered. 'You leave him alone. He's mine.'

'You don't own him, Tracy,' said Mavis, holding onto the back of a chair for support. 'He's had enough of you and your temper tantrums. He's a decent man. He wants a quiet life.'

Ben stood up, pulling the woman to her feet. I could see that she wasn't going to let go of whoever it was in the middle of this tug-of-love. Her black-rimmed eyes were flashing venom and in the fraction that Ben relaxed his grip, she grabbed a wine bottle off the table and flung it at Mavis as if she was competing at the Commonwealth Games.

Mavis saw it coming and had a split second to evade its aim – her face. The bottle hit her on the shoulder, shattered, drenching her in wine. Lucky she was wearing red.

'Cuff her,' James shouted.

So one crime was solved. Tracy Jones confessed down at the station that she had arranged for Chuck and his mate to bash up Mavis. Via the Latching crime grapevine, Tracy had found

189

out they did the Mexican and thought it would be simply listed as another robbery. She paid them £250, she said.

'Is that all my face is worth?' said Mavis long after.

Tracy wouldn't say where Chuck was now. They moved around. How would she know?

Tracy was bound over to keep the peace for the party incident but charges were going to be pressed on the GBH.

My hands and feet healed fast but I had to buy a size larger trainers to accommodate the dressings. I returned the hospital dressing gown the next day. It was time to call on Francis Guilbert.

Francis was amazed at how much I had discovered. I thanked him for the flowers.

'Sisters! Even twins maybe? Jordan, I do congratulate you. It puts a whole different aspect on the claim, or fraud, as I think it is now. Are we ready to confront them?' He knew I had been injured at the watermill but not that someone had pushed me in the river.

'No, not yet. I need video footage of the two of them together. I lost the video at the watermill. My visual evidence is not enough. Also we need something that confirms that Sara attended the medicals and not Sonia. What, I'm not really sure. Often, even with identical twins, there is some minor difference. I'd like to see the medical reports again.'

'I'll get you copies. And, I must tell you, the vanishing stock has stopped. It's a relief to me but I wonder if they have wind of what you discovered here?'

'DI James is sure they are going to nail the gang soon. They have so much evidence now. You see, it wasn't just Guilberts, but all the big stores in Sussex were targetted. So it was well organised.'

'Good, the sooner, the better. Jordan, I notice that you haven't picked up your pay packet from Guilberts.'

I was confused. I hadn't sent him an invoice yet.

'But I haven't worked out an invoice for you or for Oliver's work yet,' I said. It still hurt to say his name. So sad. I had to charge for that time.

'I know that. But you were so good as a seasonal temp, there's a pay packet for you in Personnel. And what about the New Year's Day sales? It's a big event. Can you come in for that? We'd be glad to have you. Miss Kent raves about you. And New Year's Eve . . . are you doing anything? I don't want to be in the house alone.'

He looked so forlorn. I could not turn him down. It would be too cruel.

'Yes . . . to both invitations. I'd love to spend New Year's Eve with you. I'd bring a bottle except that I know you have a better cellar. And I'll be a temp for the sales event. I might even spot a bargain for myself.'

'You get a staff discount, you know, on anything you buy.'

'Don't tempt me.'

I walked along the seafront. It was packed with children trying out their Christmas presents: scooters, skateboards, roller skates, zig-zagging in all directions. Such bright colours, handlebars fringed with tinsel. Plastic has a lot to answer for. I fed stale bread over the side of the pier to flocks of greedy seagulls. The young birds were a squabbling carpet of flecked white and brown feathers. I was still feeling frail after my influenza and went into Macaris for a coffee, very cappuccino, piled high with froth. I could afford it.

DI James sat down beside me on the bench, facing the window to the receding sea. He had a cappuccino too and a Danish pastry on a plate. He studied both for some moments.

'Jordan,' he said. 'It's time we pooled information. I know we are not a team. I know you were treated badly on the force and I am not apologising. It was before my time and I was not responsible. But you know things and I know different things. And we might be able to solve a few cases if we had a deal going.'

'But James,' I said, making room for him on the bench. He suddenly seemed very broad or had I shrunk? 'It's not logical. When cases are solved, I no longer get paid. You are on a monthly salary. I have a daily rate.'

Stella Whitelaw

He broke off a piece of glazed apple and pecan pastry and put it in my mouth. It was so unexpected. 'How can I tempt you?' he said, his blue eyes brilliant.

Of course I couldn't answer because my mouth was full.

Twenty

I mmediate action: take footage of the two sisters, preferably front facing. This was crucial. My focus was in gear and I was determined to get this evidence. My reputation depended on it.

Somehow I had to follow both women at the same time in order to get this shot. I had no idea of Sara's surname or address. A trip to the Family Records Centre in London would confirm if they were sisters or twins.

I went up to London. It was a terrible journey. The train service was up the creek, running late or bits not running at all, not enough carriages, luggage and backpacks cluttering the corridors, people stepping on your feet. Commuters had my sympathy. The underground was crammed with bodies and dirty floors littered with bottles rolling about and food wrappers. The bacteria must be rampant. Latching at least had clean air.

I had noted Sonia's date of birth and maiden name from the documents Oliver lent me to read when I took on the case so it did not take long to find the entry in the Births Registry. Tippett was a pretty unusual name. Bingo. Legs eleven. There it was in faded script. They were twins, Sara being the elder. They must be working a scam. I was a hundred and ten percent sure. I had to prove it.

After I had ordered copies of the birth certificates, I made some random searches through Marriages, hoping for a miracle, but Sara drew a blank. But I found Sonia's marriage to Colin Spiller, got a photocopy and two words leaped off the page. Occupation of groom: airline pilot.

The uniform . . . that was the uniform of Sonia's stalker. An airline pilot or steward. It had that distinctive well-cut look. But surely her own husband wasn't stalking her? I'd never actually seen him or met him so how was I to know? Had her companion in the Mexican been her husband? I should have to check with Miguel. If he'd paid by credit card, there would be a name on record.

I fought my way through the crowds milling about Victoria station to get the train back to Latching. A promotions stand was offering tiny tastings of Bordeaux wine in plastic thimbles and I knocked back two. This gave me the courage to say no to the blanket boy asking for change. I usually take the coward's exit.

London exhausted me or maybe that bout of 'flu was lingering. And my feet hurt. It was the cracked pavements. I'd checked that Ben Frazer was still working at the sandwich bar near the Records Centre, but I didn't speak to him. That first call home was a fragile link and I didn't want to rock the dinghy.

It was gathering darkness before we reached the Sussex coast. The train trundled over the aqueduct into Haywards Heath station and I could barely see the fields below. When we bridged over the Adur river at Shoreham, I realised with relief that I was nearly home. The countryside had flashed by in a kaleidoscope of lights, shadows and shapes and I had not taken in anything.

Sometimes fate helps you out; more often it hinders. There was still time to collect my pay from Guilberts. They were holding it for me in Personnel.

'We thought you didn't want it,' said the girl clerk cheekily. 'I was just going to put it in the charity box.'

'I'm the charity,' I said. 'But thanks all the same.'

The envelope was flat and slim. A cheque, unlike Miguel's wholesome wad of notes. I opened it in the corridor, leaning on a wall. Francis had been more than generous. He had paid the going rate for a temporary seasonal plus my daily rate for the four days of investigation. It was a nicely rounded-up sum. Plus the dress and the shoes, I'd done rather well. I could afford a cappuccino. It spurred me on to resolve the Spiller case.

Fate threw me a lucky charm on my way out of the store. The wet streets were still busy with late shoppers and people leaving work early. The air was sharply cold after the heated store and I blinked hard. Sonia Spiller was ahead of me or was it Sara? The woman had long black hair, flowing and blowing, wearing the usual sheepskin jacket and neck collar covered with a chiffon scarf. The downside was that I didn't have a video camera with me.

On went my sunglasses (in the middle of winter, very pop star), up went my collar. I decided a limp might be over the top. It was all I could do in the way of a disguise.

Sonia stopped to shop in Superdrug. She was buying hair dye. Mahogany Black: permanent. It was on offer, two for the price of one. She was either Sara making her hair look like Sonia's or Sonia touching up some grey. I bet those two had spent their lives confusing people.

I pretended to read the instructions for Deep Chestnut: semi-permanent. Then I noticed something else about this Sonia/Sara. It was the smallest detail that no one had noticed. I had spotted a difference. This was gold dust.

I had to get hold of Sonia Spiller's X-rays. Both the hospital plates which were taken right after her fall and the insurance company's independent report. She would have had X-rays taken again at the private clinic that did the report. My friend at Latching Hospital was happy to look up attendance and admittance records for me on the computer, but finding an X-ray plate was stretching a favour.

Francis Guilbert would have the muscle. Surely he could demand to see both sets? Maybe he already had them. His solicitor would advise him. But we had to have both sets of plates.

I put Deep Chestnut back on the shelf and peeled away. I did not have to follow the sisters any more. I could prove there were two of them. It was such a relief. It had got a bit tedious and I was running out of disguises. There was a limit to my charity box.

Time to celebrate. Another cappuccino and a Danish. It was treats non-stop and going to my head and my waist. I cruised Latching, trying to make up my mind where to hitch my horse. My brain was cafe hopping.

The warmth of the coffee bar and the sweetness of the Danish, apricot and apple, helped to sort out my plans. I had to make an uninvited entry into number eight Luton Road, and not merely to admire her stencilling. And I had to do it this evening, before my courage evaporated with the frost and before I saw in the New Year with Francis.

I parked the ladybird in the health club car park, well out of sight of number eight and strolled upstairs swinging my bag. I could watch the lights in the house from the gym window. I sat on an exercise bike, keyed in a programme, uphill, level five, for six minutes. The calorie usage might knock off half the pastry.

Lady Luck was certainly on my side tonight. Sonia came out of the house, all done up, got into her white Toyota and drove away. I wondered if she'd fixed her hair. There were no lights left on in the house. Then I remembered there was a forties band on at the Pier to bring in the New Year. She wouldn't want to miss some jiving.

New Year. I had almost forgotten that this was the last day of the year. It always made me feel sad. Time passing, parents gone, etc. I wondered if James had been invited to a party. And my trumpeter . . . where was he? All those jazz musicians would be having a rave-up somewhere, playing their hearts out, telling their outrageously silly jokes.

And I was pretending to cycle uphill, watching an empty house, planning how to effect an entry. New Year's Resolution: unmince words, i.e. say 'break in'.

I marched up to the front door and rang the brass bell.

196

Surprise: no answer. I rang again and then walked round the side. It seemed deserted. No Jasper now. No Colin Spiller either. Perhaps he was on a long haul. I climbed over the garden wall and tried the back door. She had locked it.

A small window had been left slightly open. It was enough. I climbed on a dustbin and managed to get my arm down inside. My fingers were still sore but I made them reach the catch of the larger window and open it.

Once inside I wasted no time on Sonia's DIY work. I knew exactly what I was looking for. I raced upstairs to her bedroom. I remembered an array of framed photos on the chest of drawers. It was not the wedding photo that I wanted, nor the childhood pictures of the twins. I didn't need them. I had their birth certificates. But what I did want to look at was the photo of a group of young women in army fatigues, sleeves rolled up. One service woman was definitely Sara, her hair scrapped back into a pleat. I slid it out of the frame. On the back was written: 'Sara, Sierra Leone 1999.'

The neck collar was abandoned on a chair. I scraped off some fragments and put them in a specimen envelope.

Sonia had a jewellery box covered in seashells. I raked through the contents. Again it told me exactly what I wanted to know. I was making a quick count when I heard a sound. A key turning in a lock.

For a second I froze then I moved fast. Someone was coming in. I closed the lid of the box then I crossed the landing in a flash and went into the small back bedroom. The window opened easily and I swung myself over the sill and let myself down, hung on with my fingertips and then with a brief look below, let myself drop. My WPC fire training helped.

I fell into a flower bed and rolled over. It only hurt a bit, but I didn't hang about. I hobbled for the wall and climbed over into the twitten. Head down and face covered, I hurried towards the centre of town. I needed merge in with booze-buying crowds.

I vaguely heard someone shouting, 'Stop, stop.' My car

would have to wait. I'd go back for it later. Anyway, it was New Year's night. No drinking and driving.

My feet were hurting by the time I got to Francis' house in the back of town. Perhaps he'd let me take my trainers off. I wasn't dressed up, only London gear. There had not been time to change. I brushed down my clothes. Francis opened the door.

'I hope I'm not too early,' I said with a smile now my breathing had steadied.

'Not at all, just about right. Come along in, Jordan. There's some supper. Knowing you, I don't suppose you've eaten.'

I'd lived on coffee all day but I didn't tell him. 'That sounds lovely. And thank you for the pay cheque. You were very generous.'

'Not at all. You earned it. Good staff are hard to come by.' He looked pleased to see me. Perhaps he had thought I would chicken out, get a better offer.

I remembered how much I had nearly charged that poor woman for two pillowcases and hid a smile. I took off my anorak and hung it on the old-fashioned hallstand. The house was warm and welcoming in its jewelled colours. There was a stained-glass window at the turn in the stairs. I didn't mention my feet but Francis had noticed my ungainly stance.

'How are your poor feet? I heard what happened. Do you want to take your shoes off? I could find you a pair of slippers.'

'Thank you,' I said. 'That would be far more comfortable. My feet are not healed yet. The cuts keep breaking open.'

'Would you mind putting these two garbage bags outside by the bins first, Jordan? I don't want to go out.'

'Sure. OK. Give them to me.'

So I saw in the New Year wearing Francis' second-best slippers and drinking his best champagne. Supper had been ample, cold turkey pie and salad; apple cheesecake and cream. His housekeeper had done us well.

'She's been having a really bad time with her daughter lately.

The girl's in trouble with the police, GBH, I think she said the charge was.'

'Grevious Bodily Harm,' I said. It clanged a big bell and I hoped I wasn't right. 'Not very nice.'

'Husband problems,' Francis added, helping himself to Stilton. 'He's a local fisherman.'

Oh dear.

Then we watched the New Year coming in all over the world on telly, fireworks lighting up a dozen skies and people linking arms and drinking and singing, and I could see Francis was thinking of his son and there was nothing I could do.

'Happy New Year, my dear,' he said, toasting me, remembering I was there.

'Happy New Year, Francis,' I said.

My keen ears caught the nuance of a noise, a foreign, close-by noise, despite all the celebratory racket on the box. 'Did you lock the front door?' I asked.

'No, I rarely do. This is a safe neighbourhood. Nothing happens here.'

'I think something is happening now,' I said.

It was like the fish and chips party all over again. The door burst open and two men came in, faces hidden in black balaclavas. Eyes behind slits. They'd been drinking. I could smell it.

'Don't move,' shouted the short one. 'This isn't what you think it is. We aren't going to hurt you. Shut up and do nothing.'

'How dare you . . .' Francis began, but he was quickly silenced by a knife brandished in his face. He went pale. I hoped he didn't have a heart condition.

'Great joke, well done, joke finished now,' I said, waving my glass. 'And a Happy New Year to you! Would you like a drink?'

The shorter one hit my hand and the flute went flying, shattering on the floor. All that expensive cut glass, no longer elegantly cut.

'Hold on,' I protested.

'Just you shut it,' he said. He did not recognise me. He had no reason to. But I knew who he was. 'Sit down here, both of you. And keep quiet.'

The other man had tugged two chairs together, back to back, and we were bundled onto them. I knew what was coming next. I'd seen it on the films. I closed my teeth and blew out my cheeks so that the adhesive tape would slacken a fraction across my face. My heart was racing.

They tied us tightly to the chairs with thin rope. I stuck out my elbows and put fingertips touching so that the rope would loosen when I relaxed. Now my feet hurt and my hands hurt and my wrists hurt. This was becoming an epidemic.

'Wanna know what this is all about?' The shorter one was obviously the brains. I nodded but no eye contact.

'Well, Mr Guilbert. It's all about your contribution to a nice little pastime we got going on with collectables, i.e. leather goods, household, CDs, videos . . . you name it, we collect it.'

Now I knew for sure. The two men were Chuck and his mate. And they were involved in the organised store non-deliveries, the midnight boots, the truck loads of stolen goods going north. Full-time criminals. They'd done the Mexican, the fair kiosk, Mavis's face. They were versatile. It was time they were caught and serving secure time.

'We don't want no trouble with the police so we thought they might take a bit of notice of a few demands if we keep you under wraps, Mr Guilbert. A bit of luck there being a young lady friend with you. Now she's going to be our trump card, know what I mean? Wouldn't want anything happening to her, would you?'

Francis started to say something but he was shut up with more tape slapped across his mouth.

A hostage situation. My mind ran through the police procedure. It could take days, bugging the walls, experts brought in to set up a rapport with the men, food packs sent in. Meanwhile Francis Guilbert and I would be roped to chairs, tape across our mouths, longing to go to the loo.

I was already desperate to go to the loo.

Twenty-One

T rying not to think about wanting to go to the loo was agony. I had taken in far too much liquid . . . coffee, champagne, water. My bladder was objecting. It was a misery. Pass me a catheter.

The two men were making themselves at home, finishing up the turkey pie and cheesecake, swigging champagne in tumblers. I had no idea what to do. My new cheapo mobile was in my bag. It was on the far side of the room. Spiralling panic blurred the distance.

Thought transference? I thought of DI James with intense concentration. I sent random thoughts to Jack. Then I thought about my jazz trumpeter even though he would not have the slightest idea what to do. He could not play me out of this situation even though the magical notes would be a comfort. Comfort stop.

'I m-ave to mend a penny,' I mumbled in desperation.

'No way.'

'M-m-urgent.'

'Let her go,' said the other one. 'I'll stand outside the door. She won't escape. I'll make sure.'

'Mank you,' I nodded with drowning relief, humble and grateful as they untied the rope. I jerked my head upstairs, as if I knew the layout of the house and grabbed my bag on the way out of the room.

'Stop that! Leggo the bag!' spluttered Chuck.

'Period. Mime of the month,' I mewed back, mouth still strapped with tape. 'Tampon.' He seemed to understand. Perhaps he had a wife.

I found the bathroom upstairs. My guard stood outside, stance grim, looking at his watch. 'You got one minute, sister,' he said.

One minute. I sat on the loo. I keyed in the DI James code on memory and let it bleep. I didn't have the time, or steady enough fingers to text him a message. I flushed the loo several times. He would hear cascading water again.

'Francis Guilbert,' I mumbled inarticulately. 'We've been taken hostage. Hostage. His house. Help us. Please, James.'

I came out of the bathroom, relieved at least. 'You've taken a long time,' he said.

'Had to wash my hands,' I mimed.

I was tied up again and we were left alone. The two men were rifling the kitchen again, opening the fridge door, looking for beer now. They were not champagne drinkers. The knots were pretty secure. There was no way I was going to wriggle loose before starvation reduced my wrist size.

We were sitting back to back so I could not send Francis encouraging eye signs. I wondered how he was coping. Nothing had prepared us for this.

The two men came back with opened cans in their hands. It was a warm house and they were beginning to sweat. They'd shed their bomber jackets but couldn't take off the balaclava helmets. I hoped the itchy wool was making their acne worse.

'Now, Mr G, we'll tell you exactly what we want. We want the combination to your safe. It's not your wife's jewels we're after though we might fancy a couple of baubles for souvenirs. A little birdie told us that your Securicor van didn't make its usual pick-up last night. Funny that, it broke down on the way from Brighton. So that's a whole day's takings unbanked. Pity. Quite a tidy sum, I should think.'

I tried some quick maths in my head. A lot of customers paid by credit card or cheque but the cash transactions would still be a hefty sum. Multiply by the number of tills in the store . . . wow!

'We'll also take the keys to your car. We've got an order for a Mercedes.'

I was pretty sure it was Chuck. All the same signs as the other hold-ups. These two men looked the same heights as the bandits who held up the funfair kiosk. It was cash they were after. I felt Francis stiffen and wondered what was going through his mind.

'You ain't got anything we want,' said Chuck rudely, twisting my arm. 'Though if Mr G has trouble remembering the numbers, we might start burning those pretty eyes out.'

I remembered Mavis's face and believed them. They were a nasty pair. He got out his lighter and flicked it on and off. Not a nice sound. I wanted to go home. I'd even settle for cooking a meal for Joshua.

People were celebrating the New Year in all the capitals of the world. The television screen was still bright, but they'd turned the sound right down. I could see small flickering figures dancing around, waving sparklers.

I tried to remember my WPC training; gain their confidence, begin bonding. Not easy with tape across my mouth. I started coughing.

'Shut up,' said Chuck.

I couldn't. The coughing was for real. Perhaps they thought I was going to choke. Chuck whipped off the tape.

'Ouch,' I spluttered. I was wheezing. 'I've g-got asthma.'

'My kid's got asthma,' said the other one. 'Where's your inhaler?'

'In my bag.' I always took it to London.

He rummaged in my bag. He knew what he was looking for and did not seem to notice the mobile. Not surprising since I was using a soft suede spectacle case as a cover.

I used the Ventolin, two puffs, and my breathing steadied. 'How old is your kid?' I asked. 'Boy or girl?'

'Boy. He's seven. He's got asthma, quite bad.'

'Poor little soul,' I said sympathetically. 'Does he have to take his inhaler to school?'

'The teacher keeps it in a cupboard. Let's him have it when he needs it.'

'That's all right in theory,' I said, keeping the talk going. 'But do the teachers know what they are doing? After all they are not medically trained—'

'Shut it! No more talking,' snapped Chuck, advancing with the roll of tape. 'Shut your mouth.'

'I'll keep quiet,' I said quickly. 'I promise. But don't put the tape on me, please. I can't breath with it.'

'She can't breath,' said the other one. 'She's got asthma like my boy, Gavin. She could choke. Then where would we be? We'd have a stiff on our hands.'

Chuck saw the defeat in letting me choke to death. No lever. He paced about, growling.

'OK, but don't talk.'

I shook my head and sent a genuine thank-you look to Gavin's father. He nodded once, briefly, and glanced away, not wanting to be caught. Chuck was in charge.

'Good idea, actually,' said Chuck. 'Mr G'll be able to hear her scream if we have to use a little persuasion.'

His mate laughed, relieved at being let off the hook. 'That's for sure, she'll scream all right.'

It was difficult to bond with either of the men when I'd promised not to speak. I tried expressions, sweet, humble, friendly, co-operative. The room was getting very warm and the two men were sweating and agitated. I knew Francis was sweating. His hands were close to mine and I could feel the dampness.

'Where's the safe?' Chuck said to Francis. 'No funny business now. Untie him.' They untied Francis and I took advantage of the activity to smile at them, then at Francis. His appearance shocked me. Francis was looking poorly, sick and pale and I was seriously worried about him. He'd had a rough enough time with his son dying, working so hard at the store and now this.

'Look, Mr Guilbert isn't feeling well,' I said, but I was

205

stopped with a smart slap across the face. It stung. 'He's ill, can't you see it?' Another slap nearly sent me sideways flying, me and the chair.

'He don't look right.'

'Give him a drink,' I ordered. This time the slap did send me and the chair onto the floor. I used the impetus to move my arms so that the rope was twisted round a thinner part of the chair than before. The rope immediately became looser. I was now lying with my back against the chair on the floor and they could not see what I was doing.

But they did take off the tape and get some water from the kitchen. Francis nodded his thanks and drank. Some of the water spilled down his shirt. It was humiliating. My heart wept for him. I'd got to do something.

My red hair exploded. I boiled over with indignation. How dare they do this to Francis? The soreness of my fingers was forgotten as I mentally planned the strategy required to untie the knots. There was now a slackness of about an inch giving me extra space in which to wriggle my fingers. I pushed the extra inch through the knot to loosen it.

I could move a finger through one loop. Promising. They were taking Francis through to another room. He had a study and the safe would be there. He might refuse to open the safe.

But not too much guts, please Francis. I'd rather he lived to see another day. The knots round my wrists were changing shape under my manipulation though whether they were becoming undone, I couldn't tell. They might be creating a different tangle. I couldn't see, I couldn't feel and I didn't have a clue what I was tackling. It was all part of my driving fury. Francis was my responsibility and he was paying me.

There were shouts coming from the study. Shouts, loud threats and my blood chilled. They dragged Francis back. He was hardly on his feet. The tape had been removed from his mouth though his wrists were still tied behind his back.

'I tell you, I don't know where the money is or who took it home. No one knows.' Francis was gasping but the words were coming out. 'We had a sort of sixth sense about the security van breaking down. It seemed just too convenient. So we drew lots as to who would take home the bulk of the store's cash.'

'You're making this up. We'll tear the house apart!' Chuck was choking with rage.

'It isn't here and I don't know who took it home,' said Francis. 'Nobody does. So you might as well untie us and let us go.'

'It might be true,' said the other man miserably. He looked as if he'd rather go home. 'Why don't we give up?'

'Give up? We can't give up now, you fool! These two know too much about us.' Chuck was chewing on the hem of his balaclava.

'We don't know anything about you,' I put in meekly. 'We can't see you. Why don't you just go and we'll forget all about it.'

This hit home. He seemed eager. 'I've had enough of this,' he went on. 'We're wasting time. Leave'em tied up and let's get out of here, Chuck.' He'd let the name out. I hoped Chuck wouldn't notice. It would be curtains for us if he had. But he was pacing the floor, trying to think where the money was.

'Right! We'll leave'em tied up. Bloody useless! Why didn't you find out about all this? You said the money would be here.'

'How was I to know?' he said, finishing his beer. 'I'm not a bloody mind-reader. I'm not the brains of this outfit.'

'You haven't got any brains, you moron . . .'

I lay very still. They were on the verge of going and nothing must change their minds. Francis had slumped onto the floor and I prayed that he realised the importance of not doing anything.

I closed my eyes as if I had passed out with fear/exhaustion/ asthma attack. There was nothing I could do but hope that DI James had understood my call. He might be off-duty, raving it up at some New Year party, surrounded by adoring WPCs ready to unbutton their uniforms.

Silence drifted down into the house. All I could hear was the ticking of various clocks and Francis's breathing. It was too early to dare to move. They could be anywhere, rifling the fridge, seaching the house, looking for car keys.

I heard the noise of vehicles being started and driven away. It sounded like two vehicles, different engine noises.

'That's my Mercedes,' said Francis in a low voice. 'I'd know those revs anywhere. I gave them the keys so that they would go.'

'They've gone then?' I whispered. 'Are you all right?'

'Nothing that a good malt whisky won't cure,' he said, sounding remarkably cheerful. 'I don't mind about the car. I wanted a new one anyway.'

'I'll soon be free,' I said, struggling with more vigour. 'Nearly there . . . I'll be done soon . . .

The front door burst open, icy cold air streamed in, and I froze. Detective Inspector James and Detective Sergeant Evans stormed in followed by a thrash of uniformed police.

'Freeze,' shouted DI James.

'I already have,' I said.

'What have you been doing?' DI James said, kneeling on the floor beside me. 'Is this some heathen way of bring in the New Year?'

'We've been waiting for you, that's what we've been doing,' I stormed. 'What took you so long? I phoned ages ago. Didn't you get my call?'

He sat back on his heels, looking bemused. 'What call? Oh, all that loo flushing? Was that you? I thought it was a hoax call.'

'So why are you here?'

'We got a call from a Miss Kent. She was worried. Apparently Mr Guilbert always calls her after midnight on New Year's Eve to wish her a Happy New Year. And this year, he hadn't called.'

'Miss Kent . . .' I breathed.

'And she told us about the security van breaking down.'

'Two and two . . .'

'Exactly. Move over. Let me untie the rope.'

I sat up straight. It took an effort. My wrists were free. 'Too late,' I said, rubbing at the marks. 'I've done it myself.'

DS Evans was freeing Francis and I was relieved to see that Francis was looking better already. He went straight over to his drinks cabinet and poured two stiff whiskys.

'Drink this, my girl,' he said. 'You were wonderful. What a woman. Such courage. I'm full of admiration.'

I glowed in the praise. I couldn't think exactly what I had done but if Francis thought I'd been Joan of Arc, then it was OK by me. The whisky went down in small fiery droplets. It made me cough.

'And the money, Mr Guilbert,' said James. 'Perhaps we ought to put it into safe keeping.'

'But it's not here,' I said. 'Nobody knows who took it home.'

Francis Guilbert was smiling, a mixture of sheepishness and satisfaction. 'The money is safe. It's outside by the bins, in the garbage bags you so kindly carried out, Jordan. The story about the secret draw . . . well, I lied. Sorry.'

Twenty-Two

T he police arrested the two crooks at the Newhaven ferry
terminal, trying to book the Mercedes on to a Channel
crossing. There was enough on them both for charges of
robbery with violence on three counts, car theft and attempted
robbery and holding two persons against their will. DI James
was pleased with events. It was a well-organised swoop.

He told me that Chuck Waite had a record of petty crime.
Chuck Waite? The name seemed familiar but I could not think
where I'd heard it before. Then I remembered and more pieces
fell into place.

The syphoning of goods from Guilberts was part of a wider
operation and had passed out of the hands of West Sussex. It
was no longer an isolated crime, but referred to several Metropolitan county forces. I wondered if there was a reward. A
mercenary streak.

I clocked in for the New Year sales. It was the least I could do
for Francis. No detective work, no being taken hostage. It
seemed like a holiday. Francis decided to call by later in the
afternoon, which seemed sensible after what he had been
through.

The creases had fallen out of the black dress. I took care
with my appearance. DI James might call by to thank me for
my help, bravery recommendation etc. The sales pace in the
store was frenetic. Where did people get the money? Or the
energy? Christmas should have cleaned them out of loose
change.

When Francis Guilbert eventually made a tour of the store, I stopped him discreetly near Electrical. It was noisy enough to drown what I was saying.

'Are you all right?'

'A bit shaken,' he admitted. 'How about you?'

'Annoyed more than anything. The police caught them at Newhaven.'

'So I heard. DI James phoned with the good news.'

'Mr Guilbert, I have to ask you something which may be distressing. Can you tell me what Oliver was doing during the afternoon before he died?'

I expected him to say Oliver was working in the store, checking accounts, at a board meeting, anything but what he did say.

'Oh yes, I know where he was. He'd gone to visit Mrs Sonia Spiller, the woman who was suing us.'

'That's extraordinary,' I said, taken aback. 'Why on earth would he go to visit her? Surely everything was being conducted through your solicitors.'

'I sent him,' said Mr Guilbert reluctantly. 'It seemed a good idea at the time. I wanted it to be settled out of court. Oliver was against a settlement as he was convinced it was a fraudulent claim. But I felt she might be satisfied with a modest payment and no costs.'

'And did she accept a settlement?'

'I don't know. I never spoke to him again.' His voice broke and he turned away. 'If you'll excuse me, Jordan, I have a lot to do.'

Both feet well in that time. Knee deep. Mr Guilbert had known all the time that Oliver went to see Sonia and I'd been trying to keep it from him. But Sonia and Sara had certainly not been arguing about a settlement at the watermill. They had been going for the big one. There was a chink of transparency on the horizon.

'Before you go,' I said, hating myself. 'I need to check Oliver's briefcase. He did use one, didn't he?'

'Of course. It's in my study, at home. No one has touched it.

Funnily enough, he didn't take it with him that afternoon. I don't know why. Come by anytime. Don't look so worried, Jordan. I know you have to ask these things.'

I'd seen the study. I'd been there, sat in the tapestry armchair, drinking wine. And Oliver's briefcase had probably been there all the time, within reach. I had no instinct, no intuition.

'I must look in his briefcase. And there's news about Sonia Spiller. You remember that I told you that there are two of them, twins, Sonia and Sara. They are identical except for one thing. Sara has her ears pierced and wears two tiny gold studs in the lobes. If you look at the shoulder area X-rays and see tiny metal pin-point studs, then the woman examined is Sara, not Sonia. Sara hurt her shoulder last year, skiing on holiday in Austria. She was skiing off-piste, at her own risk, and took a tumble.'

'Is this true?'

'Yes, and I think Oliver had spotted the difference. He was very observant. I've checked on Sonia's jewellery. She wears all clip-on style earrings. Maybe they decided to get rid of him. I think one of them engineered his death.'

Francis Guilbert seemed to stagger, but then righted himself. He leaned against the edge of a counter. 'But to kill him? Could a woman do it?'

'An army-trained woman could do it. Or maybe it's tied up with the stock disappearing. Oliver was on the track of that, too. We must look in his briefcase, find out what he had discovered. Your son was very bright. He employed me to follow Sonia but he was also doing his own investigating. He did not want to worry you. He was going to solve the thefts on his own.'

'I wish he had told me.'

I touched his arm. 'Be proud of him, Francis,' I said.

The briefcase was hand-stitched black leather, the best. It had a coded lock. Brilliant. I had to find four numbers out of millions which would open it. I tried Oliver's date of birth; his father's date of birth; his phone number, his mobile, silly numbers like

1234 and 3333. I could feel a familiar headache coming on when I thought of his pride and joy, the red Aston Martin.

It worked. I tapped the three numbers of his personalised registration plus the initial of his name. The briefcase lock clicked open and I gazed at the sheaf of papers inside. Oliver had a file of delivery notes. He had scribbled on them, non-deliveries, empty boxes, van numbers, names of delivery men, staff on duty. He had not needed me. He was a one-man detective agency.

Daffy's name cropped up, again and again. The man still off sick after a liquid Christmas. Was he Chuck's mate?

Chuck sold stolen goods. Maybe Chuck had also stolen the Aston Martin and taken it to the midnight boot. He'd beaten up Mavis, paid for by a fisherman's wife. But why the Mexican? Or the cinema? Or the funfair kiosk? Were they just a pair of small-time opportunist crooks?

So, who had killed Oliver? Put a cool arm round his throat and broken his neck? Who'd driven him down to Hell's Revenge, manoeuvred him into a ride seat in the dark, taped his head to the brace, sat beside a dead man for the whole nightmare spin, then untaped him and disappeared into the gloom. Chuck? Sara? Or Chuck and Sara? Sonia? Sonia and Colin? I was no nearer the truth.

I gave the facts to DI James that evening. Guilberts had closed to the sound of credit cards whooshing. Maeve's Cafe stayed open. We were drinking tea at a table by a darkened window.

'You solve it now,' I said. 'It's your case.'

'I have,' he said complacently. 'Do you want to hear some more facts? Daffy made a confession, i.e. he shopped Chuck.'

'A confession is hardly solving a case.'

'There speaks the voice of jealousy.'

'Convince me.'

DI James was looking far too pleased with himself. 'Chuck and Daffy followed Oliver Guilbert to Sonia's house in Luton Road, knowing they had to do something to stop his investigations. They found him talking to a woman about money. They didn't know what was going on, but she didn't try to stop them when Chuck crept up on Oliver with a head blow. However, they told her that he was only knocked-out and would soon come round. Of course, we know he didn't.'

'Was that when Sonia Spiller offered them the use of a neck collar? Instant first aid?'

'Right. She seemed anxious to get rid of some holdall, wanted to get down to the front. Daffy said she became distraught, tried to leave. They couldn't resist taking the Aston Martin, lifting Oliver's keys. They took Oliver to the funfair, all three of them, propped him up in Hell's Revenge for some air. Chuck rode alongside Oliver, then untaped him and left him to be found by the attendant.'

'And they knew Sonia wouldn't talk because she was a silent accomplice. That is Sonia or Sara, whichever one it was. And did you find fish scales in the Aston Martin?' I asked.

'Odd question, Jordan, but, yes, huss scales in the boot.'

'I got a car load of huss, very dead, delivered to my shop. And Chuck is the brother of a woman, Tracy Jones, who has a sexy husband. And this bronzed husband happens to be a fisherman with a roving eye. Does that add up?'

DI James nodded. 'Mavis? A brother tempted to help out a grateful sister and get some ready cash? Chuck wouldn't care.'

'That's my guess. And Chuck's mother is Mrs Waite, Francis Guilbert's housekeeper. She may have overheard something or seen papers at the house and passed the information on to her delightful son.'

'Possible. Chuck was once sacked from Miguel's restaurant for helping himself to the till. Although Miguel didn't recognise him, revenge could again have been the motive. Nasty.'

'And he was one of the waiters at Brenda Hamilton's party,' I added. 'No connection, but weird . . .'

'I'm surprised you can remembering anything about that party,' said DI James.

*　　　*　　　*

It was a still winter's night. So still even the stars had stopped winking, no dancing with frost. The pier was deserted. The nightclub was belting festive rock and noisily serving drinks. No one saw the woman at the end of the pier, walking along the lower angler's level, then climbing down the girders.

She lowered herself into the dark sea, not flinching at the coldness. Then she let go of the slippery bars and let the waves bash her against the ironwork till the tide took her out and the cold claimed her body.

No one was ever sure if it was Sonia or Sara. The studs, if there had been any studs, would have fallen out of her lobes and drifted down to the sea bed. The female body was washed ashore in January somewhere near Shoreham.

'Are you going to arrest Sonia/Sara for not reporting Oliver's death?'

'We've been round to number eight Luton Road. The house is empty. The birds have flown.'

'The husband was her stalker. He's an airline pilot.'

'So they have flown indeed.'

'What about the JCB rally driver?'

'A good local doctor, retired, momentarily not of sound mind who was denied membership because of a change in rules. So he took it out on the clubhouse. He has been charged. He'll probably get community service.'

A doctor? With knowledge of amputation? I shuddered.

'What about the two arms? Brenda Hamilton's missing husband.'

DI James made no comment about the name slip. 'On the files, Jordan. Case left on file.'

But DI James was not right. Facts nagged at me. Daffy's confession didn't ring true. OK, parts of it happened. But not everything. Sara/Sonia were shielding someone.

I could guess who it was. Colin Spiller. Both sisters were in love with him. Perhaps he married the wrong one, was having an affair with the other. Sonia had said Sara was greedy, always wanted the best. Perhaps she wanted Colin, too.

Maybe he had been in Austria, on holiday with Sara when she had her accident. That holdall may have contained the tickets, the brochures, the photos, the souvenirs of that illicit holiday. Evidence that now had to be destroyed.

It was Sara who was at number eight Luton Road that afternoon, meeting Colin, when Oliver unfortunately called by. Maybe he spotted the pierced ears, said so. It was Colin who killed him, not the two thugs.

Chuck had been telling the truth when he said Oliver was only knocked out. Colin, or was it Sara, who finished him off with a highly trained throat chop while the two thugs were outside, trying to start the Aston Martin. They never saw Colin, although he followed them down to the seafront to make sure everything went according to plan.

How could I prove it? Well, I couldn't. It was all instinct but one day I would tell James. After all, that's why Jasper was shut in the car. They hadn't wanted any interruptions.

The Bear and Bait was full. I had no real hope that the jazz would be good that evening, but there was always a chance. Then my special trumpeter walked in as if he had never been away, pushing back his floppy, silky brown hair and adjusting his glasses. His black clothes were crumpled and creased from a trans-Atlantic flight . . . but his jet-lagged eyes lit up at the sight of me.

'Jordan, sweetheart,' he said, closing his arms round me and kissing my cheek softly. 'Long time. How are you?'

'Where have you been?' I asked.

'Blowing a few notes, across the pond,' he said. He opened his case and took out his trumpet. It was an instrument to die for. The brass gleamed in the smokey light. The mouthpiece was dry. He blew through it and winked at me. I folded myself into his presence. It was crowded and the only place to sit was on the floor, my back against a pillar, my eyes closed against the storm of sunlight.

The sound was magic, heart-stoppingly melodic. 'Joanna', 'Little Darlin'', 'Embraceable You' . . . this music cleared my head of cobwebs and took my soul soaring to paradise. I lived for this music. It flowed from one note to another. The plaintive melodies shifted through tempos and harmonies, through improvised jazz that managed to cling to the original tune with drifting harmonics and sounds that defied description.

He was healing me with suspended wanderings, notes that turned my body into molten music with a treasure of surprise. 'Satin Doll', 'Shiny Stockings', 'Call Me Irresponsible' . . . my blood was only an emotion. There was nothing I could do but sit and listen.

My toes were tapping each other in time without my knowing. The trumpeter smiled at me again. His eyes were teasing, saying that he liked a woman who sat at his feet.

It was not easy to stay rooted to this earth. I was already drifting away to some other place when the temperature changed in the crowded pub as the door opened. DI James came in, collar turned up, frozen-faced with cold.

I could not believe my eyes. How could this be happening? James appearing in this pub (which he never came to) at the same time as my magical jazz trumpeter? Please, fate, don't do this to me.

'Jordan, what are you doing here? Why are you sitting on the floor?' He stood over me like a custodian.

'I'm listening to music,' I said staring at the red patterned carpet. There were worn patches. 'You know I like jazz.'

'Get up. Come and have a drink.'

'No, thank you.' But I couldn't let him go. 'I'll take a rain check on that invite.'

'I don't do rain checks,' said James. 'It's now or never.'

He turned his back on me, went over to the bar to order and I was flattened. My stomach contracted. A bubble of dread coursed my veins like an embolism. I could die from this.

The door opened again. Still the music flowed in an ethereal golden stream, but I was losing the magic of the blues and was sinking under it. My head was spinning. I was trying to stay afloat in an alien sea.

'Jordan, *señorita*! My beautiful lady. I see you have put my red rose in your window. How perfect, how enchanting. I must kiss you for the New Year blessing.'

Miguel Cortes strode into the crowd, pulled me to my feet and planted a warm Latin kiss on my cheek. Twice in one night. Perhaps the drought had broken.

But I was a woman condemned to endure a nuclear device exploding my dreams. Would I ever find the energy to pick up the pieces and start again? Would the painful debris littering my feet, cut and shred forever?

Were they really all here, all three of them? Surely I was dreaming.

DI James was leaving, beer barely touched. He'd had enough. He jammed the glass on the counter like a full stop. The music had come to an end. The jazzman was taking a break, shaking moisture from the mouthpiece, coming towards me, a man of sweetness and charm, eyes full of warmth, ready to talk music for hours. Just what I wanted, what I needed.

Miguel had his arm protectively round my shoulder, very amorous. '*Bella señorita*, lady of the rose,' he murmured into my ear.

'Excuse me,' I said, heading for the ladies' loo.

I climbed out of the window, jabbing awkward arms and legs, and slithered to the ground. I stood outside in the night air, leaning against the cold wall, howling into the harsh wet bricks. I wanted to bury myself inside my own body. It was too much to bear. The roughness cut my skin.

'I thought you'd try some hair-brained escape,' said James, strolling casually towards me, hands in his pockets. 'That was the men's window you climbed out of. They put little drawings on doors to help people like you.'

It was like getting the last after-dinner mint.